Only the extraordinary women of Athena Academy could create Oracle—a covert intelligence organization so secret that not even its members know who else belongs. Now it's up to three top agents to bring down the enemies who threaten all they've sworn to protect....

Kim Valenti:
An NSA cryptologist by day, this analytical genius and expert code breaker is the key to stopping a deadly bomb.
COUNTDOWN by Ruth Wind—April 2005

Diana Lockworth:
With only twenty-four hours until the president's inauguration, can this army intelligence captain thwart an attempt to assassinate him?
TARGET by Cindy Dees—May 2005

Selena Jones:
Used to ensuring international peace, the FBI legal attaché has her biggest assignment yet—outwitting a rebel leader to avert international disaster.
CHECKMATE by Doranna Durgin—June 2005

Dear Reader,

You're about to read a Silhouette Bombshell novel, one of the most engaging, exciting and riveting books on the shelves today. We're pleased to bring you fast-paced, compelling reads featuring strong, admirable women who will speak to the Bombshell in you!

In *Sophie's Last Stand* by Nancy Bartholomew, Sophie Mazaratti's trying to start over after her marriage ends *very* badly—but it seems her slimy ex has left her in a sticky situation involving the mob, the Feds and one darned attractive detective....

Get ready for a thrilling twenty-four hours as military author Cindy Dees continues the powerful Athena Force continuity series with *Target*, featuring an army intelligence agent on a mission to save the President-elect from being assassinated. To gain his trust, she'll give the villain someone new to chase—herself....

It's a jungle out there when a determined virologist races into the Amazon to stop a deadly outbreak—a danger that authorities seem determined to cover up, even at the cost of Dr. Jane Miller's life. Don't miss *The Amazon Strain* by Katherine Garbera!

And a protected witness must come out of hiding after her sister mysteriously disappears, in Kate Donovan's adventure *Parallel Lies*. It's up to Sabrina Sullivan to determine which of two charismatic men is lying—or if they both are—to save her sister's life.

The stakes are high and the pressure is on! Please send me your comments c/o Silhouette Books, 233 Broadway, Suite 1001, New York, NY 10279

Sincerely,

Natashya Wilson
Associate Senior Editor, Silhouette Bombshell

Please address questions and book requests to:
Silhouette Reader Service
U.S.: 3010 Walden Ave., P.O. Box 1325, Buffalo, NY 14269
Canadian: P.O. Box 609, Fort Erie, Ont. L2A 5X3

CINDY DEES

TARGET

Silhouette®
BOMBSHELL™

Published by Silhouette Books

America's Publisher of Contemporary Romance

Special thanks and acknowledgment
are given to Cindy Dees for her contribution
to the ATHENA FORCE series.

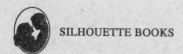 SILHOUETTE BOOKS

ISBN 0-373-51356-9

TARGET

www.SilhouetteBombshell.com

Printed in U.S.A.

Books by Cindy Dees

Silhouette Bombshell

Killer Instinct #16
The Medusa Project #31
Target #42

Silhouette Intimate Moments

*Behind Enemy Lines #1176
*Line of Fire #1253
*A Gentleman and a Soldier #1307
*Her Secret Agent Man #1353

*Charlie Squad

CINDY DEES

started flying airplanes while sitting in her dad's lap at the age of three and got a pilot's license before she got a driver's license. At age fifteen, she dropped out of high school and left the horse farm in Michigan where she grew up to attend the University of Michigan.

After earning a degree in Russian and East European Studies, she joined the U.S. Air Force and became the youngest female pilot in its history. She flew supersonic jets, VIP airlift and the C-5 Galaxy, the world's largest airplane. She also worked part-time gathering intelligence. During her military career, she traveled to forty countries on five continents, was detained by the KGB and East German secret police, got shot at, flew in the first Gulf War, met her husband and amassed a lifetime's worth of war stories.

Her hobbies include professional Middle Eastern dancing, Japanese gardening and medieval reenacting. She started writing on a one-dollar bet with her mother and was thrilled to win that bet with the publication of her first book in 2001. She loves to hear from readers and can be contacted at www.cindydees.com.

This book is dedicated to women everywhere
who work in their own way—as mothers, professionals
or role models—toward making this world a safer place
for all our children. Thank you for your vision
and your quiet heroism.

3:00 A.M.

Diana Lockworth lurched bolt upright in bed. She blinked, disoriented, at the blanket of darkness around her. Something had ripped her from a deep, dreaming slumber to full consciousness. But what? Even the street outside was quiet, deserted at this hour. Silence pressed against her eardrums. *Nothing*.

Sheesh. She was letting work get to her again. But then paranoia was the logical price of sitting around day after day hunting for conspiracies for Uncle Sam. At least Don Quixote had real windmills to joust with. She tilted at shadows and innuendoes, vague rumors and possibilities. Maybe that was the problem. The reason her predictions had gone sour lately. She'd moved so far away from concrete reality in her thinking that she could no longer tell the difference between the possible and the actual.

She flopped back down on her pillow in disgust. The telltale whirl of disjointed thoughts in her head did not bode well for getting back to sleep anytime soon. Crud. She propped herself up on an elbow to plump her squashed eiderdown pillow. And heard a noise. Either the biggest mouse in the history of mankind was in her house, or else someone had just bumped into something in her living room.

Intruder. Autonomic responses programmed into her relentlessly since she was a child kicked in. Adrenaline surged through her veins, sending her brain into high gear and preparing her body to fight. She rolled fast, flinging herself off the far side of the bed. Counted to sixty in the thunderous silence. Nobody opened her door. But no doubt about it, someone was out there. She could *feel* it.

She reached up onto her nightstand for the telephone, her hands shaky, and dialed 9-1-1. She whispered into the receiver, "There's someone in my house."

The 9-1-1 dispatcher efficiently asked her address, name, physical description, and current location in her home. He was in the middle of telling her the police would be there in under five minutes when Diana heard another noise. The distinctive metallic squeak of her computer chair as someone sat down in it. She heard a faint, rapid clicking. Typing! *On her computer full of sensitive and highly dangerous material.*

She pushed upright, the phone forgotten, her bare feet silent on the hardwood floor. On bent knees, she moved catlike to the bedroom door. She opened it inch by cautious inch. A fast spin out into the hall. *Empty.* She plastered herself against the wall and tiptoed toward a blue glow emanating from the computer workstation in her living room. She leaped forward, surging into the living room on a wave of fury and fear.

One male, dressed in black. A ski mask over his face. He jumped to his feet and spun to face her in a fighting crouch. Wiry body. Hands held open and ready at shoulder height.

Weight centered and balanced. A trained martial artist. Fortunately, so was she. In Krav Maga, the deadly system developed by Israeli Defense Forces for street fighting. Dirty, deadly street fighting.

She settled herself before the intruder. He rocked on the balls of his feet, noncommittal about attacking. She didn't want this guy to flee. She wanted to know who he was. Why he was poking around on her computer. She needed him to stand and fight.

"You think you can take me?" she taunted. "Think again. You're not man enough."

The guy snarled audibly. Excellent.

"Go ahead. Try me," she urged.

Another growl, but no attack.

She laughed derisively. And that did it. The guy came in with a fast roundhouse kick aimed at her face. Impressive in a Bruce Lee movie, but completely impractical in a real fight. She ducked under it easily. While he was still regaining his footing from the kick, she stepped in and stiff-armed him in the sternum. He staggered backward. But to his credit, he came out swinging. Fast hands. She blocked three quick jabs, but took a glancing hit from the fourth on the nose. Pain radiated outward from it, making her eyeballs ache. She blinked fast to clear the involuntary tears oozing from her eyes. And as she did so, she lashed out with her foot toward his knee. A solid hit. The guy cried out. Staggered. But righted himself and charged.

He was too close. She couldn't avoid the tackle. They both went down on the floor. She got an elbow between them, but the guy was pissed off now. He went for her neck with his gloved hands. She heaved and came around hard with her elbow. And clocked him in the jaw. The guy reeled back. A mighty shove and he was off her. She jumped to her feet.

"Who do you work for?" she demanded.

The guy's only answer was a nifty back-bend-and-jump-to-his-feet move. Damn. She should've stood on his head while she had him down. He launched at her with a flurry of kicks and punches that forced her to give ground. She banged into the coffee table. Knocked it over. Stumbled over it and righted herself barely in time to get a hand up as his foot came flying at her face with lethal intent. She grabbed his ankle and yanked, using the momentum of his kick to propel him into the sofa. But she was off balance herself and crashed to the floor flat on her back. She rolled, pulled her feet under her and shoved vertical. And felt faintly nauseous as the room spun around her. She saw double images of her assailant bouncing off the cushions and spinning to face her. She huffed hard a couple times to clear her head and focus.

His gaze flicked over her shoulder for an instant. Toward the front door. Either he had a partner who'd just walked in and she was hosed, or the jerk was contemplating getting out of Dodge. With a wordless shout, he charged her. But at the last second, he veered left. She dived for him as he ran past and wrapped her arms around his legs. They fell hard, his heels jamming into her gut until she nearly barfed. He kicked furiously, twisting and wriggling frantically. She hung on as best she could, but he slipped through her grasp. He jumped up and took off for the door. She pushed up and gave chase, bursting out onto her front porch. There! To the left. A sprinting figure.

She charged after him, the concrete sidewalk rough and cold beneath her bare feet in Maryland's January chill. He screeched to a stop by the door of a car. Ripped it open and jumped in. The car peeled away from the curb. She dived between two parked cars as the getaway car sped past, both to take cover and to get a closer look at the vehicle. Silver, midsize foreign sedan. The license plate was covered with something black.

Maybe a plastic garbage bag. It rippled as the car accelerated away from her into the night. Helplessly, she watched the vehicle turn onto River Road. Her Bethesda home had ready access to major highways in several directions, no telling where her assailant had gone. The bastards had gotten away.

And she was standing in the middle of the street on a freezing January night, with snow on the ground for God's sake, in nothing but a cropped T-shirt and soft cotton short-shorts.

In the two more minutes it took the police to arrive, she hurried back inside and threw on a pair of slim black jeans, a bra and a slightly longer and less tight T-shirt that nonetheless hugged the slender curves of her body. She pulled her wavy, shoulder-length blond hair back into a ponytail and checked the spot on the back of her head where she'd hit the floor. No goose egg forming. She examined her eyes in the bathroom mirror, and the aqua-blue rings of her irises were identical in diameter. No concussion, then. Her nose was a little red, but that could be as much from the cold as the glancing blow it had taken.

A chiming noise sounded. The doorbell. She moved carefully through the living room so as not to destroy evidence and opened the front door.

"You reported an intruder in your house, ma'am?" the officer asked tersely.

She nodded and stepped aside to let the pair of policemen inside. Quickly, she relayed what had happened.

"And you fought him off?" the guy asked, sounding surprised.

"That's right."

"Are you injured, ma'am?"

She shook her head in the negative and flinched as her nose twinged. She'd been clocked worse than that by her big sister in a boxing ring more times than she could count.

"I'm Officer Grady and this is my partner, Officer Fratiano." The pair of big men stepped into the room. "Tell us exactly what happened again, and this time include every detail you can remember."

The poor cops scribbled busily until she was done with her trained observations, and no doubt they had a good case of writer's cramp. Grady moved around the room, notepad in hand, walking through the events she'd described. And then he looked up at her, skeptical. "I've never seen a victim of an attack who could describe it in such perfect detail. Your account jives exactly with the evidence. Almost too exactly." He paused and then added slyly, "That usually indicates the crime scene was a setup."

The guy thought she was lying about the intruder? She frowned and looked around the living room. It did look shockingly undisturbed given how violent a fight had just taken place in it. The upended coffee table and a few sofa pillows on the floor were the extent of the damage. She explained carefully, "I'm an Army Intelligence officer. I'm trained to notice details, even under duress."

"Mind if we have a look around, ma'am?" Grady asked dryly.

"Not at all," she answered coolly. Jerk.

Grady wandered down the hall toward her bedroom while the second officer checked her computer for fingerprints with a special flashlight. Fratiano looked up at her regretfully. "Do you have long fingernails?" he asked.

"Yes," she answered cautiously.

He nodded. "That explains why there are no complete fingerprints on your keyboard. You don't leave full prints when you type, and your intruder didn't leave any, either."

"I told you he was wearing gloves. Of course he didn't leave any prints," she retorted. The beginnings of desperation tickled the back of her neck.

"What kind of gloves did he have on? It's not like you can type in most gloves."

She thought back to the sight of his hands coming up to fight. "They looked like driving gloves. Thin material. Maybe Lycra or very fine leather. Can't you check the keyboard for fibers or something?"

The cop nodded reluctantly. "But we usually don't call out a full-blown evidence collection team for a simple B and E when nothing was taken and nobody was hurt."

"Look," she explained patiently. "I'm not your usual random victim. I work for the government. I uncover conspiracies and predict terrorist activity. I have enemies. No break-in to my home, particularly when my computer is the target, is a *simple* B and E."

"Then I'd suggest you call the Army Criminal Investigation Division—"

"Hey Vinny!" Officer Grady shouted from her bedroom. "Come have a look at this!"

Cripes. She winced. He found her wall of pictures. She hastened after Officer Fratiano to explain herself before they hauled her in as a stalker. She rounded the corner into her bedroom and sure enough, the two cops were gaping at her massive collection of pictures of Gabe Monihan, President-elect of the United States. She had literally hundreds of pictures of him pinned up on the wall of her bedroom opposite her bed, the entire space wallpapered with images of him. They were taken mostly in the final months of last year's Presidential campaign—the months leading up to and immediately after a thwarted terrorist attack at Chicago O'Hare airport that he'd nearly been caught in the middle of. The planned attack, a suicide bombing, had occurred just a couple weeks before the Presidential election, and many pundits credited sympathy votes for Monihan's election. Monihan and the incumbent, now-outgoing President James Whitlow. Had both been in the area to campaign. Reports had it that Monihan's presence there had been a bonus for the terrorists, but his death was not their goal. She had other theories on the incident, however.

"Are you some kind of sicko, lady?" Grady demanded.

She schooled her voice to patience. "I told you. I'm a conspiracy theorist for the government. I'm investigating the attack on Monihan last October. These pictures are part of my research."

"Research. Right," Grady growled. "Then you won't mind if we photograph all…this?"

"Go right ahead," she replied evenly. But her gut churned at the way they were blowing her off. They thought she was a kook who staged an attack on herself to…what? Get attention? Get caught? She supposed it fit the profile of the kind of person who'd build a shrine to a famous politician in her bedroom.

God, she hated not being taken seriously. It was endemic to her work that people routinely thought she was crazy. But that was her job. To cook up crazy ideas and build contingency plans to respond to them. First the army thought she was nuts, and now these cops. Did the entire flipping Establishment feel that way about her? Did she have some sort of tattoo on her forehead that identified her to the authorities as a weirdo? At least the army had the excuse of the notorious Lockworth name as a reason to doubt her. But these cops didn't know her from Adam. What was it about her that inspired such antipathy? It wasn't as if she *tried* not to fit in. Well, okay. She rebelled against the system sometimes. But that was just because they all made her so mad!

In a decidedly rebellious frame of mind, she stood by silently while Grady and Fratiano painstakingly photographed her wall of pictures. They took their sweet time finishing the job. Finally, Grady said casually, "Any chance we could take those pictures with us?"

"No!" she answered sharply. "I told you. They're part of

an ongoing investigation I'm conducting. Get a warrant if you want to seize any of my stuff."

Any pretense of pleasantry between them gone, the police left quickly after that. Some help they'd turned out to be. But, she did take Officer Fratiano's advice and give Army CID a ring. A night sergeant took down the information about her break-in and, after she assured him no classified information had been stored on her home computer, seemed totally unimpressed by her urgency over someone attempting to break into said computer. When the guy asked which of her files had been accessed, she jolted. That was a darned good question. She promised to check out her system and get back to him on it. In turn, he suggested she come down to the CID office in the morning and make a written statement.

She hung up the phone and sat down at her computer. As always, a sense of joy and adventure at connecting to the vast electronic universe of the Internet tingled through her fingers. She checked out her basic operating system first. Yup, the code had been tampered with. The guy had been trying to gain access to her encrypted notes on dozens of possible conspiracies. *And that would be why they're encrypted, buddy.* The new commands the hacker had inserted into her system were spare. Elegant. Coldly logical. This guy had a distinctive flair for his work. A strong signature to his programming style. Unfortunately, she didn't know the individual to whom it belonged.

In the hacker community, certain computer programmers became cult celebrities. They had legions of fans who followed their exploits with breathless awe and emulated their spectacular break-ins. She cultivated relationships with informants and outright criminals in this cyber underground as part of her work gathering intelligence off the Internet.

She highlighted the intruder's code, then cut and pasted it to a new file. She'd have to show it around. See if any of her cyber pals recognized the work. In the meantime, it was wicked late and tomorrow was a big day. January 20. Inauguration day for her favorite poster boy.

She climbed into bed wearily and reached for the lamp beside her bed. "G'night Gorgeous," she mumbled at the wall of pictures of Monihan.

She closed her eyes gratefully and let her mind drift toward sleep.

She was just on the verge of slipping into unconsciousness when a sound jolted her rudely to full awareness. An insistent electronic chirping. *Now* what? Surely she didn't have an alarm clock set somewhere in the house for this insane hour. Reluctantly, she sat up in bed. If it was a smoke detector in need of a battery, she was going to rip the damned thing right off the ceiling.

She padded out into the living room and stopped cold at her fully lit computer screen and the bold announcement across it in large letters that she had an incoming e-mail. When in the Sam Hill had her Internet server started announcing incoming messages like this? She was bloody well turning the new feature off this instant. Irate, she sat down at her computer and pulled up her Internet server. She went to the mail screen and gaped at the address of the e-mail's sender. Delphi@oracle.org.

Holy…freaking…cow.

Oracle? To her home address?

And *Delphi?* Personally?

An involuntary shiver passed through her. Oracle. An idea. A database. A secret organization. Her secondary employer and the tool of a shadowy figure known to her only as Delphi.

She'd been recruited for her ultrasecret work for Oracle and Delphi straight out of her army intelligence training. Although, she always suspected it was more her attendance at the ultraexclusive Athena Academy for the Advancement of Women than her position in the government that earned her the nod from Oracle. Her first mission for Delphi had been to plant the Oracle computer program in the army's vast computer network, where it collected data on everything from crop patterns in Africa to political unrest in Europe, terrorism threats to DOD research programs, and anything else that might prove useful to Delphi.

She didn't know if Delphi was male or female, a person or a computer program, or maybe just another layer of protection shrouding in mystery the identity of the person or persons behind Oracle. At any rate, Delphi took inputs from a wide variety of government and nongovernment sources and analyzed the staggering mass of information, combing through it all for hints of possible threats to the United States. The ultimate conspiracy theorist, as it were.

And tonight, Delphi had something to tell her.

Since when had her secret employer started contacting its agents personally in the middle of the night? Not that she ever had any contact with other Oracle agents to compare notes, but it certainly had never happened to her before. Hastily, she opened the e-mail from the mysterious Delphi.

Have been working on the database and it came up with a rather alarming bit of information. Could you please look into it immediately? —D

Attached was a reference number for the particular analysis Delphi wanted her to check out.

She assumed "immediately" meant this very second. What in the world could be so urgent? Thoroughly alarmed now, Diana accessed Oracle's database, or at least the superficial levels of it available over the Internet, and plugged in the reference number. She waited, tense, while the system retrieved the analysis in question. Most of the assessments the Oracle database had fed her recently were bogus, and her repeated proposals of these eventually unfounded threats to her superiors had earned her a host of rumors that she'd lost her edge completely. But this one… Straight from Delphi? Did she dare believe it, if this "bit of information" turned out to be yet another wildly off-the-wall speculation?

The threat analysis popped up onto the screen. She scrolled down through the lengthy write-up to the end where the thumbnail summary of the problem was traditionally placed. Tonight, this section was surprisingly short. She scanned the words quickly. And lurched upright in her seat at the report's terse conclusion.

A person or persons will attempt to assassinate President-elect Gabriel Monihan within the next twenty-four hours. You must stop them.

4:00 A.M.

A rather alarming bit of information, indeed! Urgently, she paged through the rest of the report, scanning the facts and assumptions the massive Oracle database used to arrive at its conclusion. Of course, large sections of the analysis were not transmitted to her here. They were deemed too sensitive to transit the Internet where they risked being intercepted. If she wanted to read the full text, she'd have to go down to the Oracle office and do it in person. But, at a glance, the logic looked sound. Not that she seriously expected anything else. Despite its recent flubs, the program was a masterpiece of computer software engineering.

She grabbed her black leather duster, a nearly ankle-length coat that billowed menacingly when she strode along a windy street. It made her feel like a gunslinger straight out of the Wild West. Plus, it had great pockets that stored a host of doo-dads and gadgets. Heck, it could swallow up an automatic rifle if it had to. Not that a desk jockey like her needed that feature often, of course. The coat also helped her blend into the gothic subculture of hackers and society dropouts from whom she got some of her best intelligence tips. Best of all, it drove her ultraconservative boss at the Defense Intelligence Agency crazy. And that was all the reason she needed to wear it.

She climbed into her sporty German coupe and backed out of the driveway. She steered down the winding, tree-lined streets of Bethesda, Maryland southward toward Alexandria, Virginia and its Old Town neighborhood where Oracle made its home.

Rock Creek Parkway and the gorgeous park it wound through was deserted at this time of morning with only a few delivery trucks and graveyard shifters on the road. And that was probably why she spotted the piece-of-shit sedan tailing her about a quarter-mile back. She'd lay odds it was Army Intel. The driver's movements were so precisely according to the Army training manual that it couldn't possibly be anyone else back there. Besides, no self-respecting FBI agent would be caught dead in a gutless heap like that. And surely the intruder from her house wasn't so brash that he'd follow her this soon after his getaway. He'd been worried about getting caught. No way would he expose himself openly again. Especially if her hunch about his identity was correct.

She could weed out anybody else by process of elimination. She had no other major investigations open. Every thug she'd helped catch in recent memory was safely behind bars. The other conspiracy theories she was developing at the moment involved political or economic forces that had no human face. But, she'd spent the last three months on the Internet day and night, slowly worming herself inside a terrorist organization known as the Q-Rajn, or Q-group. After that bunch had nearly killed her Athena Academy classmate and NSA code-

breaker pal, Kim Valenti, she'd been put on the trail of the
Q-group as well. Kim had cracked a code the terrorists were
using and foiled a suicide bombing the group was planning
in Chicago, but was nearly killed herself in the process. Immediately after the incident, Delphi had assigned Diana to
take over the hunt for Q-group and search for any possible reason the terrorists might want to kill Gabe Monihan. Personally, she thought the link between the Q-group and Monihan
was tenuous at best. Until tonight. Now, all bets were off. And
despite recent busts of local Q-group headquarters in several
states, they were still capable of mounting a break-in at her
house. And they were certainly capable of trying to kill the
President-elect of the United States.

The Q-group was comprised of ex-patriot citizens of a tiny
country called Berzhaan, which made up for its small size by
brewing bucketloads of international political upheaval. The
Q-group was devoted to overthrowing the current regime in
its homeland. Historically, they operated only on Berzhaani
soil. But all that had changed last October, when they'd taken
over a Chicago news station as a diversion and then attempted
to set off a bomb at Chicago O'Hare, one of the busiest and
highest profile airports in the world. The Q-group had claimed
that the attack was an effort to stop U.S. aid to rebels in Berzhaan who wanted to overthrow the country. But she'd never
bought that explanation. Why wouldn't these guys just protest on the steps of the United Nations or hold press conferences demanding a change in U.S. foreign policy? No, they'd
had some other goal in mind.

And that's what she'd been trying to pinpoint for the last
couple of months. She'd found a chat room on the Internet
where she believed these guys reported to their superiors, received instructions and obtained the money and resources for
their activities. Of course, an elaborate series of code word

and phrases was employed, so a perfectly innocuous chat about World Cup Soccer scores or a visit with family members might actually be a discussion of which target had been chosen for their next attack. But gradually, she'd been able to identify different combinations of meaning until the hidden subtext of the chats was becoming clear to her.

In fact, she'd turned her attention to ferreting out the real identities of the terrorists in the last few days. It was painstaking work, tracing the electronic transmissions backward through layers of Internet servers to their points of origin. But, once she nailed down the home server for each terrorist, she'd be able to approach that server's operator with a warrant and obtain the actual customer account information, complete with names, addresses and credit card numbers. Given another couple of weeks, she ought to be able to name everyone in the Q-group's American network.

Except, if Delphi was right, she didn't have that long.

Her gut instincts screamed that the Q-group was not only behind the break-in at her house, but also any attack that might be imminent against President-to-be Gabe Monihan.

She rolled down Massachusetts Avenue and its stately rows of foreign embassies, and took surface streets toward Route 1, which ran south past the Pentagon and down into Alexandria, passing through the Old Town section of that Virginia suburb. She watched her rearview mirror carefully as she turned onto the wide semihighway. Yup, the sedan behind her made the turnoff. Damn. She couldn't lead anyone to Oracle's doorstep! Not the Q-group, and definitely not the Army. Oracle existed outside of the government, outside of private enterprise, outside of any system, in fact. It was a force unto itself and needed to stay that way, buried deep where nobody but a select few even knew of its existence.

The good news was she had a fast and maneuverable car

and her followers did not. She approached a major intersection in the multilane road and turned off it at the very last second, crossing a couple of lanes of traffic at high speed to do so. The street was deserted so the maneuver wasn't dangerous per se, but it was darned hard to miss. If her tail was going to stay with her, he'd have to pull a similar stunt and point himself out to her in spectacular fashion. The Army training manual on a one-car pursuit said he'd go ahead and make that highly visible turn if it was more important not to lose the quarry than to be stealthy. In her experience, Army Intel wasn't too hung up on stealth and generally adhered to the brute-force theory of doing business.

Her car held the sharp swerve of the turnoff beautifully. The tail didn't follow her. Which meant one of two things. Either he had a partner vehicle she hadn't spotted and had handed off the pursuit, or he had some other means of tracking her. And as soon as the second option occurred to her, she knew without a shadow of a doubt that it was correct.

Change of plans. She caught a red light, so she turned right on red and sped away from the next intersection. She proceeded several blocks into the tall office buildings of Fairfax, Virginia. City ordinances in Washington, D.C., prevented any buildings from being taller than the U.S. Capitol's dome or the various monuments that defined the D.C. skyline. So, the necessary vertical sprawl of a major city had spilled over to this side of the Potomac. She drove until a stoplight was kind to her and turned yellow just ahead of her. She punched the accelerator and shot through the light as it turned red. She made a couple more quick turns, reversing direction and heading back west toward the Potomac River that dissected the metropolitan area in half, north to south. If a tail was still back there, the guy was better than she was.

She pointed her car toward the Beltway, the eight-lane

highway that ringed Washington and its environs. Somewhere along its perimeter, she'd no doubt find a truck stop.

Why in the world was the Army following her? There'd been rumors for years that she was on her way over the edge to la-la land. Yeah, she'd made a couple of bad calls the last few months. Or more accurately, the Oracle database had made a couple of colossally bad calls. The kind that embarrassed the Army big-time when, one after another, the theories were proven wrong. She'd been eating a steady diet of crow for about the last three months. But that still didn't explain why the Army was following her now. The only reasonable explanation she could think of was that her bosses had finally had enough of her. Maybe they were building a file of documentation to use to pull the plug on her!

Right. And now who sounded paranoid and delusional? She needed a vacation. Bad. Or maybe a new job.

Unfortunately, she couldn't breeze into her boss's office and resign her commission just like that. It was a lengthy process that could take months or be denied altogether, especially in a critically undermanned field like hers. Which was to say only a handful of other people in the Army did what she did, and Uncle Sam wasn't about to let any of them go.

The traditional intel community valued slow and steady legwork. Gradual, careful case building. Unassailable logic. Hard evidence. But she was a maverick. She speculated on the unknown. She *guessed,* for God's sake. The brass couldn't abide her style of doing business. It wasn't that she objected to traditional intelligence collection. She just believed both methods of thought were necessary to build a balanced picture of threats in the world. Maybe it wasn't so surprising after all that someone in the Army saw fit to keep close tabs on her.

She pulled into a sprawling truck stop and got out of her car. She knelt down and peered underneath the back end of her car. Nothing. Okay, maybe she really was losing her mind. She moved around to the front and laid down on the cold ground to peer underneath her car's front axle. And saw it. A round, metallic disk about the size of her palm. Shiny in contrast to the vehicle's black metal frame. The bastards had put a tracking device on her car. She pulled a screwdriver out of the tool kit in her trunk and pried the radio transmitter off the bottom of her car, then strolled past a semi with California license plates, unobtrusively popping the magnetic locator beacon onto the underside of its front bumper as she walked by. There. That should keep the Army busy for a while. Cheerfully whistling Wagner's "Ride of the Valkyrie," she made her way back to her car.

She took a circuitous route through Old Town, passing the pub where George Washington used to go to hoist an ale and the shop where Paul Revere's silver had been sold when it was new. And, of course, the ice-cream shop that made the best hot fudge sundaes this side of the Potomac. She turned down a tree-lined residential street of narrow town houses, dating back some two-hundred-fifty years. After one last check in her rearview mirror to make sure no one was behind her, she turned into a driveway beside one of the historic homes. A tall, iron security gate swung open silently. Only one Oracle agent at any given time was allowed into the town house that acted as their headquarters. Agents were required to park behind the house. Had another agent already been inside, the gate would not have opened and she'd have had to come back later. Delphi was nothing if not fanatical about secrecy.

She parked her car and hurried up the steps to the back door. A simple key lock got her inside the enclosed porch. But then the real security measures started. A retinal scanner checked her eyeball with a tiny red beam of light. Next, she entered a security code into a number pad and swiped one of her normal-looking credit cards with its secretly embedded computer chip. Last, she announced her name and password sentence to a state-of-the-art voice recognition system. And finally, a heavy steel door disguised as a regular porch door unlocked, granting her access to the interior of the house.

She stepped inside, moving quickly past the kitchen and down a narrow hallway toward the front of the house. Tonight she needed the full Oracle database. And that was housed in the library.

She stepped into a large room that dominated the entire front half of this floor. It was lined to the ceiling with shelves crammed with books on every subject under the sun. She'd love to just sit in here for a year or so and do nothing but read. Stripping off her duster, she dropped it into the nearest chair and moved to the desk at one side of the room. An innocuous-looking computer monitor and keyboard stood on top of it. And in fact, it was innocuous. This system was purely for controlling access to the actual Oracle mainframe. In and of itself, it had no real functionality.

She booted up the computer and entered the triple passwords required to get into its operating system. Then, she placed her hand flat on the system's perfectly normal-looking mouse pad, which proceeded to light up and scan her palm print. The computer screen announced that she was, indeed, Diana Lockworth. A quiet swish on the other side of the room heralded the slow glide of a pair of bookcases as they slid backward on hidden tracks and then moved to the side behind the other bookshelves. A computer terminal and a half-dozen monitors lined the secret alcove. The Oracle mainframe.

Diana moved over to the hidden computer terminal and logged on. She typed in the reference number of the threat analysis Delphi had sent her and, in the blink of an eye, the computer displayed the full text of the report on the center monitor. She read it quickly.

Oracle had made a careful analysis of the tactics used by the Q-group in its Chicago attack and determined that the plan had to have been developed by...*holy cow!*

She blinked in disbelief. The CIA? No way. That bunch would never stage a terrorist attack against Americans, and certainly not on their home turf.

Except this was one of the great strengths of Oracle. It was dispassionate. It ignored the beliefs and value judgments that humans injected into their analyses and it looked purely at facts. Of course, the flip side of that coin was the intuition and leaps of logic the human mind could make that Oracle could not. Reluctantly, she conceded the point to the computer. Technically it was possible that the CIA had trained the Q-group terrorists. The idea made her gut clench, but she read on.

The Q-group attack closely matched a training scenario the CIA had developed more than a decade ago that had proven to be highly effective and difficult to neutralize. Oracle was 97.4 percent certain that this very scenario was the basis for the Q-group's tactical plan in Chicago. Lovely. She read on grimly.

Furthermore, the original CIA scenario was *not* aimed at taking over an airport or large public space. It was designed to assassinate an individual, specifically a political figure protected by a team of highly trained bodyguards along the lines of a Secret Service detail. An extravagant explosion with maximum loss of life was used to cover up the true target of the attack.

Like Gabe Monihan. No wonder Oracle thought he was going to be killed! She continued reading, her jaw tight. If, in fact, the Q-group's mission in Chicago had been to kill Monihan and not to protest U.S. involvement in Berzhaan, which was almost a certainty according to Oracle, they were 89.9 percent likely to try again within a year. The Q-group was extremely motivated by patriotism and zealotry, and Oracle noted that such people rarely gave up if a first attempt at a goal that furthered their cause failed.

She scrolled down to the next page. And jumped as a sound intruded upon her concentration. She frowned. Nobody else should be here if she was in the building. The noise came again. It sounded like something hitting the front door. Was someone knocking on it? Who in the world would be at the door at this hour? A nosy neighbor? The Army? The CIA? Q-group?

She stood up to check it out. Then leaped for the library door as a massive sound of rending wood came from the vicinity of the front hallway. She looked out and saw splinters of wood lying on the floor, and great cracks splitting the wood trim around the door.

Ohmigod. Somebody was forcing his way into the building!

She raced for the desk and smacked the button on the access computer that closed the book panels, then jumped for the library door again. A ponderous swishing noise began behind her. *Hurry, hurry!* she begged the panels. She should've brought her service pistol with her. But who'd have guessed there'd be a break-in here of all places? She slammed the library door shut and locked it as a great tearing sound on the hallway side of it announced the failure of the front doorjamb.

Someone tried the doorknob at her hip.

"Over here," a male voice called out.

She checked behind her. The panels were about halfway closed. She threw her shoulder against the wood door to bolster it against whatever assault was about to come. She gasped as a sharp object burst through the wood beside her head. An ax! That answered how they'd gotten inside the front door so easily. Brute force, indeed. A second ax blow thumped through the door near the doorknob. This interior door wasn't made to withstand an assault like this. It would splinter into matchsticks in a matter of seconds.

She certainly didn't need to get a finger cut off or her head cleaved in two in a fruitless attempt to hold the door together. She backed away from the door as axes chewed through it like cardboard. The secret panels began their ponderous slide forward into place. She looked around frantically for a weapon. Nothing. She tipped over a delicate Queen Anne chair and stomped on it, breaking off a leg and scooping it up in her hand. It wasn't much, but it was better than nothing.

An arm reached through a jagged hole in the wood for the lock, and she jumped forward, bashing it with her makeshift club. A howl of pain and the hand withdrew. Diana jumped as she heard three sharp spits in quick succession. Crud. A silenced pistol.

The bookshelves behind her shut with a soft pop. And the hallway door exploded inward.

She backed away from the entrance quickly, her hands heading skyward, as four masked men burst into the room. She dropped the chair leg and, hands on top of her head, announced immediately, "I'm unarmed."

She stood motionless as two of the men headed for the computer at the desk and the other two rushed over to her. They grabbed her arms and yanked them behind her back, slapping on a plastic restraint and pulling it painfully tight around her wrists. She stood passively as one of the men frisked her roughly and thoroughly. But she did flinch when one of the men across the room pulled out the computer's component tower from its cabinet inside the desk and took out a baseball bat. He swung violently at the computer. Pieces of plastic flew everywhere. Another swing and the tower split open. A third swing and pieces of circuit board and wire went flying. A swift yank and he pulled the entire hard drive free of its mooring.

He grunted, "Got it. Let's go."

A voice snarled in her ear, "Back off, bitch."

And then something hard and heavy smashed into the back of her head.

5:00 A.M.

Something scratchy rubbed her cheek. She moved her head slightly and groaned as pain throbbed outward from a point at the back of her skull. Man, that hurt. She sat up carefully. Her wrists were tied together behind her back. It felt like a set of plastic handcuffs.

Dang, her head throbbed something fierce. How long had she been out? She looked at the mantel clock at the far end of the room. Ten minutes, maybe. Oh, Lord. Oracle! She whipped her head around to check the bookshelves. Piercing pain shot down her neck. *Oww.* The panels that hid the Oracle mainframe were still intact. Thank God.

The first order of business was to get her hands free. She climbed awkwardly to her feet, a bit of a trick with her hands tied behind her back. Cautiously, she stepped into the hall. The entire front door frame hung askew, the wood and metal ripped out of the walls. She headed for the kitchen, praying it actually contained some kitchen implements, like, oh, knives.

She found what she needed in a drawer beside the sink. Turning to face away from the drawer, she fished around with her fingers until she grasped the handle of a paring knife. It took some maneuvering, but she worked the blade between her wrists and sawed at the tough plastic until it burst free. She rubbed the circulation back into her hands and hugged herself to stretch her aching shoulder muscles. First order of business: clear the building and make sure the intruders were gone.

Scooping up the biggest butcher knife in the drawer, she ran upstairs and checked the conference room and equipment lockers that took up most of the second floor. She'd never been to the third floor, but she went up there and cleared the plush offices and single, small bedroom that turned out to be housed there. Empty. And interestingly enough, the computer work-stations in them were undisturbed. The intruders had specif-ically targeted the computer in the ground-floor library. Had the Oracle Agency been breached? Its security broken? How else could anyone have such specific targeting information on where Oracle could be found?

She sat down at the desk in the largest office, facing the street. The phone still worked. She dialed the emergency number she'd memorized years ago but had never had occa-sion to use. Until now. The direct contact number for Delphi. Her curiosity to hear the voice of her employer almost over-rode her urgency to report the break-in. The phone rang once. A second time. And then the receiver clicked.

An answering machine intoned a standard "leave your name and phone number at the beep" message. The female voice sounded like the same one the phone company used to announce its various automated messages. Drat. No help at all in learning more about Delphi.

She left a quick message describing the break-in and declared her intention to stay here and guard Oracle until help arrived. She hung up, staring at the dark, blank computer screen before her. Who were those four men? They were all tall, fit and strong. Efficient. Focused tightly on their mission. Pros for sure. She closed her eyes and replayed the break-in again in her head, allowing the tiny details to flow past her mind's eye. These men were distinctly different from the guy who'd broken into her apartment. She compared the two attacks. The man at her house had been slighter of build. Trained in classical martial arts. He'd relied on speed and skill rather than sheer brawn.

And then her memory registered something new about his masked face. *The skin around his eyes had been nut-brown.* Not Caucasian. But the men in the library, at least the two who jumped her, showed glimpses of fair skin. One of the men had pale blue eyes. Caucasians for sure. She'd been certain the first attack at her home was the Q-group. But this second attack? It didn't have any of the hallmarks of having been executed by the same people. Then who in the world were the *second* intruders?

A snippet from the Monihan report popped into her head. The Q-group bombing had mimicked a CIA exercise. Was it possible? Had a group of CIA agents just broken into Oracle's headquarters? An ex-CIA agent had been in Berzhaan a year or two back, making deals with some Q-group rebels. He'd been caught working with a Q-group cell in Baltimore just after the Chicago O'Hare incident. In fact, Kim Valenti had been part of the raid resulting in his capture. What was his name?

She turned on the computer in front of her, accessed the Internet and typed the access codes for Oracle. Nada. It was locked down tighter than a drum. The destruction of the access computer in the library must have triggered some sort of alarm. She turned off the computer on the desk in front of her and headed downstairs, back into the library. The access computer in there was a shambles. She went over to the mouse pad and tried to activate the secret panels. Nothing. There had to be some other method to get to the Oracle terminal. But darned if she knew what it was.

She needed the identity of the American agent who'd worked with the Q-group, but it was at home, along with her cell phone with Kim Valenti's phone numbers in it.

As she waited for someone to show up to guard Oracle or at least fix the front door, something else came back to her. One of the men said something to her right before he knocked her out. She frowned and tried to remember the growled threat. He told her to back off. *In a distinctly American accented voice.* Since the Q-group was comprised entirely of Berzhaani natives, that pretty much ruled out the Q-group as the second set of attackers.

Back off. Of what? Her assailants had made a tactical mistake. They'd in essence told her she was correctly on the trail of something or someone big. Big enough to send in thugs to stop her and Oracle. Of course, the attack might have nothing to do with her investigation and could be related to some other pot Oracle was stirring. Except her gut said otherwise. The timing of an attack on her home computer and then an immediate attack on Oracle was just too big a coincidence to be random. She jumped to the next logical conclusion. Oracle had to be right. The Q-group was working with someone else. Someone who'd staged this attack on Oracle's headquarters. But who?

She was startled just a few minutes later to hear the rumble of a truck not only coming up the street, but stopping in front of the house. She moved to the front window and peered outside cautiously. A man carrying a carpenter's belt in one hand was headed up the sidewalk. She grabbed her leather duster coat and threw it on, hiding her knife in its folds as she headed out of the library.

"Can I help you?" she asked around the remains of the front door.

"I'm here to fix your door," he replied impassively. "Wouldn't want all your Greek antiquities to be exposed to the cold air and get damaged."

Greek antiquities—Delphi. Whoa. It hadn't been more than fifteen minutes since she reported the break-in to Delphi. And there was already a repairman here? She stepped back into the library and closed the door. Quickly she pulled out her cell phone and dialed Delphi's emergency number again. She waited impatiently for the answering machine's beep.

She said with quiet urgency into the phone, "Hi, it's me again. I don't mean to be dense, but a repairman already showed up at the house to fix the door. That seems awfully fast to me. I just wanted to verify that this guy is who he says he is before I let him in. Call me back—"

The line clicked. Someone had just picked up the phone. Another click as some sort of electronic device connected. And then a strangely modulated voice spoke in her ear. "If the repairman made a reference to Greek antiquities, then he's legitimate."

The voice was neither male nor female, human nor inhuman. Computer generated, or maybe run through a scrambler. Damn. No clue as to Delphi's identity.

Diana blinked. "Uh, okay then. Should I stick around until he's done and lock up, or may I leave?"

A pause, and then the strange, disembodied voice asked, "Do you have somewhere pressing to go?"

"Yes. I think I may have a lead on who's backing the Q-group. Or at least I may know someone who has a lead."

Another pause. "Then by all means, go ahead and leave. You don't have much time to stop these people."

Even through the filter of the electronic voice alterations, Delphi's concern was clearly audible. A chill raced across her skin. It could not be a good thing if her employer, whose stock-in-trade was global-scale crises, was so worried.

Delphi's urgency latched on to the back of her neck and clung to her with sharp talons as she drove back to her house. Fortunately, no one appeared to follow her or otherwise attempt to assault her between Alexandria and Bethesda. When she got home, she did a quick walk-through to verify that nobody had been inside since she left. The hairs across doorsills and other signals she'd left behind were still in place.

She retraced her steps to the kitchen and put a pot of coffee on to brew, then pulled out her thick folder of newspaper clippings on Gabe Monihan. She sipped at a mug of strong, hot coffee while she spread out copies of the *Chicago Tribune* for the week immediately following the October Q-group attack. Kim Valenti's name appeared several times as the heroine who'd worked with FBI bomb squad member Lex Tanner to stop the terrorist's plans. The headlines all shouted about the attempted terrorist bombing in Chicago and Gabe Monihan's brush with death. Pictures of the presidential candidate splashed just beneath the headlines.

Lord, Monihan was a handsome man, in a clean-cut, All-American kind of way. The sort of guy she'd found wildly attractive until she got burned by a jerk who looked just like that in college. Three years she'd been desperately in love with Robert Danforth. She'd practically done his law school for him. And the bastard had dumped her cold the minute he made *Law Review* and graduated with honors. Told her she wasn't wife material for a man with a bright future like him. Said she wasn't classy enough—wouldn't fit in at the country club. To hell with him and the snooty crowd he represented. Who wanted to fit in with a bunch of snobs anyway? At least she'd gotten her revenge. He was a lousy lawyer without her to do his reasoning for him. He'd crashed and burned at the high-powered law firm that hired him based on his—her—grades in law school. Served him right.

She blinked away the memory, and Robert's casual, blond good looks were replaced by Gabe Monihan's serious, patrician visage on the page in front of her. Unlike Robert, the next president had dark hair, a rich, warm brown shade. And instead of blue eyes, Gabe's were light brown, a dancing golden color that hinted at dry humor beneath the keen intelligence of the man.

Work, girlfriend, work. Someone was trying to kill Mr. Wonderful and she was supposed to be figuring out who it was. Quickly, she skimmed the portions of the articles she'd highlighted. There it was. Richard Dunst. That was the guy's name. An ex-CIA agent suspected of doing arms deals with a group of Berzhaani rebels awhile back. He'd been part of the group that had taken over the UBC TV studios in Chicago to divert security attention from the airport. The newspaper article said he was being held in jail without bail under provisions of the Homeland Security Act.

She went to her computer, plugged his name into a search engine and sat back to wait. It didn't take long. Only one recent hit. He'd been arrested in a raid of a suspected Q-group headquarters in Baltimore over Columbus Day weekend and was being held by federal authorities.

Which meant Dunst was here, in Washington. The CIA was probably debriefing him now that they'd caught up with him. Typing quickly, she poked around the federal prison database but didn't find what she needed. And so, like any good Athena Academy graduate, she took matters into her own hands and engaged in a little quick extracurricular activity, hacking into the restricted portion of the federal prisoner database.

Bingo. He was being held at Bolling AFB, a gray and unobtrusive spit of land sitting in a curve of the Potomac on the south side of Washington, D.C., and home of the Defense Intelligence Agency. The prisoner database indicated only that Dunst was under investigation for possible un-American activities. Yup, the CIA was still working him over.

She needed to talk to him. ASAP. He wasn't likely to give up any significant information to her in a single interview, but she had to try. He was her only potential link between the Q-group and the CIA. The more she thought about it, the more sure she was that the Berzhaani terrorists were behind any forthcoming assassination attempt on Gabe Monihan. And if they'd gained access to more CIA training and techniques, she bloody well needed to know it if she was going to save the President.

6:00 A.M.

She stared at the clothes in her closet, pondering the perfect outfit. She opted against her Army uniform. The idea was to get Dunst to talk to her, not put him off by coming across as yet another government flunky out to milk him for information. Even if that was exactly what she was. She needed to strike a tone that would put him at ease. Professional yet casual, with a touch of sex appeal.

She settled on a pair of tailored, brown suede slacks and a pale yellow turtleneck that hugged her figure in all the right places. She brushed her golden blond hair into soft waves around her face and reached for her makeup kit, which looked more like a fishing tackle box than anything else. But then between her work and real life, she wore so many different faces that maybe it wasn't surprising she'd put a clown to shame with the array of cosmetics she used.

Today, she went for a classic look. A little eyeliner and understated eye shadow, enough mascara on her extravagant lashes to draw attention to her big blue eyes, a hint of blush over her flawless skin and coral lipstick to match the peaches-and-cream color of her complexion. This wasn't a face she put on often. Her big sister, Josie, would call it her about-damn-time-she-cleaned-up face. Her mother, vacant soul that she'd been until recently, would have patted this cheek and called her such a pretty little thing. As if she wasn't five foot seven and twenty-seven years of age. And Dad. Dad would flash her the dimples that exactly matched hers and nod in silent approval at this face. She sighed and sprayed on one of the expensive, elegant perfumes her sister was prone to giving her as gifts.

There. As good as she could manage on half a night's sleep before the sun was even up. Hopefully, the look would work on Richard Dunst. She drove down to Bolling AFB, suffering through the early phase of the morning rush hour. Washington, D.C.'s streets were designed for horses and buggies, and she was firmly convinced everyone would get places faster if the residents went back to using horse-drawn conveyances. The many government agencies downtown staggered their work hours to ease the daily gridlock, but the result was a morning rush hour that stretched from before 6:00 a.m. to nearly 10:00 a.m. She eventually wound her way past the Jefferson Memorial and its now skeletally bare promenade of cherry trees to her destination.

The gate guard at Bolling didn't raise an eyebrow at her civilian clothing in concert with her military ID. Many of the Defense Intelligence Agency staffers headquartered here worked out of uniform. But the guard did raise a brow when she asked for directions to the prisoner holding facility on base. Its very existence wasn't something most people knew about, let alone visited. He pointed to her right and rattled off a confusing series of street names and turns. Ah well. She'd find it. At least he'd given her a decent description of what the building looked like. She'd fake the rest.

A few minutes later, she pulled into a parking lot and climbed out of her car. She pulled the collar of her leather coat up around her ears. The Capitol had been in the grip of an arctic cold spell for a couple of days, and the deep freeze wasn't showing any signs of letting up today, either.

She hurried into the brown brick, three-story building and was immediately confronted by a glass security wall. She signed a stack of forms and affidavits, submitted to a body search by a female guard, was metal detected, x-rayed and thoroughly scrutinized before she was allowed to pass through the glass partition. Then there was a delay while it was determined whether or not the prisoner in question was awake yet. Frankly, she didn't care if it was a violation of Richard Dunst's civil rights to disturb his beauty rest or not. She needed to talk to the guy. Now. Eventually, a combination of sheer insistence and winning charm got her the final signature she needed to interview Dunst, awake or otherwise.

She carried her documents to a second, double-doored security area watched by guards sitting behind bulletproof glass. One guard buzzed her through while the second guard met her on the far side and walked her down a hallway as sterile as a hospital. The floor was linoleum, the lights bright and fluorescent behind steel mesh covers. Gray steel doors flanked her on either side, pockmarked with heavy, shiny steel rivets.

The guard stopped in front of one such unmarked door and punched a lengthy sequence into the number pad beside it. A green diode lit on the pad's face. Putting his weight into it, the guard pulled on the door. It slid open ponderously, its soundproof rubber stripping rubbing on the floor. She stepped into the dim room and blinked in surprise as the guard flipped on the lights. The walls were blindingly pink, an intense pep-permint shade that assaulted the eye.

"What's with the wall color?" she asked the guard.

"The shrinks-from-on-high say that Pepto-Bismol pink calms down prisoners. Makes 'em less likely to be violent."

She rolled her eyes. "Too busy puking to fight with each other?"

The guard grinned, then said more seriously, "I'll bring the prisoner to you here." He pointed at the pair of surveillance cameras in opposite corners of the small room. "We'll mon-itor the meeting with the audio feed turned off like you asked for. Dunst knows the rules. If his hands disappear from plain sight at any time, or he makes any move that might be con-strued as aggressive or threatening toward you, a guard will step in immediately. If you want a guard to come in, just look up at one of the cameras and nod. You sure you want to be left alone with this guy?"

"Yes," she answered firmly. She needed Dunst to feel as though he could talk freely. Off the record.

The guard shrugged. "Don't offer the prisoner any item whatsoever, not even a pen or a paperclip. This guy's a trained killer. Got it?"

She nodded.

"Okay then. I think they've already got Dunst out and are searching him. I'll be back with him in a couple of minutes."

The heavy door swung shut behind the guard as he left her alone in the vaultlike interview room. She tried to imagine liv-ing boxed up in a place like this for the rest of her life. And shuddered. She'd go crazy, pink walls or not.

She'd been sitting at the steel table for about three minutes when, without warning, the room plunged into darkness. Inky, cavelike blackness without a hint of light. She waited several seconds for the backup power to kick in, but nothing happened. The room stayed dark. What was going on? The blackness and the walls pressed in on her, heavier and heavier, until she thought she was going to suffocate. She *had* to get out of here.

She felt her way around the table and stretched an arm out, groping for the door. A step into the void. And another. And then her hand encountered cold metal. With both hands, she felt for the door handle. Please God, let her not be locked in here. They'd told her they would lock her in here with Dunst once he arrived. She found the latch and pushed down on the thumb lever. Putting her weight into it, she leaned on the door. It moved. Thank God. It slid open to reveal another void of total darkness. Jeez. Didn't they have any emergency generators or something in this place? Using the wall as a guide, she turned to her right and began to make her way down the hall toward the exit.

Something brushed against her in the dark. And instantly, a powerful blow slammed into her collarbones. A human arm contracted, snakelike, whipping around her neck and yanking her off balance. Scared out of her skin, she screamed as loud as she could. The piercing noise echoed weirdly, amplified to an almost inhuman pitch by the long hallway. A sweaty hand slapped over her mouth, cutting off the sound. It yanked her down violently. She crouched awkwardly, still wrapped in the man's powerful grip.

A voice snarled in her ear in a bare whisper, "Shut up if you don't want the bastard to kill you."

No sooner had the words left her assailant's mouth than a deafening explosion cracked. The hard body against hers lurched spasmodically and the arm around her neck went slack. The guy toppled over, knocking her to the floor with him.

"*Shit*. Shit, shit, shit, shit, shit," the man now sprawled half on top of her chanted under his breath. "Can you shoot, lady?" he ground out.

"Yeah," she gasped under his crushing weight.

"I dropped my pistol. I think it fell against the far wall. Find it, will you, so the prisoner doesn't grab it."

Prisoner. This was one of the guards. And someone must be trying to break out of the jail. She wiggled out from under him, which was no small feat. Crawling on her hands and knees and feeling around on the floor in the dark, her hands encountered something slippery and wet. A metallic smell announced that it was blood. She jerked her hands away. Who'd shot the guard beside her? And where was that blasted gun? On this highly waxed linoleum, the darn thing could've slid halfway down the hall.

And then she heard a rhythmic noise above the rasping breaths of the wounded guard. Slapping. Like feet hitting the floor. Running. Toward her from the direction of the cell block. In this dark, it was impossible to tell if it was another guard charging to the rescue or the prisoner making a break for it.

She froze, crouched by the wall, straining to gauge the running person's distance from her. To tackle or not to tackle. That was the question. A door opened at the far end of the hall and a sliver of light spilled into the narrow space. Several voices shouted. They echoed so loudly she couldn't understand a word. But they sounded furious.

Another shot rang out from the direction of the running man, and the door slammed shut once more, plunging the hall back into blackness, made all the thicker by the brief exposure of her eyes to light.

Acting purely on instinct, she reached out as the running footsteps approached. Something hard cracked into her forearm. Felt like a shin. A grunt and a thud. She dived for the guy, but he threw her off violently. She grabbed again, coming up with nothing more than a fistful of hair as he jerked away from her grasp. She wrapped her arms around whatever she could grab. Felt like an ankle. What must have been a fist connected with her left ear. She lost her grip on the guy's leg, and heard him scramble off in the dark. Where were the damned emergency lights?

She couldn't go anywhere for now, so she crawled back to the injured guard. Maybe she could help him, at any rate.

"Where are you hit?" she whispered.

Nothing. The guy must've passed out. Not good. She prayed it was pain that had knocked the guy out and not blood loss. His breathing sounded terrible. He was shot in the chest cavity, then. She felt around on his upper body, following the wetness on his shirt to a small, round wound under his left arm. Lucky shot. It had just missed his bulletproof vest and hit him in the armpit. She couldn't tell the angle of entry in the dark to take a guess at the damage he'd suffered. Based on the sucking noises coming from him, his left lung was collapsed at a minimum.

She jumped as a barrage of shots exploded from the direction the prisoner'd just gone. Hopefully, the guards had just killed the jerk.

Meanwhile, the guy beside her sounded bad. It was damned hard to render first aid by feel without any supplies or equipment whatsoever. For lack of anything more to do in the inky dark, she put her hand over the hole and applied pressure to it. The sucking noise abated some.

It seemed to take forever, but the overhead lights finally flickered back on. Oh, God. There was blood *everywhere*. Her guard was breathing but unconscious, his face deathly pale. Probably a combination of blood loss and shock. She shouted for a medic and prayed someone heard her in the chaos that erupted as the doors opened and a SWAT team burst into the hall.

"I'm Army," she cried out. "This guard's been shot. Someone ran past me that way in the dark." She gestured with her head.

An EMT took over care of the guard's chest wound while another guard helped her to her feet.

It seemed unfair somehow that *she* ended up being escorted into a room and interrogated herself. A crime-scene investigator examined her hands under a magnifying glass and picked tiny fibers off her palm with tweezers.

"As I suspected," the guy announced after examining the fibers closely.

"What?" Diana asked.

"A wig. This is fake hair. Won't get any DNA from it."

Nonetheless, the guy took away the bits of hair she'd grabbed for analysis. Finally, after she'd given the same statement to no less than four different people, a man in an expensive suit stepped into the room. Not a beat cop in threads like that.

"Captain Lockworth, I'm Agent Flaherty. Thank you for answering our questions so patiently. How are you doing?"

She noticed he didn't say who he was an agent of. Fine. She could play that game, too. "I'm all right. Ready for a few answers of my own."

He perched a hip on the corner of the room's lone table and smiled pleasantly. "Fire away."

"Who raced by me in the dark?"

"A prisoner trying to escape. Name's Roscoe Dupree."

The guy watched her intently as he said the name. As if it was supposed to mean something to her. In fact, it did tickle at the edge of her memory. She'd heard that name somewhere before. "Did he get away?" she asked curiously.

"Unfortunately, yes. But I have every confidence we'll pick him up soon. And what did you say brought you here today?"

Her mind snapped back to business. "I'm here to speak to

Richard Dunst. It's a matter of great urgency. While I realize you've just had an escape and things are crazy around here, I still really need to speak to him."

"That would be difficult, Captain. Roscoe Dupree *is* Richard Dunst."

Memory flooded her. *Of course.* Roscoe Dupree was yet another name for the man known as Dunst. He'd used the Dupree identity in Berzhaan when he'd dealt with a Berzhaani rebel group that was trying to overthrow the government there. He'd worked under the Dunst name when he obtained a bomb and gave it to the Q-group to use to kill Gabe Monihan in Chicago. And he'd *escaped?* Today of all days? Could Dunst, a trained killer, be involved in the plan to assassinate the next President of the United States on this, his inauguration day? Surely that was no coincidence. *Not good. Not good at all.*

"What can you tell me about how he escaped?" she asked the agent urgently.

Flaherty shrugged. "We don't know for sure."

She took a calming breath. No sense making this guy any more suspicious than he already was. "I'd like to hear your best guess," she asked quietly. "It's important. National security important."

He looked her in the eye and she held his gaze for a long moment. She saw him weighing her words. Weighing her. This guy smelled like FBI all the way. And clearly, he didn't trust her completely. But she saw with relief the instant when he decided for reasons of his own to answer her question. Frankly, she didn't care what game he was playing as long as she got what she needed.

"Dupree—Dunst—got a knife and a disguise—presumably to wear once he got out of here—from somewhere. Overpowered a guard in the hallway while en route to the interview with you. Took the guard's gun and ran down this hallway, briefly impeded by you."

"How'd the power go out? Doesn't this place have emergency power of some sort?"

Flaherty's jaw rippled. "We don't know yet how both the primary and backup power systems went down."

"How did Dunst get out the door? Surely it fails to a locked mode in a facility like this."

An outright clench tensed Flaherty's jaw this time. He gritted out, "The lockdown mode on the exit Dunst used never engaged properly. He ran up, pulled the damn door open and shot his way out."

"How'd he egress the area? Surely you'd have caught him by now if he were on foot. How did a getaway car get through the front gate?"

"Good question. We've got film but the license plate was intentionally obscured."

Just like the car the guy who broke into her house used. She asked sharply, "Did they use a black plastic garbage bag over the plate? Drive a late model silver sedan? Four doors? Foreign make?"

The guy lurched to his feet. Paced a lap of the tiny space and came back to the table, planting his palms on it and leaning toward her aggressively. "And just how in the hell did you know that? Are you working with Dunst? It's pretty damned convenient that you showed up at this ungodly hour, insisting that Dunst be dragged out of his cell and brought out here."

She reared back in shock. "I am *not* working with Richard Dunst! I'm here because I believe he's involved in a conspiracy to kill Gabe Monihan. I want to nail this bastard!"

Flaherty stared at her in silence. She knew the technique. Guilt makes people babble to fill the silence. She used the moment to think hard. Flaherty was right about one thing. Dunst must have had inside help to slip him the weapon. He also needed technologically advanced help from outside to hack into the building's electrical system. How else would both systems have failed at once? This building was undoubtedly hooked into the DOD power grid, which was hardened against all manner of attacks from without. It was a favorite target of hackers, and a damned hard one to get into.

Inside help. High-level hacking. Getaway car in place. Prison locks tampered with. And the whole thing precisely timed and executed. Not the work of a few radical yahoos. Somebody smart, powerful and knowledgeable planned and executed Dunst's escape. She seriously needed to run all this through Oracle's analysis program.

Flaherty's cell phone rang, and he listened briefly before pocketing it again. "The getaway car was just found. It was abandoned down by the river. Apparently our man got away by boat."

Damn. Dunst was free. She looked up at the agent. "Am I free to go, now? This escape just increased my workload for today dramatically."

"Not a chance, lady."

She winced. Time was the one thing she couldn't spare right now. But she also couldn't afford to get combative with this guy if she wanted to get out of here anytime soon.

He fired a question at her aggressively. "How long have you been working for the Q-group?"

She lurched. "Q-group? Me? You've got to be kidding."

"Answer the question," he snapped.

How was she supposed to respond to an absurd accusation like that? It was a Have-you-stopped-beating-your-wife-yet sort of question. "I do *not* work for the Q-group," she stated emphatically.

"Then why is your e-mail address plastered all over the Q-group chat room?"

She stared in undisguised shock. Who was this guy? How in the world did he even know what her e-mail address was, let alone that she'd been visiting Q-group hangouts online? And how was it that he was here, now, at an obscure prisoner facility, questioning her? Alarm bells clanged wildly in her gut.

Flaherty commented smoothly, "Army pay doesn't go too far in an expensive town like this, does it? A nice car, a nice house, nice clothes—" he eyed her sleek suede pants pointedly "—they all cost big bucks. How does a girl like you do it?"

He was accusing her of going over to the enemy for money? Betraying her country in the name of designer fashion? She answered the guy's slimy innuendo through gritted teeth. "I have a trust fund. A big, fat one from my grandfather."

The agent crossed his arms. "Ah, yes. Joseph Lockworth. Former director of the CIA. Pretty handy to be related to someone like that who can hide the family skeletons."

A memory surged forward in her brain, unbidden.

Crouching at the top of the stairs in her flannel nightgown, clutching Lammy, her precious stuffed lamb. She'd hauled that poor toy with her everywhere in those first days after The Incident.

Something bad had happened to Mommy. One day she was her laughing, smiling, soft-smelling self and gave the best hugs in the world. And the next day, she got all sad and had a funny look in her eyes all the time. And stopped hugging.

Men in suits kept coming to the door. Daddy tried at first to make them go away, but they never did. They yelled at Mommy sometimes and asked her questions that made her cry. One time, Gramps came over and yelled at Mommy, but he stopped after a while. He said he supposed every family had a skeleton in the closet. He said he'd do his best to cover up this one.

For weeks after that, she'd been terrified of closets. She kept expecting a dead, bony body to jump out of one at her. Her big sister, Josie, was terribly brave and didn't mind opening closet doors, which was the only way she ever got clean clothes to wear. Daddy was too sad to notice whether or not she wore the same thing to school three days in a row.

"How much is Q-group paying you?" Flaherty barked.

She enunciated each word clearly. "I...do...not...work...for...Q-group. I work for Army Intelligence and I'm trying to apprehend those bastards. Now, are you going to charge me with something or may I get out of here and go try to track down the killer *you* just let escape before he kills someone?"

"You do not have jurisdiction to pursue an escaped fugitive, Captain. You get near the Dunst investigation and screw it up, and I'll hang you from the highest tree I can find. You got that?"

She glared at him. "Yeah, I got it. And here's one for you. You get in the way of *my* investigation of Q-group and a possible plot to assassinate the President-elect, and I'll see *you* hanged. You got that?"

Flaherty met her glare for several long seconds. He curled his lip in an ugly sneer. "Get out of here. And don't even think about leaving town."

7:00 A.M.

She wasted no time getting the hell out of Dodge before Flaherty changed his mind and decided to hold her indefinitely under the Homeland Security Act or some such loophole-ridden law.

She pulled away from the building in her car and fumbled in her purse for her cell phone. With shaking hands, she started to dial the emergency phone number to Delphi. And as she did so, the gray-white bulk of DIA headquarters, with its bristling array of antennae and satellite dishes on the roof, loomed in her windshield. She didn't dare make the call from here and risk having it intercepted. Delphi was adamant that his or her existence must never be revealed to anyone.

She guided her car off base and relaxed a bit when Bolling's guard shack disappeared from her rearview mirror. She headed south on the Anacostia Parkway for a few minutes, then turned onto a random side street and stopped in the first parking lot she came to. The apartment complex around her was disreputable looking at best and a multibuilding crack den at worst. She locked her car door and dialed Delphi's phone number.

The electronically altered voice she now recognized picked up immediately. "What did Dunst say?" Delphi asked without preamble.

How in the world did Delphi know that was where she'd been? Was *Delphi* involved with Dunst somehow? Diana asked carefully, "How did you know I went to talk to him?"

An electronic chuckle. "You are not the only person in the world who can tease information out of a computer. Your military ID number was logged into the Bolling AFB holding center's computer record of visitors. It was an easy matter once Oracle got that hit to search the holding center's list of prisoners and figure out who you were there to see. Good thinking to track down the connection between the CIA and Q-group."

She warmed at the compliment from her employer. She hadn't been getting too many of those recently from her Army superiors. "That's why I'm calling you. Richard Dunst escaped about thirty minutes ago."

The silence on the line was deafening. Finally, Delphi asked grimly, "What do you propose to do next?"

"It's time to warn Monihan."

"Agreed."

"Except," Diana added, "we don't have time to go through all the red tape of convincing the Secret Service I'm not a kook and should be taken seriously. I need to cut to the chase and get word directly to Monihan's security detail. I was hoping you could help me with that."

A short pause. "I'll see what I can do. I'll be in touch."

Diana disconnected the call and pulled back out into traffic. She made her way across Washington toward home. She needed a shower and new clothes. Her sweater and slacks were covered in blood.

She made reasonably good time across town since she was traveling against the inbound flow of people. Man, it felt good to pull into her driveway. Some morning it had already been.

She stepped out of a quick shower and pulled on a pair of faded jeans and a skinny little black sweater with just enough angora in it to make it delicious against her skin. She was bent over, head upside down, toweling her hair dry when the phone rang. Groping around on her nightstand, she found the phone and stuck the receiver under the towel.

"Hello?"

The digital voice of Delphi said briefly, "You have an appointment with Gabe Monihan in twenty minutes. He can give you five minutes. He's at the Mayflower Hotel. Go to the concierge desk and identify yourself, and they'll ring upstairs for an escort."

The line disconnected. Gabe Monihan himself? She'd only been hoping to talk to one of the guys on his security detail. Dang, Delphi was good.

Then the rest of the phone message hit her. Twenty minutes? At the Mayflower? That was downtown—a good thirty-minute trip on a normal day. Crud. She jammed her feet into a pair of soft leather boots, grabbed her purse and flew out of the house. For once in her life, she succumbed to putting on makeup in the car. No way was she walking into a meeting with the President-elect of the United States without at least a little mascara on. She turned the heater on high and blew it at her face to at least dry the hair around her face. Its natural waves formed a golden halo by the time she hit Connecticut Avenue.

She broke every speed record she'd ever set and thankfully

didn't run into any speed traps en route. She managed to careen into the parking garage beneath the ritzy Mayflower Hotel with two minutes to spare. She jumped out of the car, raced up the stairs rather than waiting for an elevator and all but skidded to a stop in front of the concierge desk exactly on time. Had it been anyone but Delphi who put her through the last twenty minutes' worth of panic, she'd have had some choice words for him right about now.

"May I help you, ma'am?" a suave man in a suit asked her pleasantly.

"My name's Diana Lockworth. I'm here to see Gabriel Monihan. I have an appointment," she huffed between gulps of air.

The concierge picked up a phone. "Miss Lockworth is here for an appointment." A pause and the guy hung up. "Someone will be down to get you."

She had just enough time to register the gilded marble opulence of the lobby before a burly man in a boring suit stepped off an elevator. Even if she'd seen this guy just walking down a street somewhere, she'd have pegged him as Secret Service. He had the alert stare that never stayed in one place, the calm assurance, the bulge under the armpit and a tall, fit physique that couldn't add up to anything else. He walked up to her, eyeing her up and down, no doubt checking for places to hide a weapon and not scoping out her female attributes.

"Miss Lockworth, come with me."

She followed the guy to an elevator, watching as he pulled a key out of his pocket and inserted it in the keyhole on the button pad inside the door. He pushed an unmarked floor button and the doors swished shut quietly. As he put it away, she noticed the key was attached to what looked like a thin, steel lanyard that disappeared somewhere inside his pant pocket. Yup. Secret Service all the way. They took being careful to levels of paranoia she couldn't even imagine.

And so she wasn't surprised when the elevator door opened and she was whisked a short distance down a hallway into a room that had been converted into a full-blown security checkpoint. She and her purse were x-rayed, her drivers' license and military ID run through a computer, and her right thumb fingerprinted on an electronic pad. Eventually, after she checked out clean, another Secret Service agent showed her through an adjoining door into a large suite.

Large being the operative word. The place sprawled like her grandfather's mansion in Chevy Chase. Desks, computers and phones that jarred against the sleek, tasteful decor of the place were swallowed up like minnows in the belly of a whale. Clusters of people stood in various parts of the main room. Several more Secret Service agents sipped coffee by the wet bar. A pair of men peered at a sheaf of papers one of them held, apparently discussing what was written on it. At least six closed doors ringed the room.

The place was quiet, but energy fairly crackled through the space. The about-to-be most powerful man in the world was behind one of those doors. She could *feel* his presence. Maybe staring at his pictures all over her bedroom wall for so many weeks had created some sort of psychic link between them. Whatever it was, it zinged all the way to her fingertips.

The Secret Service agent handed her off to a secretary who spoke quietly into a wireless headset. A door behind the secretary opened, and a face she recognized from heavy media coverage of it stepped out. Except it wasn't Gabe Monihan. It was Thomas Wolfe, the charismatic senator from California who'd been Gabe's rival through the primaries and had become his vice presidential running mate at the Democratic convention.

Wolfe was daunting in person, tall and rail thin, in an intense, ascetic way. His hair was black shot through with silver and combed back from a high, sloping forehead. His eyes glowed with even more intensity than the Secret Service agent's had, giving away the zealotry of the man's personality. No surprise he'd been one of the most feared federal prosecutors in America before entering politics.

Diana blinked as Wolfe stepped forward and held a hand out to her. He crushed her hand in a bony, powerful grip. "Miss Lockworth. What can I do for you this morning?"

"Uhh, I'm here to meet with President-elect Monihan," she replied, startled at this insanely high-powered meet-and-greet. It had been impressive enough that Delphi got five minutes of Monihan's time on less than an hour's notice, but Wolfe, too?

Wolfe cast a quick look around the huge suite and took her by the arm, leading her away from the secretary's desk. He steered her over by a window and all but hid her behind a potted palm tree. "The President-elect is extremely busy with last-minute preparations for his inauguration. What is it that brings you here today? I'm sure I can help you with it."

There was something about this conversation that didn't feel right. Maybe it was the way he'd intercepted her, or the furtive way he'd looked around the suite before tucking her over here in this corner. But her suspicions were definitely aroused. She answered Wolfe smoothly, "It's a personal matter, and I'm afraid I really must speak directly with Mr. Monihan about it."

Wolfe's cold gaze bored into her. "What sort of personal matter? How did you get in here? You're not here to try some tawdry extortion scheme, are you?"

Extortion? She blinked in shock. What ever gave the guy that idea? "Absolutely not, sir! I'm an Army Intelligence officer and I'm here on official business." Although in jeans and a sweater, with half-dry hair, she had to admit she hardly looked the part. Nonetheless, she was distinctly disinclined to tell this guy another word about her business with Gabe. Whoops. President-elect Monihan. She had to quit thinking about the guy by his first name like that. He was about to be her commander-in-chief, for goodness' sake.

Wolfe exhaled sharply. "We do not have time around here for people like you to play games. If you won't speak to me about your business, then Gabe Monihan certainly doesn't need to hear about it. I think it's time for you to leave, Miss Lockworth."

He reached out to take her arm, but she stepped back quickly. And crashed into the potted palm. She landed on her behind with a thud. Fronds waved wildly overhead, but fortunately the whole thing didn't tip over. A big pile of dirt whooshed out onto the floor, however, and several assorted aides and flunkies rushed over to clean up the mess and drag her up off her rear, which was wedged firmly between the palm's trunk and its pot.

She reached out and took the first hand that appeared in front of her eyes. Heat and electricity shot up her arm and down her spine. The hand tugged, and she popped free and onto her feet. She looked up into a gorgeous pair of amber eyes. Amusement danced in their golden depths.

Oh my God. Gabriel Monihan. In the flesh.

"How's the coconut hunting?" he asked dryly, his whiskey-smooth voice sending a whole new round of tingles shooting down her spine.

"Not good," she replied deadpan. "Turns out it was only a homicidal date palm. Not a coconut in sight."

The amused glint in the President-elect's gaze faded as he looked over her shoulder at Wolfe. "I've heard those date palms can be downright pushy. They horn in all over the place where they're not needed or wanted."

She blinked. What was up with that edge in his voice? The heavy double entendre? Clearly, it was aimed at Wolfe. For the barest instant, Gabe's gaze went a hard, crystalline gold. And then he was all pleasant smiles again. "And who might you be, ma'am? I'd venture to guess you know who I am."

She smiled back at him. "I'm Captain Diana Lockworth, Mr. President-elect. I have an appointment with you. Or at least I did. My five minutes on your schedule just expired." And as she tried to turn her wrist to look at her watch, she realized Gabe was still holding her hand. And just what was the etiquette of holding the President-elect's hand, anyway?

He tucked her hand under his arm and turned to walk toward a door on the far side of the room all in one smooth movement. *Well, there you have it. You tuck your hand under the President-elect's elbow and let him lead you wherever he wants to.*

She became aware of waves of hostility fairly slamming into her shoulder blades. Must be Wolfe back there, glaring a hole in her head. Gabe led her into a combination living-dining room. It was much smaller than the first room. Much more intimate. Only a few Secret Service agents lounged around the margins of this space.

"Have you had breakfast yet, Captain Lockworth?"

"No, as a matter of fact, I haven't, sir." And as soon as the words left her mouth, her stomach shouted its protest at being ignored.

"Dine with me."

It wasn't exactly a command, but the words were uttered by a man who clearly was used to getting what he wanted most of the time. Okay. All of the time.

She replied, "Are you sure? I know how busy you must be today, getting ready for the inauguration and all...."

He shrugged. "That's what I have speech writers for. It's

their job to panic. Besides, we finalized the inaugural address last night. I don't have a blessed thing to do today except go talk to a judge at two o'clock."

"Well, you do have to look pretty and smile nicely for the cameras. Maybe have a little lunch. Go to a parade. Oh, and become President of the United States," she retorted. Dang it! When was she going to learn to stop and think before she just blurted out the first thing that popped into her head?

He laughed aloud. "You make it sound like I'm taking some sort of monastic vow for the rest of my life. It's not a prison sentence, you know."

Every head in the room swiveled at the sound of his laughter. From the surprised expressions on people's faces, she gathered it wasn't a sound they'd heard much lately.

She grinned back at him, enjoying the sparring. "Monastic vows? I should hope not. A good-looking guy like you ought to—" She broke off sharply. Holy cow, she'd done it again. She felt heat creep up her cheeks in a telltale blush. The curse of her fair skin.

"Ought to what?" he asked wryly.

"Nothing, Mr. President-elect," she mumbled. "Never mind." She ventured a peek up from her crisply starched napkin. Yup. Grinning like the Cheshire Cat, he was.

"Call me Gabe."

Uh, right. On a first name basis with the man who was about to be President.

The butler saved her. He served her a bowl of fresh strawberries just then, ladling clotted cream over the dewy red globes. She ordered an omelet stuffed with the works in a muted voice, while Gabe ordered French toast with extra syrup.

"I'm sorry," she murmured. "You must think I'm a complete bumpkin."

"Not at all," he replied smoothly. "I think you're charming."

She smiled reluctantly. "I don't deserve that, but thank you."

His gaze met hers for a moment, but then slid away as the butler stepped between them to pour coffee. Whoa. That had been a definite spark of interest in his eyes. Of course, it wasn't as if he was an old man or anything. For Heaven's sake, he was only thirty-eight. Younger than Jack Kennedy by seven years when he took office. *Business, Diana. Business.*

"Uh, sir, I came here today because I believe your life may be in danger."

Gabe's fork paused for the barest instant before it continued its path to his mouth. He responded utterly casually, "Of course my life's in danger. Do you have any idea how many enemies I inherit with this job? At any rate, let's finish breakfast before we talk about anything serious."

She frowned. For all the world, she'd swear he'd just blown her off. Except he looked her square in the eye and nodded reassuringly the moment the words left his mouth. Now what was that all about? But it wasn't as if she was about to tell the next Commander-in-Chief he couldn't eat his breakfast in peace. He didn't want to talk with wagging ears around, maybe?

She studied him surreptitiously as she ate her fluffy omelet. Her bedroom wall didn't do justice to him in the least. The pictures didn't capture his energy, the sense of purpose that radiated from him. This was a man on a mission. Not that it was any surprise. Everyone knew about his past. His alcoholic father died in a fiery car crash when Gabe was eleven. Rumor persisted that the wreck had been a suicide to escape crushing gambling debts that were coming due. Gabe had stepped up to the plate and become the man of the house, working a paper route before school and mowing lawns after school to help support his devastated mother. In his spare time he'd still managed to get straight As and quarterback his high school football team to the State Championship. The All-American boy.

Their backgrounds weren't so different. She'd lost her mother to a drug-induced haze, he'd lost his father to booze. Although where his old man had died, her mother had just languished in a clinical depression so deep and so irreversible she might as well have been dead. So how was it he came out of the experience as bright and shiny as a gold coin, while she came out of it running in the opposite direction from the very system that embraced him?

"That's a pretty grave look on your face, Captain Lockworth. Am I going to have to solve world hunger for you after breakfast?"

One corner of her mouth lifted reluctantly into a smile. "Oh, that you could. And please, call me Diana."

His gaze waxed serious for a moment. "I wish it were that easy to solve world hunger. But even the office of President can't put a dent in that particular problem." He wiped his mouth and laid the linen napkin down on the table beside his plate. "But maybe I can fix your problem."

"Actually, I'm the one trying to fix *your* problem," she replied.

One sable eyebrow lifted. "Indeed?" He got up from the table and came around to hold her chair for her, cutting off the butler who'd stepped forward to do the same service.

She took the hand he offered her and stood up. When was the last time somebody helped her up from breakfast in such gallant fashion? She thought about it for a second. That would be never. And there weren't even any paparazzi or reporters around to justify the display. Was he actually one of those guys who did such things out of a natural impulse to do so?

He led her away from the table and over toward a wall of floor-to-ceiling glass windows that lent a panoramic view of Connecticut Avenue below. "Great view, isn't it?" he said rather more loudly than necessary.

Not especially. It was just a gray street on a cold day with dirty cars hurrying by, along with a few pedestrians bundled up to their ears. "Uh, yeah. Great."

Under his breath, he asked, "So who harbors this dark plot to assassinate me that you're so worried about?"

She had no idea why they were practically whispering, but she mimicked his tone. "I'm convinced the Q-group rebels who tried to bomb Chicago O'Hare were not there just to make a statement about U.S. involvement in Berzhaan. I'm convinced that was a smoke screen to hide the real target of their attack—you."

A pulse abruptly throbbed in Gabe's temple and his eyes blazed. He put his hand on her elbow and reached for the sliding-glass door in front of them. With her peripheral vision, she caught the alarmed jump of the three Secret Service agents across the room. But then Gabe's fingers closed on her arm in a painful vise that left her no choice but to step outside with him or have her arm wrenched out of its socket.

She stumbled to a stop as a biting wind swirled around them. Gabe pulled the door shut behind them and pointedly turned his back on the room behind them. Worried about lip-readers, maybe? He demanded, "How in the hell do you know the Q-group was out to kill me that day?"

She pivoted until her left shoulder touched his right shoulder, her back squarely to the room behind them. "I can explain that to you in more detail later. What's important right now is that they're going to try again. Today."

Eavesdroppers and lip-readers forgotten, he turned to stare down at her in shock. He bit out a single terse command. "Start talking, lady."

8:00 A.M.

She took a deep breath. "The database I use to gather and compare intel made a definitive match between the tactics used in Chicago by the Q-group cell there and an old assassination training scenario. Of a single target. One that's surrounded by bodyguards and heavy security. And it was developed by the CIA."

The full brunt of Gabe Monihan's intelligence bored into her as his gaze went nearly black. "Do you have any proof that the CIA was behind the attempt on my life?" he bit out.

"None," she replied quickly. "Nor am I making that allegation. However, as you probably know, Richard Dunst, an ex-CIA agent who's been known to mess around in Berzhaani politics, was involved in the Q-group attacks last October. I think he may have trained the terrorists who attacked you. He's a trained killer himself."

Gabe's gaze narrowed. "And?"

Perceptive guy. He assumed, accurately, that she had to have more news than that to have asked for five minutes of his time today of all days.

"And Dunst escaped from the detention facility at Bolling Air Force Base a little over an hour ago."

"Jesus." Gabe ran a distracted hand through his hair. "Does Owen Haas know this?"

"Who's Owen Haas?"

"The agent-in-charge of my security detail."

"Ah. Actually, I was expecting to speak to him this morning when I asked for a meeting. And no, he doesn't know, yet. But I'll be glad to tell him everything I know."

Gabe stepped forward and grabbed the wrought-iron railing in front of him, gazing down at the street below.

"Sir, if you don't mind my asking..." She hesitated to interrupt his intense concentration.

"Ask," he ordered tersely.

"Do you have any idea why the Q-group might have tried to kill you last fall?"

He frowned. Shook his head. "None."

She asked, "What's your policy on Berzhaan? Have you said something specific that would inflame the Q-group?" She'd read everything she could get her hands on about Gabe's stance on Berzhaan, and nothing she'd run across had struck her as inflammatory enough to cause the Q-group to come after him. If anything his policies promised to be significantly more to the Q-group's liking than Whitlow's had been.

"I've argued against sending American troops there. I'm in favor of economic and educational aid sent to them via a neutral government of the Berzhaani people's choosing. Nothing that should've sent the Q-group tearing over here to off me."

"What about the Secret Service? Do they take this threat seriously?"

He exhaled sharply. "Oh, they took the Q-group seriously, all right. Except every last one of the terrorists who staged the Chicago attack is safely behind bars. The Secret Service considers the threat neutralized, and so did I until about a minute ago."

"I've been tracking more Q-group sympathizers online for a couple of months now. The FBI caught their cell in Chicago, but that's far from the last of the Q-group's operatives. I'm convinced they've got another cell here in Washington that's going to attack you today."

"I wouldn't be surprised if you're exactly right," he said quietly.

She frowned. "I don't mean to be impertinent, but if that's the case, then why are we standing out here alone having this conversation with our backs to the door so no one can read our lips?"

He looked at her in surprise for an instant, and then spit out a single word. "Wolfe."

Okay. There must be a leap of logic in there somewhere, but she'd missed it. "What about Wolfe?" she asked cautiously.

"He's convinced I'm not fit to be president. That I'm suffering post-traumatic stress disorder as a result of the attack and won't be able to make rational decisions regarding national security or foreign policy."

Yikes! She recalled abruptly the cold exchange of looks over her head between the two men while she sat in the potted palm.

"I need you to do me a favor," Gabe asked abruptly.

"Of course. You're the Commander-in-Chief…."

He cut her off with a sharp, short hand gesture. "Not yet, I'm not. I'm asking this of you, personally. Not because you're about to work for me."

"Anything," she replied promptly. "You name it."

"Don't tell anyone about your suspicions."

"But—"

"No buts," he interrupted firmly. "If Wolfe gets wind of the fact that I think the Q-group's going to try to kill me, he'll eat me for lunch. He'll go to Congress so fast it'll make your head spin and insist that I'm crazy. Not Presidential material. I barely dodged that bullet right after the election. Did you know the bastard actually went to the Supreme Court and asked them under what circumstances he could have me removed from office or block me from taking office?"

Whoa. No wonder there'd been such a glacial chill between the two men.

"And he's your second in command why?"

"I needed the votes to get elected. The party was split between him and me, and our respective constituents would be damned before they'd vote for the other guy. It was the only way to cobble together the numbers we needed to win the White House."

She looked up at Gabe candidly. "For what it's worth, he tried to waylay me when I first got to the suite this morning. Insisted that I tell him my business instead of you. Said you were too busy getting ready for the inauguration. I refused to talk to him and he was in the middle of throwing me out when you fished me out of the palm tree."

Gabe nodded in stony silence as if that information didn't surprise him. Their gazes locked in silent communication and understanding flowed between them. Oh yes. She knew exactly what it was like to be wrongly accused of being crazy. She knew exactly how the injustice of it twisted and roiled like a serpent in Gabe's gut, galling him to no end as long as he was helpless to combat the charge.

Finally, she broke the charged silence. "Will you at least tell Agent Haas to be on his toes, today?"

"I will," he promised solemnly. "But you've got to do something for me, as well."

"Besides go against my better judgment and keep the plot against you to myself?"

He reached out and took both of her hands in his. "Be careful. These Q-group guys are the real deal. They're serious terrorists."

His golden gaze was mesmerizing, his touch pure seduction tracing down her spine. Whether his attraction to her was genuine or just a slick politician's blatant manipulation, she couldn't tell. And at the moment, her pounding pulse didn't care. "Of course."

His hands tightened on hers. "Thank you. I'm sorry you got sucked into this mess."

She smiled back and said lightly, "Last time I checked, it's my job to investigate conspiracies. And I'm the one who came to you."

He released her hands, but his fingers trailed across her palms as though he was reluctant to lose the physical contact with her. His withdrawal left her feeling cold and vulnerable, all of a sudden.

He fished in an inner pocket of his suit coat and emerged with a business card. "Here's my personal cell phone number. I'll be carrying my phone with me today."

She took the card and commented, "Remember to turn off the ringer while you take the oath of office?"

He smiled. "Thanks for the tip." His smile faded slowly, leaving a residual glow between them. More seriously, he added, "Keep me updated on any new developments."

She pulled out one of her own cards and scribbled her cell phone number on the back of it. And was just reaching out to hand it to him when something caught her attention over his shoulder. Something that didn't belong there. Something that set off an alarm in her head.

A window in a building across the street had just slid open

a few inches, and something was coming out of it. Something circular. Made of blue-black steel. A metallic gleam caught the dull morning light.

Holy shit.

She dived for Gabe, tackling him around the waist with the full weight of her body, driving him down to the ground in a single heavy fall. In the millisecond it took her to register that she was lying full length on top of him, something incredibly heavy landed on top of her, squashing her flat and forcing all the air from her lungs.

Gabe grunted beneath her, as well. Three Secret Service agents plastered themselves on top of her and Gabe, acting as human shields for their charge. One of the men ordered tersely, "Don't move, either of you. We'll neutralize the threat before we try to get you inside. It's too damn exposed out here to move you."

As the seconds ticked by and no gunshots were forthcoming from across the street, she became more and more aware of the intimacy of her situation with Gabe. She was learning some fascinating things about the next President of the United States. He was in hard, athlete's condition underneath his conservative suit. His body actually filled out the suit's broad shoulders, not bulky pads. She also learned she fit against him perfectly, their legs intertwining as if they'd been lovers for years. And when she shifted her weight a little, his stomach contracted into a rock-hard washboard beneath her belly. Up close, his eyes could blaze brighter than the noonday sun, incinerating her from the inside out.

"Sorry about that," she murmured.

His mouth curved up into a wry grin. "No need to apologize for reacting to what I assume was a threat to my life?"

She answered brightly, "Actually, I always throw myself at hot guys like this."

His chest shook beneath hers, creating the most amazing sensation in her breasts, which were smashed against him in a blatantly sexual fashion.

One of the Secret Service agents growled, "Stay still, you two."

Gabe replied dryly, his gaze still locked on hers, "Diana, allow me to introduce you to Owen Haas. He's the agent-in-charge I told you about earlier."

"Pleasure to meet you, Agent Haas," she responded politely. "Is that your belt buckle or your pistol digging into my side?"

The guy scowled and didn't reply. Which was just as well. He needed to concentrate on his job at the moment. The guy was jammed up against her left side closely enough that she could hear the chatter coming over his earpiece. A team of Secret Service agents was clearing the offices across the street room by room. So far, no assassin.

Gabe smiled up at her and commented conversationally, "You know, I haven't been this crushed since my last football game."

"And were there cheerleaders in that pile, too?"

Ah, the delicious feel of a chuckle tantalizing her chest again. "No such luck."

She retorted, "You wanna talk about luck? Lucky will be no paparazzi getting a picture of this. Can you imagine the headlines the tabloids would cook up for the five of us?"

Gabe opened his mouth to reply when Agent Haas interrupted. "Ma'am, Agent Willis, he's the guy on top of you, is going to roll to your left and take over covering my position. I need you to stay on top of the President-elect for a little while longer. We're going to bring out bulletproof shields before we let him get up. Got it?"

Oh, hurt her. Make her lie some more on top of the sexiest guy she'd met in nearly as long as she could remember. "Sure, Agent Haas. Consider me plastered to the boss."

A phalanx of burly men rushed out onto the balcony, door-size riot shields in hand. They quickly formed a wall of polycarbonate resin and flesh between Gabe and that window across the street.

Owen Haas's voice growled from above her, "You can get up now, ma'am."

A strong hand on her upper arm lifted her to her feet. She looked up wryly at Agent Haas. "Aren't you at least going to offer me a cigarette after that, Owen? I mean, it's practically time to take you home to meet my parents."

Coughs and snorts sounded all down the line of agents. The giant man scowled down at her, not amused. As Gabe climbed to his feet, Haas hustled his charge inside the hotel room. The agent's shoulders sagged in relief when Gabe was safely behind closed curtains and bulletproof windows. She felt a flash of sympathy for the Secret Service man.

"Is the threat neutralized?" she asked Haas seriously.

"Yeah. It was a secretary emptying an ashtray out the window. Her boss came in to work unexpectedly and she didn't want to get caught smoking in the office."

Diana couldn't help grinning at how shocked the poor woman must have been when an armed team of Secret Service agents burst into her office to arrest her for sneaking a lousy cigarette. She remarked dryly, "I bet she never smokes again in a Federal office building with that kind of response to it."

The Secret Service agent's smile disappeared as quickly as it appeared.

She looked up at Haas. "Hey, I'm really sorry if I gave you a fright."

The guy's gaze softened slightly, from granite to, oh, cement. "Don't sweat it. I'd rather have you tackle the President-elect and be wrong than do nothing and me be out there right now scraping his brains off the windows."

"You take care of him," she said quietly. "Stay sharp today."

The guy gave her a long, hard look. Finally, he answered, "I will, ma'am. Count on it."

One of the other agents escorted her out of the suite. As she passed through the main room, she felt several pairs of eyes following her progress toward the exit with open antagonism. She glanced around casually. Yup. Wolfe was over in the corner, in a huddle with several men. As his gaze drilled into her, she looked away hastily from what appeared to be a strategy-planning powwow of some kind. Lord, she didn't envy Gabe the backstabbing and political maneuvering that was going on inside his own administration. What a lousy way to have to enter office.

She sure hoped he had someone he could trust to watch his back.

9:00 A.M.

She sat in her car and stared at nothing. Now what? She was supposed to save the President-elect's life, but she didn't have the foggiest idea what to do next. Dunst was missing. A Q-group cell was out there somewhere, getting ready to kill the amazing, wonderful man upstairs. How was she supposed to find either target in this city of millions? Her only connection to Q-group was the Internet, and it was a tenuous link at best. Anonymous e-mail addresses and a series of seemingly innocuous messages.

Unfortunately, it was all she had.

She started her car and headed back up to the street. She guided the vehicle west toward the funky chic of M Street in Georgetown and an Internet café located there where she had a standing expense account. Several of her best informants liked to hang out there and wreak havoc upon "The System." Of course, at this time of day they'd be home in bed after surfing the Web all night, or they'd be at grindingly mundane day jobs that masked and financed their alternate lives.

She parked the car and glanced in her rearview mirror yet again. Still no sign of any tails. But then something else caught her attention in the mirror. Her own face. She couldn't walk into the Chaosium Café looking like this! She'd wreck her reputation as an antiestablishment chick in two seconds flat. Fortunately, her clothes looked the part. Although, she could not believe she'd just seen the next President of the United States in sloppy jeans and a shabby sweater. It pushed even her sense of flaunting propriety.

She dug in her purse for a wet wipe and scrubbed all the classy makeup off her face. She layered on heavy black mascara and eyeliner, dark brown lip liner followed by a coat of maroon gloss and white powder over the rest of her face. In broad daylight like this with her fair skin, the vampire-wannabe look was particularly glaring.

She dug around in the bottom of her purse and came up with a small tin of gel hair paint. She dipped out a little of the red goop and smeared it through a strand of hair down the left side of her face. Then, she pulled the rest of her hair back into a severe ponytail, put on a pair of so-ugly-they had-to-be-cool horn-rimmed glasses, and her goth, cyberpunk look was complete.

Hard to believe she'd been sprawled all over the next president of the United States less than an hour ago. Harder still to believe that someone who looked like this might be responsible for saving the guy's life today.

After what had happened to her mother, to her whole family, truth be told, a person would think she'd know better than to dive into deep waters full of big, hungry sharks. Her mother had tangled with bad guys who'd sabotaged her work and made it look as if her incompetence had resulted in a man's death. She'd resigned from the military and suffered a mental breakdown, existing in a nearly catatonic state for twenty years. She supposed she ought to be grateful the bastards who'd drugged her mother hadn't killed her outright, but living with the empty shell of her mother for so long had been worse in some ways than losing her completely.

It had torn apart her family. Josie had sided with their mother, Diana with their father in the first months after what they now knew to be sabotage to halt her mother's research on stealth technologies for military aircraft. When their father finally sent the girls away to a boarding school, the destruction of the family had been complete. Although she loved her sister, she'd never been able to understand Josie's fanatical loyalty to their clearly crazy mother. Maybe it was because Josie was older when The Incident happened, while she'd only been four. Josie had many more memories of their mother from before the drugs that she didn't have. Practically her only recollections of her mother until last year were of a gaunt, ghostlike woman only tenuously in touch with reality.

At least at the Athena Academy she'd found a measure of acceptance. The girls and staff there were unanimously too bright to blame her and Josie for their mother's problems and gave both girls a chance to find a place for themselves. Beautiful, outgoing, confident Josie had fit right in at the Academy. But, unlike her big sister, she'd struggled to find an identity that suited her.

She'd envied her older sister. Wanted to be just like her. But she never quite measured up to the standards Josie set. It didn't take long for her to head in a completely opposite direction rather than compete with her and lose every time.

If Josie joined a team sport, Diana quit sports altogether. If Josie decided makeup and fashion were important, she threw out every stitch of decent clothing she owned. If Josie studied French, she studied Arabic. If Josie went to swimming camp, she went to horseback-riding camp. And the hell of it was she still ended up just like her big sister. A pale, unsuccessful shadow of her, but *just like her.* Both military officers, both beautiful women in their own right, both highly intelligent, both with wildly promising futures. Of course, unlike Josie she did her damnedest to hide both her beauty and her brains most of the time, and she was rapidly throwing away her career and her future.

But she couldn't break away from her family completely. Last year, when Josie set out to clear their mother's name once and for all, Diana had come running to help Josie. She'd even taken a bullet for her big sister when the same guy who'd sabotaged their mother's work went after Josie's research as well.

Was she doomed to repeat her mother's fatal mistake and take on forces too big for her to handle? Was she headed down the fast track to her own destruction by tangling with the Q-group all by herself?

She pushed the car door open and stepped out. A couple of pedestrians looked away from her hastily. It was amazing how a change of makeup could make her completely invisible to respectable people. Maybe that was why she had so little respect for most of them in return. She stepped inside the surprisingly quiet Internet café. A half-dozen guys dressed in varying degrees of grunge lounged at the coffee bar to one side of the room. Most of the computer terminals were empty at this time of day. The coffee server waved a hello at her and she waved back. Damn. None of her regular hacker buds were here.

She made her way to the back of the room and picked a terminal facing the entrance. She logged on quickly, using the Arabic handle she'd hidden behind to infiltrate the Q-group chat room. No new activity in the chat room since yesterday afternoon. That was odd. They yacked up a storm most evenings. But last night had been completely silent. Like maybe they were all away from their computers. Maybe breaking into her house and getting into position for today's assassination attempt.

She highlighted the e-mail handle she believed belonged to one of the cell's leaders. It translated roughly from Arabic to English as "Glory Seeker." She attempted to trace it back to its source and immediately ran into a firewall, a blocking command by Glory Seeker's Internet server that prevented her from seeing any further into the source of the transmission. Quickly, she typed in a protocol to circumvent the firewall. No problem. She sailed right past the routine antihacking protection.

She dug into the server's memory, searching for any trace of Glory Seeker and his point of origin. And hit another firewall. A big, fat honking one this time. She tried her protocol again and it bounced like a Super Ball. Hmm. Time to pull out the big guns. She uploaded a program one of her hacker pals had written a few months back that purported to bust through any firewall anywhere.

She watched the spinning hourglass icon on the computer screen as the program did its magic. This sure was taking a while. It was taking way too long, in fact. At this rate it'd be next week before she got the name of a single Q-group member. She needed more computing power. Or more hacking power, to be precise.

While the firewall buster continued to batter away at the barrier to her progress, she pulled out her cell phone. "Hey, Dynamo, Die Hard here."

A sleepy voice complained, "Do you know what time it is?"

"Yeah. I'm sorry I woke you up. But I've got an emergency. The mother of all hacking jobs for you."

The voice perked up to vaguely human standards. "Anybody done it before?"

She couldn't help but grin. It was all about status. Be the first guy to break into an unbreakable system and your fame was assured within the secret world of hackers.

She replied, "Nope, it's a virgin system. A bunch of virgin systems. I'm at the Chaosium. Can you be here in ten minutes?"

"Are you kidding?"

"No, I'm not kidding. It's really an emergency. I'll owe you huge if you help me out."

"How huge?" the guy asked, distinctly interested now.

She laughed. "Not that huge. No sexual favors from me. But hey," she added casually, "Don't sweat it. I'll call CrystalMeth. I bet she can get what I need if you can't." It was a dirty trick. Dynamo and CrystalMeth were ex-lovers and archrivals. They hated each other's guts.

"I'll be there in five," Dynamo announced with a definite fire in his pants now.

She repeated the call a half-dozen more times, pleading and wheedling the best hackers she knew into coming down and helping her out. True to his word, Dynamo walked into the café, in his pajama bottoms and a Def Lepperd T-shirt in five minutes flat. She stood up to greet him and leaned over his shoulder as he settled in and signed on at a terminal near her. Several more of the hackers trickled in over the next couple of minutes. They looked startled when they took note of the team she'd assembled. It was a who's who of East Coast hackers.

She told the late arrivals, "I've got eight more hackers on-line. They're signed in and waiting for you guys to join them."

"Jesus," Dynamo exclaimed. "Are we taking over the Federal Reserve today or what?"

CrystalMeth, the only other woman in the room, retorted, "Been there. Done that. Got the T-shirt."

The woman also was on probation because of that particular stunt. Before the pair could erupt into a full-blown spat, Diana directed everyone, "Log on to your most powerful server while I tell you what's up. Time is of the essence, here."

"What's so urgent?" Dynamo asked as his fingers flew across the keyboard.

"I need to find some guys. Track them back to their points of origin, break into their servers and get actual, real-world identities on all of them. And I need it done like yesterday."

One of the other hackers spoke up. "That's kid stuff. It's time consuming, but any garden-variety hacker could do it. Why all this firepower, Die Hard?"

She'd promised Gabe she wouldn't tell anyone what was afoot. Besides, these guys wouldn't believe her if she did tell them. Not to mention they might very well refuse to help her. "I can't give you the details, but this is no-kidding save-the-world stuff. The sort of stuff that could get all of your records cleared."

That got their attention. Well over half of them had had run-ins with the law. She had no authority to promise such a thing, but she'd bet Gabe did.

She gave them the address of the known Q-group chat room and assigned a user of the room to each of them to track down. In a matter of minutes the café had gone silent except for the clacking of keyboards as eight hundred-word-a-minute typists body-slammed their way through the Internet.

"Hey, Die Hard, mind if I ask a friend to help us?" Crystal-Meth called out.

Diana replied quickly, "Not at all. In fact, all of you, invite anyone you want to jump in."

Before long, word had gone out literally all over the world, and hundreds of hackers jumped on the bandwagon. Most of them would be no help at all, but with that many operators at work, somebody was bound to stumble across back doors into the right server systems.

She jumped as her own computer beeped. The firewall protocol had worked! She was inside the next layer of protection surrounding Glory Seeker. She typed in a few commands and scanned the code scrolling down her screen. Wow. Nice program architecture. But permeable, nonetheless. She started to type in a set of instructions to get past it. And noticed something funny. The original code at the top of her screen was degrading. Literally eroding before her very eyes! Crud. Somebody was counterhacking.

She typed furiously. She had to get in the final command before the entire grid imploded in her face. She stabbed the Enter button on her keyboard and prayed she'd been in time. The hourglass icon blinked steadily for several seconds.

And a new set of code scrolled down her screen. Bingo.

Reading fast, she identified the type of encryption this layer of security used. She'd seen something like it before. Casting back in her memory, she recalled the command set to bypass it and typed fast. Again, the code started to erode. Whoever was chasing her through this server was good. Damned good.

A fork in the path of the logic loomed ahead. She had to choose one direction or another. And fast. The counterhacker was right on her heels. Abruptly, one of the forks in the path started to erode as she watched. Well, that made the decision easy. She dived in front of the erosion, down the disappearing pathway, racing across cyberhighways like the wind.

Hunched over the keyboard, her fingers fairly flew across the keys as she flung commands into battle like electronic warriors against her foe. She paused just long enough to send a couple of commands designed to confound whoever was tracking her, and then she went back to work attempting to break the encryption. She entered the final command. And sat back to wait. If she didn't miss her guess, this was the last layer of protection inside this server. If she'd sent the right commands, and if she'd been in time to beat the counter-measures, she ought to see names, addresses, phone numbers and credit card information on her screen when the hourglass went away.

The wait was agonizing. Each second that ticked by was one closer to Gabe's possible death. The idea of all that vibrant energy, that intelligence, that sex appeal, being snuffed out made her faintly sick to her stomach. She had to get through.

The computer screen went dark. Her heart dropped into her feet. Damn!

But then a small, rectangular window opened in the middle of her screen. Would the server administrator please enter a valid password?

She sagged in relief. A simple password block? No sweat. She typed in the standard protocol for bypassing a password request. This shouldn't take more than a minute or so. She couldn't believe how many people thought their computers were actually safe because it took a password to get to the data. Every twelve-year-old hacker wannabe in the world knew how to get past that.

The screen flickered. And lit up.

Hot damn! She'd done it. A system administration screen opened in front of her. Quickly she entered the handle, Glory Seeker, into a search field. And moments later, the screen began to erode. Data melted off of it like butter off a hot knife.

C'mon, c'mon, she urged the search engine. Just a name. A lousy name, and then the whole damn server could implode for all she cared.

The search window began to melt.

But then a name flashed up in the reply box. For no more than a second. But it was enough. Tito Albadian. In New Jersey. And then it was gone.

Rapidly, she accessed the Social Security administration and broke into the system through a back door she could drive a Mack truck through. No record of a Tito Albadian in New Jersey. She frowned. Maybe she was looking in the wrong place. She tried the Immigration and Naturalization Service and got an immediate hit. She called up a copy of the guy's work permit. Using an illegally obtained police code, she requested a picture of this Albadian guy.

A laser printer behind her spit out a sheet of paper.

"I've got a name, folks," she announced. "Could a couple of you help me look for known associates of this guy?"

Every pair of shoulders hunched higher around their ears. Hackers were nothing if not competitive. Over the next several minutes, assorted curses and crows of triumph were heard. Finally, Dynamo shouted out, "Gotcha!"

Diana moved over behind him as he traced a credit card number to a driver's license in California and called up a picture of the owner. "Way to go!" she congratulated him.

He sat back, rolling his shoulders. "Man, that was close. I had a counterhacker on my heels the whole way."

"Same thing's happening to me over here, too," Crystal-Meth spoke up. "But I'll beat the bastard."

One by one, the hackers, some working alone and some working in teams, broke into Internet server systems all over the world and harvested names and faces from the participants in the Q-group chat room. In all, fourteen faces printed out on the printer to go with the handles of the Q-group chat members. Undoubtedly, not all of these guys were part of an active Q-group hit squad. Some of them were innocent people, just looking to connect with a few immigrants like themselves and going about their lawful daily lives. But some of them were here in Washington, right now, planning to assassinate Gabe Monihan. Of that, she had no doubt.

Diana picked up the sheaf of printed photos and took them over to the copier machine in the corner. Quickly she made a duplicate set of the pictures and stapled them together. She put a yellow sticky pad on them and scribbled the name, Owen Haas. How she was going to get the pictures to him, she had no idea. But she had faith he'd know what to do with the pictures once he got them. He was a sharp cookie and hadn't missed her veiled warning to him that someone was out to get Gabe Monihan today.

What she really needed to do now was run these names and pictures through the Oracle database. It was plugged into computer systems that these hackers didn't even dream existed. She scooped up both sets of the pictures and her purse and headed for the door.

"You guys are the best. I won't forget this," she called out as she exited the café.

And was grabbed around both upper arms by a pair of powerful men, one on either side of her.

She struggled in the men's grasps to no avail. "Hey!" she shouted. "What do you think you're doing? Let go of me!" It was women's self-defense 101. Make a very loud stink if someone tried to snatch her. Most kidnappers, rapists and murderers weren't looking for a troublesome public confrontation.

Several people on the sidewalk were staring at her, and a couple of passersby looked as if they were reaching for cell phones. Three cheers for civic-minded citizens!

"Sorry ma'am," one of the men intoned, deadpan. "We can't let you go."

"Why the hell not?" she shouted back at him, still trying to draw attention.

"You're under arrest."

10:00 A.M.

"**I**'m *what?*" Diana exclaimed.

"You're under arrest, ma'am."

"And you might be *who?*" she demanded of the men holding her.

"Army Criminal Investigation Division. If you'll come with us, ma'am. We need to ask you a few questions."

She cursed under her breath. She *so* did not have time for fun with CID right now. Gabe would be inaugurated in a scant four hours. "Look fellas. Can I take a rain check on this? I'll be happy to talk to you later this afternoon. But right now I have extremely urgent business to take care of."

"That's what we'd like to talk to you about ma'am," one of them replied stolidly.

She cursed under her breath. Their questioning could take hours. She thought fast and yanked back hard on the guy's hands. She didn't break their grip on her, but in the ensuing tussle, she managed to drop one of the photocopied sets of pictures on the ground and kick it behind them. It was the best she could do. Maybe someone inside the café would see Owen Haas's name on the photos and get them to him somehow. It was a long shot, but it might be all she had.

Capitulating abruptly, she walked forward rapidly, all but dragging the Intelligence officers away from the Chaosium Café and the sheaf of papers on the ground. She stuffed the remaining set of pictures into her purse.

"Where to, boys? Do you have a safe house around here somewhere or are we going for a ride?"

The poor guys seemed confounded by her abruptly cavalier attitude. "Uh, our car's right here."

They stopped beside a black sedan and put her in the back seat.

She groused, "Sheesh, aren't you going to handcuff me or anything? I'm a pretty dangerous character, you know. Us desk-jockey analysts are real beasts."

The driver rolled his eyes at her in the rearview mirror but didn't rise to the bait. She caught the other guy eyeing her surreptitiously and grinned. "Whatchya staring at, Sergeant? Haven't you ever been inside an Internet café before and seen how the other half live?"

The guy glared. "I'm a captain, not an enlisted schmuck."

She leaned back in her seat. "Dunno that I'd be casting aspersions on enlisted personnel, Captain. They're the backbone of the Army. They outnumber commissioned officer *schmucks* by something like twenty-five to one."

The guy scowled at her openly. She definitely had him off balance now. Of course it probably helped that she was in full punker makeup, and he knew she was an officer. The guy was no doubt having a hard time reconciling the two in his mind The car pulled to a stop in front of the Pentagon and the tw men escorted her inside. They took her in the same side of the building the airliner had hit on 9/11 and downstairs to an anonymous-looking office. Several men at desks glanced up at her and did double takes as she walked past. She wasn't exactly standard Army issue at the moment. The pair who'd arrested her sat her down at a table in the middle of a one-each interrogating room and pointedly locked the door. She looked around. It came complete with the big, two-way mirror, a surveillance camera and a tape recorder.

She sat impatiently through a reading of her rights. She duly waived the right to counsel and leaned back in her chair. "Okay, gentlemen. What's this all about?"

"You reported a break-in at your house earlier this morning."

She frowned. And they were arresting her because of it? "That's correct," she answered aloud.

"Was anything stolen?"

"No." She hadn't been a rebel most of her life for nothing. She knew full well to volunteer absolutely no information whatsoever under questioning. The headmistress at the Athena Academy had often been unable to pin pranks on her because of her gift for silence during interrogation.

"Were you injured?"

"No."

"You reported that the intruder was attempting to use your computer. Did you have any classified information on your computer?"

Taking classified information home from work was a felony. She answered that one firmly. "No."

"Was any data stolen?"

"No."

"Why did you report the break-in?"

She stared at the officer pointedly, making it clear that she didn't deign to answer patently stupid questions. The guy reddened slightly.

The second officer dived in. "The Bethesda police reported finding a disturbing collection of pictures of Gabe Monihan in your bedroom."

She stared back at him as he left the statement hanging between them.

"Care to comment on that?" he asked.

"No."

"Are you obsessed with Gabe Monihan?"

Wouldn't these guys have a field day if they knew she'd spent a piece of this morning plastered all over the man in question? She answered the query. "No."

"Are you stalking him?"

"No."

"Fixated on him?"

"No."

As much as she wanted to shout at these guys that they were wasting her valuable time, that would give them power over her. If they knew she was in a hurry, they'd slowball this little interview until it was too late for her to do a damn thing to save Gabe.

She waited for the next inane question.

"Then why have you been illegally accessing information via the Internet pertaining to President-elect Monihan's personal life?"

She blinked. Huh? Now how in the world had they figured that out? She would readily admit that she'd broken into all kinds of private information about Gabe's life, college transcripts, medical records and the like, but she'd been searching purely for a reason that the Q-group wanted to kill him. Besides, the guy's life was as squeaky clean as they came. She hadn't found a speck of dirt on the man, except that he'd flunked French 101 three times in college.

The real question, though, was how did *these* guys know about it? Had a wiretap been authorized on her home computer? Except the Oracle database had protection protocols built into it that would detect something like that on any system it was using. Just within the last few hours, she'd had Oracle open and running on both her home and work computers and no alarms had gone off. They couldn't possibly be tapped!

She leaned forward in her chair. "Do you have any evidence to back up your ludicrous accusation that I'm accessing information illegally, or do I need to call my lawyer and document this interview for a harassment and libel lawsuit?"

"Do you deny the charge, then?" one of the men asked.

"I damn well insist on seeing the evidence upon which you'd make such an accusation," she retorted. It wasn't exactly an outright denial, but hopefully the indignation of her tone made up for that minor omission.

"We're not at liberty to divulge our sources, ma'am," one of the guys replied.

Sources? Now there was an interesting word choice. In the intelligence community that both she and these men came from, that particular word almost invariably meant a human source. More times than not, an informant. Had they gotten a tip that she'd been poking into Gabe's personal affairs?

If the Secret Service or the FBI had actually traced hackins of Gabe's records to her, they'd have already come to her home with a search warrant, seized her computer, filed charges against her immediately and arrested her outright. She knew enough hackers to whom that very sequence of events had happened for her to be dead certain of how it went down.

But these guys, despite their initial statement of arrest, had yet to charge her with anything and apparently had not been to her home themselves. And that meant her computer probably had not been seized. Which meant these guys had nothing but a tip of some kind to go on. *They were on a fishing expedition.*

"Why did you aggressively evade a surveillance detail upon you earlier today, Captain Lockworth?" one of the men fired at her.

So. It *had* been the Army tailing her toward the Oracle office in Alexandria earlier. "I had no way of knowing if it was the Army or the forces of evil following me. It's my job to lose enemy surveillance if I become aware of it, is it not?"

No answer to that one.

"You expended extensive military resources on a wild-goose chase."

She was tempted to tell them they should have sent someone competent to do the job, then. But she bit back the comment. No sense being more antagonistic toward these guys than she had to be. Not if she wanted to get out of here any time soon.

She asked casually, "So how did you guys catch up with me if I lost you?" Might as well let them toot their own horns for a moment to appease their bruised egos.

"There's been a police APB out on your car all morning."

Wow. She'd rated an APB? "And why did you think it was that urgent to talk to me, again?"

"We believe you may pose a threat to the safety of the President-elect of the United States."

She'd laugh if that weren't so absurd. "Me? A low-level intelligence analyst from DIA? What the heck kind of threat do I pose to anyone? I go to work every day, sit in my office, read a lot of paperwork, write reports and go home. Where in the world did you get the notion that I'm a threat to Gabe Monihan?"

"Again, I'm not at liberty to divulge our sources."

An informant pegged her as a threat to Gabe, too? The timing of it all was mighty damned suspicious. It certainly lent credence to the idea that she'd been shaking the right tree by investigating the Q-group. Look at the garbage that was falling out of it. Somebody'd sicced these guys on her to back her off of the investigation.

"May we have a look at the papers you put in your purse as you were coming out of the Internet café?"

She retorted coolly, "May I see a copy of your search warrant?"

The men scowled. After a pregnant silence, the two officers exchanged glances, got up and left the room. Great. How long was she supposed to cool her jets while they came up with Plan B? She glanced at her watch. Time was a'wasting, here. Vividly aware of the camera and the two-way mirror, she forced herself not to fidget. She painted an expression of saintlike patience on her face and sat quietly in her chair, even though her insides were fairly bursting to get out of here.

One of the men stepped back into the room a few minutes later. "Things will go better for you if you tell us what you're up to, Captain Lockworth," he said kindly.

"You can lose the good cop-bad cop routine, buddy. And furthermore, I'm not *up to* anything."

"Then why are all those pictures of Monihan plastered all over your bedroom?"

"They're in my bedroom because it was the largest blank wall in my house to put them where I could see them all. I have the pictures in the first place because I've been investigating the attack against him in Chicago last October. *Under official orders to do so, I might add.*"

"Is that so? Care to share any details of this investigation?" the guy asked. Damned if he didn't sound genuinely surprised.

"Obviously my superiors deemed that you don't have the security clearances to hear the details of my work, or else you'd already know the details. Given that, I'm certainly not going to tell you what I'm working on."

The guy stared at her, frustrated.

She sighed. "Look. I don't know who put you on this assignment. But you've been given a bum steer. I'm no more a stalker than you are. Somebody's got it in for me and is using you and your partner as patsies to harass me. Unless you guys have warrants and hard evidence to back you up, I'm not talking to anyone. And this is turning into a big waste of your time and mine. So, arc you going to charge me with something or not?"

The guy shrugged. "That's above my pay grade to decide."

"Tell you what. You let me make a phone call and I'll see if I can bring this Mexican standoff to an end." She held her breath, praying the guy would take the offer.

"Who are you going to call?" he asked suspiciously.

She thought fast. Who had the clout to call these guys' bluffs and spring her out of here fast? It had to be somebody who wasn't in her chain of command. Somebody who wasn't trying to sabotage her career. The perfect person came to mind. "I'm going to call my grandfather."

"He some kind of lawyer or something?"

She managed to keep a straight face. "Yeah. Or something."

The guy left the room. And came back in a minute later with a telephone in his hand. He plugged it into the wall socket and set it on the table in front of her. He pointedly did not leave the room. Whatever.

She dialed the Pentagon operator. "Would you mind ringing up Joseph Lockworth for me? That's right. The former director of the CIA. You may need to patch the call through the operator at Langley. Tell him his granddaughter, Diana, urgently needs to speak with him."

While the operator put the call through, her poor interrogator stared, slack jawed.

She put her hand over the receiver and said to him sympathetically, "I'm sorry, man. Like I said. Somebody's using you to screw with my career. You've been caught in the middle of some political maneuver designed to mess with me. I just hope the fallout from this doesn't take you down with it."

While dismay blossomed on the guy's face, a deep, familiar voice came on the line. "Diana! How are you, kiddo?"

"Hiya, Gramps. Actually I've been better. Something weird is going on. Army CID has picked me up and is detaining me. They're making wild accusations about me stalking Gabe Monihan. Is there any chance you could look into this and get me out of here? They've got me locked up in the basement of the Pentagon."

Her grandfather asked drolly, "Are you stalking Monihan?"

She burst out laughing. "Not hardly."

"Glad to hear it, pumpkin. Put me on the line with who-ever's breathing over your shoulder. I assume they've got someone listening in to whatever you say?"

"Of course. Here he is." She thrust the telephone receiver into the surprised hand of her interrogator. She watched in high amusement as the guy introduced himself as Captain Hammersmith and stammered out a series of names and Criminal Investigation Detachments. When he'd worked his way up the chain of command to four-star generals, he finally stopped speaking. A short pause and then a crisp, "Yes, sir."

The guy hung up the phone. "Your grandfather asked me to tell you he's sending a car and driver around front to pick you up. He said that by the time his driver can get here, he'll have you 'sprung from the pokey.'"

She sighed in immense relief.

"Uh, if you'll excuse me, I need to make a couple calls to my superiors."

"To warn them about the shit that's about to roll downhill and land on their unsuspecting heads?" she asked helpfully.

"Yeah. Something like that."

She grinned openly as the guy hastily exited the room.

True to his word, her grandfather had her out of there in under fifteen minutes. In fact, it was an impressive display of string pulling. But she wasn't going to stick around long enough to rub it in. Gabe's would-be killers were still out there, somewhere.

With a last admonishment to stay the hell away from Gabe Monihan, her two interrogators left her standing alone on the steps of the Pentagon. Dang, it was cold today! She pulled her leather duster more tightly around herself, huddling into its not-quite-warm-enough folds.

Before long, a black luxury sedan pulled up and a driver in a chauffeur's uniform stepped out. "Miss Lockworth?" he asked.

She didn't recognize the guy. Not her grandfather's usual driver. But then, maybe the CIA had assigned Jens to a real job in the agency. She gave him grief about his plush assignment every time she saw him.

She stepped forward, smiling. "That's me. I'm Diana Lockworth." She held out a friendly hand. The driver looked surprised, but took the offered handshake. "Darryl," he mumbled.

"Hi, Darryl. Let's blow this Popsicle stand, shall we? I need to get downtown. Down near the Mall and the parade route for the inauguration," she said, referring to the long grassy section of the city that stretched from the Lincoln Memorial all the way to the Capitol Building.

"Coming right up, ma'am," he replied. He held the door for her as she climbed in and shut it firmly behind her. As he pulled away from the curb he asked, "Would you like some music, ma'am?"

"No thanks," she replied. "I need to do a little thinking."

The driver nodded silently. She was surprised when a blacked-out privacy glass came up out of the back of the front seat, closing her off from any further conversation with Darryl. Gramps must have a new car to go along with the new driver.

As they headed toward downtown Washington, D.C., she had no specific destination in mind. She just knew she had to head down to where Gabe was going to be in a few hours. For that's surely where the Q-group would be, as well.

She replayed the interrogation by the Army Intelligence officers in her head. Who was the informant? Had the two intelligence officers revealed anything to her, said anything, that would give her a clue as to who'd set her up like that?

Was there a chance the incident was connected in some way to the Q-group and its assassination attempt on Gabe? The idea was ridiculous. Except the timing of it was just so blasted suspicious.

Who could be working against her like this? Or maybe the question was better stated, Who inside the government was working against Gabe Monihan like this? An image of a high, sloping forehead under black-and-silver hair and piercing, furious eyes popped into her head. Was it possible? Had Thomas Wolfe set her up? She wouldn't put it past the man. He'd struck her as having nerves of ice and steel. And she had no doubt he was capable of arranging her arrest, or at least detention.

Of course, Wolfe undoubtedly hadn't done the dirty work himself. He'd probably had a flunkie call CID and make the accusations against her. She could probably track down the phone records of the call and find out exactly who'd made the call. Where was Oracle when a girl really needed it?

She might not have Oracle here, but she could certainly try to think like Oracle. Okay. Her dislike of Wolfe aside, who else inside the government might have a reason to stop her from foiling an assassination attempt on Gabe? For whoever that person was, she'd lay down good money that he was behind, or at least involved in, the upcoming assassination attempt. Of course, the very idea of an assassination attempt from *inside* the government was outrageous. But that was her job. To imagine the outrageous and then plan for it.

Any person out to kill Gabe would have to be very high up in the government to benefit from Gabe's death. They'd need to have passionate opinions about certain foreign policies that lay in direct opposition to Gabe's. They'd have to have access to the intelligence community. How else would an old CIA scenario have turned up with a bunch of terrorists, and how else could Army Intel have been sicced on her so quickly?

She ticked off the list of requirements for the ringleader of any plot to kill Gabe. High-level government official. Ultraconservative or ultraliberal politics. Access to the intelligence community. Wealth enough to finance the historically destitute Q-group. Access to resources in the form of high-tech equipment or training.

She mentally noted every possible suspect, even if her head said they couldn't possibly be the right person. And stopped cold as a particular name came to mind. One that fit every criteria to absolute perfection.

Joseph P. Lockworth. Former Director of the CIA.

Gramps? No way.

She reminded herself to think like Oracle. No value judgments. Just the facts. Let them speak for themselves. And she was riding in his car this very second. Had she just handed herself directly into the clutches of the enemy?

11:00 A.M.

She reached for the door handle and tested it. Locked. *Don't panic.* It was probably a standard security procedure to lock all the doors from the driver's position. She looked outside. And noticed they were headed farther north than was necessary to get to the Mall, where she'd asked to be dropped off.

"Hey, Darryl," she said into the intercom on the panel in the back of the front seat. "Can you just drop me off right here? This will be perfect."

If anything, the car sped up more.

Good Lord. Was she being kidnapped? By her own grandfather? Maybe the intercom just wasn't working. She tried the button marked Up and Down for the partition. Nothing.

"Darryl," she said louder into the intercom. "Stop right here."

Still nothing. Crud. She couldn't see him through the black glass partition. She banged on it with the flat of her hands and shouted, "Darryl! Stop the car!"

Nada.

Oh yeah. She was definitely a prisoner in here. She looked outside. They were well north of the Mall and traveling east. Fast. She banged on her side window, but nobody could hear her over the traffic noise, of course. She had to get out of here! But how? For all she knew, the window glass was bullet-proof, and nothing she did would break through it. She tested the upholstery at the back of the seat. Maybe she could tear through to the trunk and kick her way out of there. The seat cushion pulled away to reveal a steel wall between the passenger compartment and the trunk. Maybe she could access the door lock itself. Tear off the inside door panel and manually release the locking mechanism of the door. She pried at the door lining and broke a couple of fingernails but didn't budge the panel. She might be able to pry it off using some sort of tool, though.

Okay. Plan A was to try to break out a window and escape that way. Plan B would be to try to take apart the door.

Now for something heavy and hard to bust the glass with. Even if it wasn't bulletproof, the window would still be made of tempered safety glass, and it took a hefty blow to damage that stuff significantly. She gazed around the interior of the car. Her purse was too soft. Her shoe was too light. She could wrap her leather coat around her fist and try to punch it out, but she doubted she had the strength to succeed. She opened the minibar contained in the back of the front passenger seat. Bingo. Bottles of liquor. She tested them and pulled out a magnum of champagne. The bottle had a thick, heavy bottom and a chunky body. The weight of the liquid and the pressure of the carbonated beverage outward upon the glass bottle might just give it enough smashing power to break the window. If not, she was about to make a really big mess for nothing.

She pulled the sleeves of her leather coat down over her

hands to protect them and herself from flying glass. She picked up the champagne bottle by the neck in both fists, closed her eyes and swung it with all her might at the right rear passenger window.

Her arm jarred all the way to the shoulder and a tremendous crashing noise of breaking glass filled the air. She jumped in icy shock as cold champagne drenched her. But a basketball-size spiderweb of fractured glass had appeared in the window. Hallelujah!

The car swerved violently and lurched forward again as if the driver had just stomped on the accelerator. Gave Darryl a fright, did she? Quickly, she lay down on her back on the seat, feet up. Using the heels of her boots, she kicked out the shattered glass. It bent outward in a sheet, and finally, under repeated blows from her foot, gave way. A cold wind rushed into the interior of the car. The vehicle slowed abruptly.

Uh-oh. Darryl was on to her.

She leaped up and ducked through the window. Her eyes watered ferociously and her hair whipped all around her face. She grabbed onto the roof of the car and sat on the edge of the door frame while she maneuvered a foot out the window. The pavement sped by underneath her at a good thirty miles per hour, but the vehicle was decelerating fast. She swung her second foot through and jumped clear of the car.

She landed on her feet in a blessedly empty turn lane, but the impact and her momentum knocked her off balance. She tucked and rolled, flinging her arms over her head to protect it as her fall sent her tumbling end over end for a good twenty or thirty feet. She lay on the ground in a ball, stunned. Still alive. Amazing. Lucky as hell, too. Thank God for the tough leather coat.

Brakes squealed ahead of her. She looked up in time to see the big Cadillac heave into a tire-screaming J-turn and stop facing her, like a bull getting ready to charge. The white flash of the license plate below the radiator looked like a fleck of foam dripping from the silver-toothed maw of the beast. The powerful engine shifted into gear. Here he came. She forced her aching body to unfold and pushed painfully to her feet, looking around frantically for cover. A couple car horns blared as cars passed her and swerved around the Cadillac, which was now facing the wrong direction. She was out in the middle of a six-lane street. No time to dive for cover behind one of the parked cars at the edge of the concrete expanse. She crouched at the ready. She'd wait until the last second and leap to the side. If Darryl was any good, he'd swerve to hit her. And then she'd have to leap back out of the way in the other direction. Fast.

It was a plan, at any rate. And it wasn't as if she had time to think up anything better. The black monster bore down upon her, gathering speed and momentum, building up deadly power. She saw Darryl's face through the car's windshield as he drew close. It was devoid of emotion, displaying only the utter concentration of a pro. He was out to kill her, all right.

She head faked left and right like a basketball player trying to go around a defender to score a basket. But the car just came on, straight at her. She waited until the car was no more than a hundred feet away and jumped hard to the left. As she'd expected, the car swerved at her, like a heat-seeking missile tracking its target.

Fifty feet.

Darryl would expect her to jump back to the right at the last second. She glimpsed his hands changing grip on the steering wheel, in fact, readying himself to yank the car back the other way.

Twenty feet.

Acting purely on instinct, she jumped again. Farther to the

left. Out of his way a second time. The car lurched and Darryl tried to correct for the sudden and unexpected movement. But he wasn't in time. The sleek metal door brushed against her side as the car went barreling past. Damn, that had been close. Bullfighters could have their job, thank you very much.

The Caddie's brakes squealed again. She had to give the guy credit for being persistent. Time to split. She took off running, scooping up her purse where it had rolled to a stop in the street not far from her. She looked up and saw a wall of oncoming traffic. Crud. A stoplight had changed and sent three lanes of cars barreling toward her. She dived out of the way between two parked cars. Fortunately, the oncoming traffic blocked the Caddie from driving across the lanes of traffic in pursuit.

"Hey, lady! Are you all right?" someone called out.

No time to stop and chitchat with bystanders. She took off running down the sidewalk. She was in a business district. Plain concrete buildings that had seen better days lined the street. She ducked into the first decent-size doorway she came across. An office-supply store. She raced toward the back of it, ignoring the startled cries of the employees. She slammed through the swinging doors marked Employees Only and into the storeroom. Looked left and right and spied the loading dock to her right. She ran for it. Out onto the chest-high cement platform. A running leap off it, and her left ankle gave out as she hit the ground. She turned it into a perfectly executed parachute-landing fall, rolled, and popped back onto her feet. The ankle felt okay. Off and running again. She raced down the dirty alley and came out on a one-way street. The traffic was heavy. She sprinted along the sidewalk, waiting for an opportunity to dive across the broad avenue.

A shout behind her. The deep baritone of Darryl's voice. Traffic or not, she jumped out into the street. A car stomped on its brakes and swerved, narrowly missing her. She darted across the next two lanes of swerving, honking cars and ducked as a metallic pinging sounded behind her. Bullets on metal. The bastard was shooting at her!

Time to change the rules of engagement, here. She had to get off the street. She took the first left turn to the south and put on an extra burst of speed. God bless the Army's stringent physical fitness standards, and God bless all those years of sports at the Athena Academy. A right turn, down another block, and another left turn.

She looked over her shoulder, panting. No sign of Darryl. She looked around fast. And jumped into a dark little Greek restaurant. She made her way, huffing, past the mostly empty tables. Too early for the lunch crowd.

The manager looked up and surprise lit in his eyes. Reacting to her unsavory punker getup, no doubt.

"Where's your bathroom?" she asked breathlessly.

He pointed over his shoulder toward the back of the place. Perfect. Beside the kitchen. She stepped into the dim bathroom. She ran a sinkful of water and rinsed the streak of red out of her hair. Paper towels painfully, albeit effectively, rubbed off her heavy makeup, leaving her skin reddened, but mostly back to its normal hue. She dug around in her purse for yet another of her punker accoutrements. A can of black aerosol hair spray. Normally she'd just do the tips in black or maybe a lone streak of black, but today she laid it on all over her head. She didn't have time to make it look nice as she covered her golden blond hair with the black spray. There. At a glance, she'd pass for a brunette.

She coughed at the cloud of aerosol propellant around her head and zipped her purse shut. Pulling out a black silk scarf she usually tossed around her neck, this time she wrapped it around her head for a total profile change.

She stepped out of the bathroom and the manager about gave himself whiplash double-taking on her. As she ducked through the door into the kitchen, he belatedly lurched and shouted something at her in Greek. The chef looked up in surprise, but merely watched, bemused, as she rushed past him toward the back exit.

She popped out into a narrow access alley and ran lightly down it until she reached the street. Slowing to a quick walk, she stepped out onto the sidewalk. Now, it was all about stealth. About blending in. As she moved toward Capitol Hill the crowds grew thicker. She thought she glimpsed Darryl well behind her, once, but she couldn't be sure. He was too far away to see clearly. Which was good news. With her new disguise, he very likely couldn't make her out in the crowd, either. Especially since he'd be looking for a pale-skinned blonde with stark makeup and that telltale blood-red streak in her hair.

She slowed down her pace to blend in with the leisurely crowd of tourists beginning to make their way toward the Mall and the Inaugural Parade. She guessed she was still ten blocks from the Capitol, whose dome peeked out above the buildings ahead. She crossed a street and turned the corner and happened to catch sight out of the corner of her eye of a man in a camel overcoat shifting to the far side of the street behind her.

Alarm bells went off in her head. That was a standard surveillance move for someone working as part of a multiman team to tail a target. Was it just some random guy crossing the street, or God help her, had someone managed to pick up her trail again? She doubled back abruptly and dived into a recessed storefront with multiple glass display windows. Using the glass as a makeshift mirror, she watched for the telltale shift of a pedestrian across the street in the middle of the block. There he went. A guy with a long, gray ponytail in a black leather jacket. Dammit.

She ducked into the jewelry store beside her.

A female clerk eyed her colossally bad hair-dye job as she approached the counter. One of the woman's hands slid unobtrusively under the counter. Reaching for the silent alarm.

Diana sighed. She still looked completely disreputable, apparently. She reached—slowly—into her purse and pulled out her wallet. She flashed her military ID card at the clerk and spoke in her most professional tone of voice. "I'm an intelligence officer with the Army. I'm helping provide security for the inauguration, and I've got a bit of a problem. There are some men moving down this street whom I need to follow. Is there a stairwell inside this building, maybe a fire escape, I could use to get to the offices upstairs? I'd be tremendously grateful if you could help me."

The woman weighed her words for a moment. "Is that a disguise you're wearing?" she asked.

Diana grimaced. "Yes. Horrible, isn't it? But it was the best I could do when I spotted these jokers."

The clerk came out from behind the counter. "Follow me."

Diana followed the woman into a small back room with a desk, a coffee machine and a door that looked as though it led to a bathroom. Diana frowned as the clerk stopped near a metal locker and stooped down inside it for a moment. Was she reaching for a weapon? Diana tensed in preparation for disarming the older woman.

The clerk emerged with a cardboard box. "Lost and found. Is there anything here you could use?"

Diana sagged in relief. "Bless you." She rooted around in the assorted items of clothing and came up with two scarves, one a vivid cobalt blue, and the other a pattern of assorted brown tones. "These are perfect. I'll return them when I'm done with them."

The clerk shrugged. "No need. They've both been in there awhile. The fire escape is this way." She led Diana to a heavy-looking metal door and punched in a code on the number pad beside it. The door buzzed and the clerk opened it. "Good luck."

Diana looked the woman in the eye sincerely. "Thanks. I really appreciate your help."

And then she was off, racing up the stairs to the building's second floor, and as she had hoped, a long office complex that spanned the entire block of stores below. Unlike the jewelry store, the fire doors onto this floor were not locked. She walked quickly all the way to the far end of the building and stepped into the corner office. A man wearing a white shirt and a sloppy tie looked up from his desk.

"Can I help you?" he asked in surprise.

"Yes. I need to look out your window for a moment."

"I beg your pardon?"

She moved past the guy as she flashed her military ID yet again. "I'm doing security for the inauguration and your office has the view I need for a minute. I'll be out of here in a flash."

She plastered herself against the wall beside the window that looked down on the street she'd just left. She watched the ebb and flow of humanity below, and sure enough, after a minute or so, three people stood out from the normal movements of the crowd. The man in the camel coat, the guy with the ponytail in leather, and...Darryl. Sonofagun.

The man in the camel coat turned the corner, and she shifted over to the office's other window. Yep, standard search pattern in progress for a lost target. *Straight out of the government training manual.* Who were these guys? More CIA trained terrorists, or no kidding government types this time?

All three men were Caucasian. Not one among them looked even remotely Berzhaani. Not Q-group material, then. Somebody else. But who, dammit?

"May I use your phone?" she asked the guy at the desk.

"Um, sure," he said cautiously. Man. Even mostly cleaned up, she still exuded some vibe that made people think she was trouble.

She leaned across his desk and dialed zero. Asked the operator for a taxi company. Got a dispatcher on the line. She held her hand over the phone and asked the poor guy whose office she'd invaded for the street address of this building. He told her quickly, as if he was relieved at the idea of getting rid of her. She relayed the address to the dispatcher. Twenty minutes, the guy said.

"Make it ten and I'll double the fare and throw in a tip for you," she said into the receiver.

"Done," was the prompt reply.

She put down the phone and smiled gratefully at the office worker. "Thank you so much for your help, sir. You have no idea how valuable your assistance has been."

"No problem," the guy said, warming up to her dazzling smile.

"One last favor, if I might. Could you tell me how to get out of this building?"

He gave her directions to the elevators down to the main lobby. She made her way to the ground floor of the building and lurked inside, partially hidden behind a big, fake fig tree. At least it wasn't a palm tree, this time. She kept a sharp eye out for her three tails, but saw none of them. Good Lord willing and the creek don't rise, they'd moved on past this area in search of her.

Ten minutes later on the nose, a Yellow Cab pulled up out front. Using the muted brown scarf to cover her head and shoulders, she hurried outside to the cab and jumped in. "Thanks for getting here so quickly," she told the driver.

He nodded in the rearview mirror. "Where to?"

She thought fast. If the Q-group was trying to make a political statement, they'd do it in front of the largest possible crowd, which meant the Mall and its teeming thousands of tourists. "As close to the Mall as you can get me," she answered.

"Which end?"

Good question. The blasted thing stretched forever. How was she supposed to figure out where they'd mount their attack along its length in the next hour? Well, it wasn't as if she had any choice but to just start looking. Gabe's motorcade would probably enter the Mall from 15th Street beside… "Take me to the Washington Monument."

"You got it."

"And could you drive conservatively so you don't call any attention to us?"

The guy's eyebrows went up in surprise, but he nodded. After all the rush to get here, he probably figured she was in some giant hurry. She was, but it was more important at the moment that her tails not spot her.

The foot traffic was heavy, and various streets were closed such that the cab could only drop her off a block north of the towering spire of the Washington Monument, but that was close enough. She paid the guy double the fare plus an extra twenty-dollar bill for his dispatcher and watched him pull away. She walked quickly until she hit the back of the crowd that was lining up ten people or more deep along Madison Avenue to watch the parade, which was due to start any minute.

A sea of faces spread out before her, stretching a mile or more to her right and wrapping all the way up Capitol Hill and around the Capitol building itself. The east end of the Mall was filling up fast with people, there to watch the inauguration ceremony and listen to Gabe's inaugural address on the huge platform that had been erected on the Capitol steps.

Where would she go if she were planning to assassinate the

President-elect, and when would she do it? Gabe would be standing still in the open when he took the oath of office and gave his inaugural speech. It would be easy to use a high-powered rifle and take a shot at him then. Except he'd be surrounded by bulletproof podiums and antisniper measures galore. The less likely option was to hit him in his limousine, which was heavily armored and protected by Secret Service to the hilt. He'd be invincible in the vehicle. *C'mon, Diana. Think like a killer.* How would *she* do it?

Everybody would believe he was safe inside the limousine. If the Q-group could pull off killing him there, the psychological blow to the country would be even greater. It would deliver a message that nobody was safe anywhere. After listening to these guys talk on the Internet for the last couple of months, that sounded exactly like the sort of logic they'd use. Okay. The limo it was. Now, where along the parade route would she try it?

She started to walk. Madison Avenue was a one-way street with traffic traveling west under normal circumstances. But today it was closed and the parade would move east along it. The cold air burned in her lungs and she breathed out a cloud of condensation as she walked quickly along the perimeter of the crowd, looking for *something*. She didn't know exactly what she was looking for, but it had to be here, somewhere. Some spot that was better than the next to make the hit. Some feature that made it the perfect place to kill a president.

The crowd continued to swell around her. Lord, there were a ton of people out here. She was so insignificant among them. One among tens of thousands. How was she supposed to make a difference? She couldn't do it. She was going to fail. Desperation settled around her, constricting her lungs until panic began to set in. *Relax. Breathe. The brain shuts down when panic hits. Keep thinking.* But the demons had her in their grip. She fought to no avail against the drowning sensation that worsened with every step she took. The Smithsonian's massive American History Museum loomed on her left, taking up a full city block. She walked even faster, nearly running past the Natural History Museum, which was no less enormous. The red brick of the original Smithsonian building loomed across the mall, ugly and factorylike.

Nothing jumped out at her. She had no earthly idea where Q-group was going to make its run at Gabe. Being out here wasn't doing any good. A man jostled her. She looked up. Focused on his face. Round. Ruddy. Caucasian. Not her man.

Maybe instead of trying to find a place, she should look for the Q-group members themselves. She had their pictures in her purse. She looked around frantically, focusing on each face until they all blurred into a sea of disembodied features.

Gabe was going to die.

She had to get help. Tell someone! Not a policeman in sight. In the far distance, she heard a band begin to play. Oh, Lord. The parade was starting. By sheer force of will, she beat down the impulse to run screaming. She had to do this. For Gabe. She fixed his face in her mind. His intelligent, compassionate, laughing eyes. And gradually, her pulse calmed. Her breathing slowed down until the steel bands around her chest loosened. *Better. Now think!*

She looked up at the buildings clustering around the Capitol ahead. If the Q-group had snipers and high-powered rifles there, she couldn't do a damn thing about it. There were so many potential perches for a gunman atop the many buildings in the area or behind an office window, she'd never find the killer in time. She'd have to leave that one up to the Secret Service and the FBI, who were much better suited to foil that sort of plan than she could ever be.

Besides, the Q-group attack in Chicago relied on direct application of force. Blowing up Gabe's car would be much more their style.

She looked around, trying to orient herself. In her panic, she'd lost track of where she was. Over there. The West Building of the National Gallery of Art loomed well ahead on her left. A huge banner down the side of the building announced an exhibit of paintings celebrating freedom and its many faces. The banner looked like a stylized American flag, and the thing was a good three stories tall. It would make a great backdrop for a video shot or a photograph.

Bingo. *That was where they'd do it!* They'd splatter Gabe's brains all over a giant American flag. What could be more ironic or make more of a political statement than that?

She took off running toward the building, scanning faces as she went.

Somewhere nearby, among these throngs of people, was a small team of men intent on killing Gabe Monihan. And she had only a little while left to find them.

12:00 P.M.

She reached the National Gallery of Art and its enormous banner. The sidewalk in front of the great structure was crammed with people packed in shoulder to shoulder. Nobody could move over there, let alone maneuver into position to kill anyone. No, the Q-group would have to operate on this side of the street with the relatively open Mall behind them.

The first band passed, a high-school drill team complete with a line of half-frozen girls in hot pants trying to smile and remember their routine. A sheriff's posse from somewhere in Pennsylvania passed by on fractious horses. They didn't like the cold any more than their riders did.

She scanned the sheaf of papers clutched in her hand and went back to watching the crowd. She moved slowly now, methodically observing everyone on this side of the street. She'd swept the area once and was making a second pass through. The faces in the pictures were burned into her brain, and this time she was trying to imagine them with disguises, either in the form of facial hair or clothes obscuring part of their features as she checked out the crowd. She had to spot one of them soon or Gabe was history.

The gnawing sense of doubt was growing in her gut again. She hadn't done enough. She hadn't cracked the code soon enough, hadn't warned the right people in time. Gabe was going to die a horrible, bloody death because she'd let him down. For the third time, she scanned the crowd in front of the art gallery. Nada. Her panic, held at bay for the moment, notched up a little higher.

She was a screwup. Always had been. Her teachers always moaned about how she was wasting her potential. What they didn't know was that her "potential" was a lie. She was not smart, competent Josie, who could fling a supersonic jet through the sky with perfect precision, who handled every crisis in her life exactly correctly, who never screwed up when the chips were down. She was the afterthought little sister. The tagalong who basked in the reflected glow from her illustrious sister but never shone on her own. And man, was she about to blow it big-time.

She jumped when her cell phone rang in her purse, emitting an electronic version of the George Thurgood classic, "Bad to the Bone." She dug it out and looked at the caller ID. "Private Call," it announced. She clicked it on and put it to her ear. "Hello?" she said cautiously.

"Hi, Diana. It's me." She about dropped the phone as the dulcet tones of Gabe Monihan's voice caressed her ear. "How's it going?"

She forgot to breathe. "Uh, i-it's going," she stammered. "I've stirred up a real hornet's nest if that counts for anything."

"Where are you?" he asked.

"I'm in front of the National Gallery of Art along your

parade route. I think this is where the Q-group will try to hit you."

"Lovely," he commented lightly. His truncated comments struck her as odd. As if maybe he couldn't talk in the company he was in.

"Can't talk much right now?" she asked.

"Exactly," he said pleasantly.

"Got it. Fine, you just listen and I'll do all the talking. I think I've uncovered the identities of the men who comprise a Q-group cell. They look to have been based out of New Jersey for the last year or so. I think they're the ones planning to kill you today." She paused in her recitation. "Lord, I hate even hearing those words said aloud."

"Ditto," he agreed.

"At any rate," she rushed on, "I got detained by Army Intelligence for stalking you…isn't that a laugh…but my grandfather sprang me. His driver tried to kidnap me, but I got away."

"Your grandfather?" Gabe asked incredulously.

"Long story. I'll tell you about it later. The thing is, I tried to get a copy of the pictures of the guys I've identified as the Q-group cell to Owen Haas. I doubt he received them, however. I expect it's too late to get them to him now, since I'd guess you're getting ready to move."

"I'm in the car now," Gabe replied.

"Are you sure I can't talk you into telling anyone that these turkeys are going to try to hit you again?"

"I'll be happy to do it after I take the oath. But not until then."

She huffed in frustration. "I was afraid you'd say that. If you get a moment alone, tell Owen to keep an eye out for six to eight men of Berzhaani descent. They all look to be around thirty years old or so. Middle height, medium builds. It's not much for him to go on, I know. But they're out here, somewhere. I can feel it in my gut."

"Me, too."

Now that she thought about it, he did sound tighter than a high-tension wire. But she only knew that because she'd heard him this morning when he was relaxed and open by comparison. The guy hid his stress well. Heck, he had good cause to be stressed out, even if there weren't a bunch of guys hanging around trying to kill him. He was about to take on one of the toughest jobs on the planet.

"How are you holding up?" she asked.

"Okay. I'm not crazy about giving big speeches, truth be told."

"And you're a politician?" Surprise made her voice higher than usual.

"I never was much for campaigning. I enjoy the work, but I'm not fond of what goes into getting the job in the first place."

"Not much for kissing babies?" she asked sympathetically.

"Actually, I like that part," he replied. "The worst part of it is having to shake hundreds upon hundreds of hands when every last person in the crowd wants to impress you with their firm grip. My hand gets so sore I can go days at a time unable to pick up a pen."

"Wow. And you had to feed and shave yourself, too." She added, "You can't imagine the visual image I'm getting right now of Owen Haas feeding you cereal while shaving you."

Gabe's rich laugh filled her ear. "Thanks. I needed that."

She asked, "So aren't you supposed to be doing something important and Presidential right about now?"

"Nah, Justice Browning will tell me what to say. I just repeat after him, and voilà, I'm President."

"How about your speech? Are you going to get through it okay?"

"I've got the whole thing memorized. Besides, all I have to do is read it off a teleprompter."

"Here's a tip for you from my high school speech teacher. Wave your arms around a bit and pound your fist on the podium a couple of times. It'll make you look passionate and will stir up a bunch of patriotic zeal in everyone's chests. Then they won't care so much what you actually say."

He sounded genuinely amused. "Wave my arms and pound the podium, huh? I think I can handle that. Any advice for me on running the country?"

"Don't get me started," she warned laughingly.

"Are you busy tonight?" he asked, shifting topic abruptly.

"Not particularly. Why?"

"Are you going to be at any of the inaugural balls?"

She blinked in surprise. "I've got a ticket to the military ball, but I hadn't decided if I was going to go or not."

"I'll save a dance for you if you'll come," he said winningly. As if he thought she might actually say no. Yeah, right. Not.

She stammered, "Uh…okay. In that case, I guess I'll be there."

"It's a date," he said lightly. The man actually sounded relieved. As if she'd turn down a gorgeous, smart, funny guy like him? Let alone the fact that he was going to be President of the United States. What was he smoking?

"Well, I suppose I'd better keep you alive if I want my dance, then, shouldn't I?"

He laughed aloud. "I'll let you go. Wouldn't want to stop you from doing that. Give me a call if there are any new developments."

"Okay," she answered.

"Promise?" he asked.

"I promise," she replied firmly.

"Thanks, Diana."

"You're welcome, Gabe."

She disconnected the phone. And then stared at it.

Whoops. She'd just committed a huge breach of protocol. She'd called the President-elect of the United States by his first name.

The reality of the crowded street pressed in around her. Face upon face. But no sign of her quarry. Looking for the Q-group cell out here was hopeless. She simply couldn't do it alone. Who could she call in to help who wouldn't arrest her or just take her for a complete kook? There had to be someone.

And then it hit her. Kim Valenti. Her old classmate from Athena Academy, an NSA agent stationed here in the Washington area, had been the woman who'd exposed the Q-group plot in Chicago and caught the suicide bomber at the airport, defusing the bomb with help from an FBI bomb squad member. She'd lay odds Kim was working the inauguration in some capacity today. She might even be in the immediate vicinity.

Diana opened her cell phone again and thumbed through its stored list of phone numbers to Kim's cell phone number. She dialed it and waited impatiently for it to connect.

"Kim Valenti," a voice answered professionally at the other end of the line.

"Kim. Diana Lockworth, here."

"Diana! Long time no hear. How are you doing?"

"I've been better. Look, this is kind of an official call. Do you happen to be in D.C. right now?"

"Yeah. I'm on the Mall. Plastered up against a family from Idaho and some truck driver who, if he doesn't get his elbow out of my ribs pretty quick, is going to lose it."

Diana sighed in relief. "I'm on the Mall, too. I need to talk to you. Now. It's urgent. National security urgent. Is there somewhere we can meet?"

Kim sounded surprised but answered evenly, "I'm at the Capitol. How far down are you?"

"Across from the West Building of the National Art Gallery. On the Mall side of the parade route."

"Got it. Stay put right there. I've got access to a guy in a golf cart and he can run me down there. I'll shift a guy to cover my position and I'll see you in five minutes."

"Roger," Diana answered, all business. "I'll back away from the crowd and be on the grass behind the bystanders. I'm wearing a long, black leather coat and my hair's dyed black. I'll put on a bright blue head scarf."

"You're in disguise?" Kim asked, surprised.

"Yeah."

"I'll be there in three minutes."

The line went dead in Diana's ear. Thank God. Now maybe Gabe stood a chance of walking away from this day alive.

True to Kim's word, a golf cart came tooling down the Mall toward her in three minutes flat. Her old friend jumped out of the cart.

Diana rushed up to her. "Thanks for coming down here."

"What's up?" Kim asked. "And by the way, your hair looks like hell. Josie would knock you on your butt if she saw what you've done to it."

Diana grinned. "It'll wash out. Look. This is going to sound crazy, but I have reason to believe that somebody's going to try to kill Gabe Monihan within the next few minutes."

"Why?" Kim replied tersely.

Diana replied equally tersely, "No time to explain it all. It's a long story, and I'll be happy to tell you the whole thing later. Let's just say I have access to—" *How to describe Oracle and Delphi delicately?* "—to unorthodox sources. But they're impeccable. Please just trust me on this. The bottom line is that the Q-group has another cell here in Washington and is going to try to kill Gabe Monihan again. Today."

"Again?" Kim asked sharply. "Monihan was not the target

of the attack in Chicago. He was just in the wrong place at the wrong time."

"I've approached Q-group from another angle since you tangled with them in Chicago and Baltimore. My source—"

"Ah." Kim cut her off. "I have a feeling we may have a similar source."

Diana stared at her. Did this mean Kim was part of Oracle, too? Kim cocked an eyebrow at her, and although they were sworn not to discuss it, Diana felt certain she knew the answer.

Diana continued hastily, "I've got pictures of the Q-group members who I believe will make the hit. They're out here somewhere. I think they're going to try to kill him in front of that gigantic flag banner over there." She pulled the sheaf of pictures out of her purse and thrust them at her old friend.

But instead of reaching for the pictures, Kim reached for the walkie-talkie hanging off her belt. "I've got to divert the motorcade."

Diana lurched. "No!"

Kim paused in the act of putting the radio to her mouth. "Excuse me?"

"The inauguration's got to go ahead as planned."

"Why?" Kim asked, frowning.

"Gabe was adamant about it. He'll kill me if he isn't sworn in on time."

Kim retorted incredulously, "*Gabe?* As in Gabriel Monihan?"

Uh-oh. "Yeah," Diana mumbled. "Like I said. Long story."

Kim put the radio back in its clip slowly. "Okay, then. So what does he want you—us—to do?"

"Find these guys and stop them."

Kim looked at her watch. "He's due through here in about ten minutes. We don't have time to distribute the pictures to the security team and fine-tooth comb our way through the crowd."

"Take a look through those pictures and then let's get moving. I figure they've got to be on this side of the street because the other side is too crowded to maneuver in."

Kim looked to the north. "I think you're right. Let's space out about fifty feet and start walking the line."

Diana nodded. "I'll call you on my cell phone if I spot them and you can call me if you see them first."

Kim nodded shortly and moved off. Diana did the same. There was something bracing about having somebody else out here helping who didn't think she was completely nuts. But it didn't put more time on the clock, and it didn't mean that the two of them would find these turkeys in the next nine minutes and thirty seconds.

As she walked the line of people, Diana did a rare thing. She said a prayer and willed whatever greater beings might be listening to lead her to the terrorists.

Her phone rang, and she slammed it to her ear. "Hello?"

Kim spoke abruptly, "It's me. We're running out of time. I'm going to run ahead and work the crowd starting at 7th Street and heading toward the Washington Monument from there. You're in charge of this area up to that point. We'll cover more of the parade route that way. When you hit 7th Street sprint ahead to 13th Street and pick up the search a block or so ahead of me."

"Got it." Good idea. By leapfrogging past each other, they'd cover a lot more ground in the next few minutes. They wouldn't hit the whole route by a long shot, but they'd look at a significant chunk of the crowd. It was better than nothing.

Yeah, but was it good enough?

The sounds around her blurred and dulled, fading into the background of her mind, so intense was her concentration on finding one of the faces burned into her mind. She *had* to succeed. She *had* to spot one of these guys. Five minutes to go. No sign of anyone from Q-group. She'd reached 7th Street. She spotted Kim in the crowd, about half a block ahead of her, walking quickly along the Mall, scanning faces with intense concentration of her own.

Diana took off running, moving ahead of Kim. She kept going until she was about a block ahead of her colleague. She slowed to a walk and took up the search again. She took a moment to pull out her phone and hit the auto dial, but resumed the search with the phone plastered to her ear.

"Go ahead," Kim bit out over the phone.

"I'm working the crowd in front of the Natural History Museum. Search up to that spot and then leapfrog me."

"Roger," Kim replied.

Diana disconnected the line and stuffed the phone in her pocket. She spared seconds long enough to glance at her watch. Two minutes until Gabe's motorcade was due to pass through here! Her urgency bubbled over into panic that she barely managed to hold in check. Every second counted now. She walked faster. Pushed herself to scan the sea of faces around her faster.

Faintly in the distance behind her, she heard cheering. Oh, God. Gabe was coming.

Her phone rang.

"Yes?" she panted, running now through the crowd.

"I've got you in sight. I'm going on ahead to the American History Museum. Turn around when you reach it and head back for that flag banner."

"Okay," Diana panted.

Strains of band music wafted to her. Definitely a military brass band. Probably the Marine Band. And it was drawing near. Her heart sank. It would be right in front of the Presidential motorcade. She was almost out of time.

Just a few more seconds. She raced forward now, trying frantically to stay ahead of that inexorable line of black limousines.

But it was useless. The first limousine pulled even with her. She spared a glance at it over her shoulder. She didn't recognize any of the Secret Service agents jogging along beside it. Where was Owen Haas?

Then she glimpsed a long line of limousines behind the first one. Of course. Gabe wouldn't be in the lead car. It would undoubtedly be full of Secret Service agents. Then there'd be carloads of hangers-on—incoming cabinet members, high-roller contributors to Gabe's campaign and Gabe's mother, of course.

She had maybe another thirty seconds or so before Gabe's car went by.

She pressed forward through the screaming crowd, dodging miniature flags being waved wildly. The crowd cheered deafeningly around her. She tried to scan individual male faces, but they blurred together in her panic. It was no use.

She looked ahead, trying to spot Kim in the crowd. She couldn't see her friend through the throngs of people pushing toward the street to see the incoming President. Diana swerved away from the parade route, farther out onto the Mall itself, to get clear enough of the heavy crowd to move.

A movement caught her attention just ahead. A moped. But that wasn't what had captured her notice. It was the second moped coming in from her left as if it planned to join the first moped. She scanned the grassy field in front of her. There! A third moped.

She broke into a full run, heading straight for the oddly moving conveyances. She had to get a look at the guys on those bikes!

The crowd ahead of her moved, swelling back toward the Mall. The first moped was forced to put its brakes on and wove through the mass of bodies, seeking a route forward. It was just the break she needed. She put on an extra burst of speed and drew near enough the moped to catch a glimpse of the driver's face.

Bingo!

She'd seen that face in her sheaf of pictures.

She veered toward him, running flat out, as fast as her body could possibly go. Her legs went numb and her lungs burned like fire as she sucked in the cold air. But she ignored the pain and ran as if her life depended on it. Or rather, as if Gabe Monihan's life depended on it.

1:00 P.M.

She was close enough now to see that she recognized both of the drivers of the other mopeds as well. *She'd done it.* She'd found the Q-group cell and correctly guessed their point of attack. Now she just had to stop the bastards. And she only had a few seconds to do it. No time to pull out her cell phone and call Kim for backup.

Which guy to jump? Probably only one of them would launch the actual attack on Gabe. If she picked the wrong guy to take out, Gabe could be killed anyway.

A wave of noise reached her ears, a traveling cheer growing louder in volume by the second. Oh, God. *That would be the crowd yelling as Gabe's limousine drove past.* She estimated the sound was only a few hundred feet behind her. Two of the men in front of her abandoned their mopeds, leaving them where they landed on the ground, and shoved forcefully into the crowd. Another hundred feet and she'd be upon the third moped.

The third guy, wearing a brown coat, looked to his right. A name popped into her head to match his picture. *Tito Albadian.* Glory Seeker. The probable leader of the Q-group cell.

She glanced to the right, as well, and saw one of the now-on-foot terrorists nod at him. Albadian stopped his scooter and got off, dumping it on the ground. Eighty feet to go until she was on him. As he turned to push into the crowd and she got a look at him in profile, she saw the brown backpack slung over his shoulders.

Weapon! her intuition screamed.

Albadian was the one. He had to be stopped!

Zeroed in on her target now, she dodged pedestrians as she barged forward. A clear space opened up in front of her and she burst into a run. Fifty feet to reach him. He made it into the front row of parade watchers and started to slide the backpack off his shoulders.

She wasn't going to make it. Time slowed to a stop around her as her brain shifted into a weird, out-of-time existence and her life flashed before her. A childhood dominated by fear and embarrassment. The backlash of that embarrassment taking the form of rebellion and anger. A flash of clarity as she abruptly saw her increasingly troubled military career for what it was. A strike back at the establishment that destroyed her family.

Thoughts drifted through her brain randomly as her body continued to move forward of its own volition toward Albadian. Why did she measure her life by its failures and not its successes? Why did she still blame her mother for being sabotaged by criminals out to stop her research? And why in the world was she sticking her neck out like this today, blatantly risking her life for a man who was the very symbol of everything she'd despised for most of her life?

Pow! A body slammed into her from the left, tackling her

and driving her to the ground like a professional linebacker. Ooompf. The air rushed out of her flattened lungs as pain plowed into her like a bulldozer. She stared at the grass from a range of approximately one inch. So much for out-of-body experiences.

What the hell had just blasted into her like that? Or rather, who? Was there a fourth terrorist out here that she hadn't spotted? Someone with the Q-group cell must have spotted her closing in on their man. A surge of fight-or-flight adrenaline roared through her and she heaved upward, throwing the attacker off her back. He was tenacious, though, and hung on as she struggled in his grasp.

She managed to half roll over in his grip and froze, stunned, as she caught sight of dark blue and a flash of brass. A uniform. This guy was a police officer!

She stopped struggling and shouted over the din of the crowd as it started to yell around them, heralding the imminent arrival of Gabe's limousine, "You've got to let me go! Monihan's almost here!"

"No crazy's getting near him on my watch, lady," the cop snarled back.

"You don't understand," she cried frantically. "I'm trying to save him!"

"I was told to be on the lookout for a bunch of nutcases trying to pull something today. You just cool your jets and hold still."

He leaned on her arms, expecting to subdue her by virtue of superior weight. Not a chance. This was exactly the sort of situation her Krav Maga training was designed to handle. She countered the guy's attempt to pin her and reversed the move, landing the cop on his back hard, with her knee planted solidly on his solar plexus. Normally she'd finish him off with a chop to the side of the head, but she didn't have time and the poor guy was a police officer. She left him gasping on the ground, jumped up and turned around facing the parade.

Where had Albadian gone? She searched over heads frantically, trying to spot his brown coat and dark hair.

There. Near the front of the crowd. She shoved toward him, ignoring the squawks of protest as she elbowed people aside. The yells around her grew into a roar. Crud. The first in another line of black stretch limousines came into view in front of her. Five more people to get past.

She all but picked up the woman in front of her and moved her aside in her panic to get to that backpack. She banged a tall, lean teenager aside. Three more people between her and her target. She could almost dive for that backpack.

A second limousine cruised past.

"Hey lady. Quit pushing back there," someone growled at her.

She'd apologize *after* Gabe was safe. She popped the complainer in the back of the knee, knocking the joint out from under him and jumping past him as he partially collapsed.

A third limousine pulled into sight. This one had Secret Service agents at each corner of it, walking beside it briskly. She recognized Owen Haas at the back left corner of the car. Gabe.

She gathered herself to jump at Albadian and watched in horror as he cocked his arm back. And threw the backpack. It sailed up in a brown nylon arc, flying straight for the side of Gabe's limousine.

"Bomb!" she screamed at the top of her lungs.

In slow motion, she saw Owen's head turn toward the sound of her scream. He registered the pack flying at him. He dived and made a catch any NFL receiver would be proud of, and in one move, rolled, popped to his feet and flung the pack under the front end of the limousine behind him.

"Satchel charge!" he roared as the next limo in line came to an abrupt halt.

A single thought pierced her panic. What a brilliant move. The backup limo's engine block and heavy, armor plating would absorb a tremendous amount of the explosion and protect not only Gabe, but the crowd, from the worst of the blast.

All four doors of the backup limousine opened, and men in suits poured out of the vehicle, stumbling and falling over each other in their haste to get away from the metal death trap their car had just become.

And then the backpack blew, sending out a blinding flash of light from under the car. A millisecond later, a tremendous orange fireball erupted, throwing the limousine's front end straight up in the air. The vehicle paused for an endless second, balanced vertically on its back fender like a rearing stallion. Then it slammed down to the ground with a tremendous crash, sending debris outward in all directions.

Burning fuel sprayed the crowd in a deadly blossom of orange, and shrapnel ranging in size from tiny slivers of glass to entire doors flew out into the crowd. Flames enveloped the vehicle and a wall of heat and concussion slammed into her, flinging her backward into a screaming mass of human flesh.

The wall of bodies collapsed behind her, and she fell softly on top of a stack of humanity at least four people deep. Oh, Lord. Somebody was going to be crushed! She scrambled forward on her hands and knees, despite the heat scorching her face from the inferno in front of her.

Dear God, please let Gabe be okay. And please let everyone have gotten out of that ruined hull of a limousine alive.

She looked left at Gabe's limousine. A dozen Secret Service agents lay all over it, using themselves as human shields. A noble sentiment, but wasn't the thing armored already? But then, she knew from the balcony earlier that Secret Service agents were all about putting their bodies between their charge and harm. The Presidential limo's engine revved powerfully and it accelerated away from the chaos behind it, laying down twin trails of rubber as it peeled out. Thank God. Gabe's limousine was unhit enough to get out of here.

One of the grim Secret Service agents clinging to the rear trunk of the vehicle, his arms splayed out across the rear window, looked her way. She'd swear it was Owen Haas. But then the vehicle tore out of sight.

Noise registered in her consciousness. Screaming. Lots of it. Bystanders by the hundreds screaming in panic. Injured people moaning and crying out. Stunned and bloody people staggering around shouting the names of lost loved ones. A handful of overwhelmed police officers trying to control the crowd by bellowing over the top of the entire din.

And then motion registered. People moving, surging backward, running away from the site of the disaster. She looked around, trying to get her bearings. And caught a glimpse of just the right shade of brick brown. Her head whipped in that direction. But it wasn't the bastard who'd done this. It was a man stumbling past her, his shirt partially burned off, its tatters covered in blood.

She scanned the crowd quickly. Where was Albadian? He'd been right up front, not far from the blast. He had to have taken some sort of damage. As people streamed away from the street, scattering in a starburst of panic across the frozen Mall, she cast her gaze back toward the explosion site.

There. Climbing to his feet. Staggering toward one of the abandoned mopeds. The dark-haired terrorist in his brown coat.

She looked around for the cop she'd dropped seconds ago. No sign of the guy. There was no sign of any policeman anywhere near her. And the few uniforms she saw were either too far away or heading straight for the burning limousine behind her.

Albadian righted one of the mopeds. Twisted the throttle

frantically. No! He was going to get away! She took off running toward him. Below the high-pitched screaming of the crowd, she heard the low cough of the moped as its engine caught and turned over. It revved up, sounding more like a chain saw than a motor vehicle. She dived for it, and her hand grazed the rear fender as the moped jerked forward. But it lurched away from her hand. Damn!

She hit the ground hard, knocking the breath out of herself. She sucked hard, dragging air into her lungs by main force. She rolled on her side, looking around frantically. Over there. One of the other mopeds. She pushed painfully to her feet, her chest as sore as if an anvil had just landed on it. Even with adrenaline flooding her body, she still had to forcibly order her feet to move toward the motorized bike.

She finally got a full breath of air and picked up speed, darting for the moped. Bending down, she heaved the conveyance upright and flung her leg over it. Where was the starter switch on this thing? She fumbled around with the controls and managed by some miracle to get it going. She twisted the hand throttle and it leaped forward, nearly unseating her. Whoops! She regained her balance and looked up.

Over there. She located the chain saw-like sound of Albadian's moped off to her left, heading toward the Capitol Building. She pointed her scooter that way and clumsily got into motion. The moped bumped over the frozen, dead grass, but she hung on grimly, gunning the thing after Albadian.

As she figured out the balance of the moped she opened up the throttle, racing across the Mall. The screams and sirens diminished behind her as her quarry raced toward the Capitol. The wind generated by her flight was arctic, and her cheeks went numb in a matter of seconds. Even inside her gloves she lost most of the feeling in her fingers.

Albadian veered to the south side of the Mall, clearing the

worst of the crowds and popped out onto Constitution Ave., which ran east-west, paralleling the south side of the Mall. The bulky white marble structure of the Smithsonian's Air and Space Museum flashed past as she opened up her moped's throttle all the way. She accelerated to nearly thirty miles per hour. Probably by virtue of her weighing less than the guy she was chasing, her moped not only kept pace with Albadian but began to gain on him bit by bit. Another couple of miles and she'd have him.

Albadian raced east around the south end of the Capitol building. People milled about like a herd of agitated and confused sheep down here, unsure of whether to head toward the fireball in the distance to help or whether to run like hell from the point of the attack. She had to slow down to nearly a walking pace to weave through the thronging pedestrians choking the streets. Fortunately, so did Albadian.

She almost missed him when he cut left on 1st Street SE toward the Library of Congress, but a tiny gap opened in the crowd and she glimpsed the red moped. Honing in on her target again, she raced north, toward the Supreme Court building. The steep uphill slope slowed him down and she spurted closer to him, but then her moped hit the hill and she lost most of the ground back. C'mon. Go! She leaned down low over the handlebars to improve her aerodynamic drag. She inched a little bit closer.

Albadian looked back over his shoulder at her as if he'd heard her back here and realized he was being chased. Crud. He turned to face front, crouched low, as well. She gritted her teeth against the frigid windchill and prayed her numb fingers wouldn't slip off the handles. Albadian's driving became erratic, filled with the desperation of a man running for his life. But then, her gut seethed with the implacable fury of a woman who'd just witnessed an attempt to murder someone she cared about. It was about an even match.

Albadian swerved around yet another milling crowd of people, and she did the same, temporarily losing sight of him. She gunned the moped past the pedestrians and searched frantically. Over there. Heading east. She yanked the moped to her right.

Cripes! Her rear tire slipped on a patch of ice, shooting out from underneath her. It was a miracle she managed to stay atop the bike. But, as she straightened out the front tire, the back end fishtailed wildly beneath her. She fought it like a bucking bronc and managed, barely, to bring the cantankerous moped back under control. Definitely *not* designed for snow-and-ice operations.

She looked up. Damn. She'd lost valuable ground on Albadian.

Of all things, her cell phone rang in her pocket. She couldn't spare a hand to answer it just now. Whoever it was would have to wait. She had a terrorist to catch before she could take any calls.

She had to do something to break this stalemate. Their mopeds were too evenly matched for one of them to win this contest. As her target led her down one street after another, she kept an eye out for something, anything to help her.

She blinked in shock as Albadian turned down a set of stairs, for goodness' sake, and rattled down the icy descent. Grimly, she pointed her bike after him and bumped and jarred her way down the staircase after him. He shot out into a residential street, and she did the same. A car swerved wildly to miss them both, its horn blaring behind her. Man, that had been close!

What the hell was she doing? She was going to get herself killed out here! But it wasn't as if the idea of giving up this insane chase was gaining any foothold against her grim rage. She was going to take this guy down if it was the last thing she did.

Albadian turned down a narrow alley and slid on a patch of loose gravel. Warned by his skidding recovery, she took the turn carefully and picked up several yards on him. But as he blasted past a row of trash cans, he reached out with his left hand and knocked over the last one, spewing trash all over the asphalt in front of her.

An empty milk jug exploded beneath her front tire, but she crashed through the mess without slowing down significantly. She shot out into the street, praying like crazy that no oncoming vehicle would wipe her out. Thankfully, there wasn't any traffic.

This guy was insane! But then, that sort of went without saying. He'd just tried to kill the soon-to-be most powerful, and arguably best protected man in the world. Maybe fanatic was a better word for Albadian. Soon-to-be-dead fanatic if she had her way. As her frustration grew, so did her rage. She was going to rip this guy's head off when she caught him.

Apparently, Albadian had a death wish of his own, however, and he led her ever deeper into residential side streets yet to be cleaned off after the snow several days ago. A packed sheet of ice covered the streets, and both mopeds slid all over the place. It was going to be a miracle if they both didn't break their necks on this damned skating rink. Even Albadian was forced to slow down on the ice, and their slow-motion chase began to take on a Chaplin-esque quality as he fled for his life and she chased him determinedly at something like fifteen miles per hour. And even that speed was suicidal in these conditions.

She knew this area. There was a police precinct house just ahead. Hmm. Ignoring the ice, she leaned low over the handlebars, opening up the throttle and urging the moped forward with every ounce of horsepower it had. *Horsepower.* She remembered abruptly that the police station in front of her was also the headquarters for a mounted police unit. She toured it a while back…

It was worth a shot. As Albadian went straight through the intersection in front of the police station, she swerved to the right just shy of it, shooting down a short alley beside the building. She roared around back, startling the heck out of several horses tied at a hitching post beside the building. A cop lounging in front of a heater by the back door lurched to his feet as she burst into view.

She dumped the moped on the ground, more thankful than she could imagine to get off the damned thing in one piece. She raced toward the biggest horse of the bunch, a long-legged chestnut that looked like a Thoroughbred-Quarter Horse cross. Perfect. She needed the fastest horse they had.

She shouted at the cop, "I'm Army Intelligence, and I'm chasing the guy that just tried to blow up Gabriel Monihan. Follow me!"

And with that, she yanked the big, red horse's reins free from the wooden rail they were looped around and flung herself aboard the animal. The stirrups were too long, but she didn't care as she jammed her feet into them awkwardly and reined the horse sharply out of the alley.

The horse's cleated shoes clattered on the hard ice, but dug in sure-footedly as she buried her heels in his ribs. He leaped forward, his haunches bunching and stretching beneath her, shooting her down the alley like a cannon. She careened out into the street.

Thank God. She glimpsed a streak of red and brown about a block ahead of her. She'd lost valuable time and distance, but she estimated this horse could do close to thirty miles per hour over this ice, and Albadian could only pull off about half that speed and hope to live.

She'd have one shot at this. Her horse would have one,

maybe two, all-out sprints in him before he'd tire, and Albadian probably had plenty of gas left in his tank.

She gave the horse his head, lying low on his neck like a jockey and urging him forward with shouts of encouragement. The horse pinned its ears back, and accelerated as if he'd been shot out of a cannon. That would be his Quarter Horse ancestry showing through. But then, he stretched out into the fluid gallop of his Thoroughbred ancestors and gobbled up the gap between her and Albadian with an impressive display of power.

Albadian looked back over his shoulder and gaped in shock. Glaring, he turned to face forward again. He accelerated to a beyond stupid pace on the ice.

But still the powerful horse gained on him. In a full-out run, now, the animal was pushing thirty-five miles per hour, and continued to gain steadily on the moped. As if he sensed what her target was, the beast stretched his neck out even lower, his head pumping up and down with his effort to overtake the moped.

His nose almost touched Albadian's back now.

But she also felt her horse beginning to strain, his muscles beginning to tire as oxygen debt and fatigue set in.

"C'mon, just a little more, fella," she urged her mount.

As if he understood her, he put on one last burst of speed and pulled up beside Albadian. Without stopping to consider the insanity of what she was about to do, she kicked her right stirrup free and let go of the reins. And slid off the left side of the horse.

She wrapped her arms around Albadian's neck and tackled him like a steer she intended to wrestle to the ground. The force of the impact knocked over the moped, slamming them both to the ground. They rolled over and over, and she hung on for dear life as they tumbled down the icy street.

"Bitch!" Albadian gasped.

"Bastard!" she snapped back.

He threw an elbow backward at her, and she absorbed the blow with a grunt, too mad to feel the pain that should've accompanied the shot to her ribs. She let go of his neck with her right hand, making a fist in front of his face with the tip of her thumb sticking out. She jabbed it up and back, into his right eye socket.

He howled with pain and fury and heaved beneath her, struggling to throw her off. He fought like a maniac on crack. She slammed her forehead forward into the base of his skull, nearly knocking herself loopy in the process. She blinked hard as she saw stars. That blow should have knocked him out cold, but still he fought on. She hung on grimly, but began to doubt her ability to subdue this lunatic.

And then she felt his coat go slack in her arms. The bastard had unzipped it and was slipping out of it! She let go of the soft fabric and rolled to her knees, popping to her feet at the same instant Albadian did. She could see it in his eyes. He was going to run. Dammit.

"Don't even think about running away from me," she bit out. "I ran the Boston Marathon last year and finished in the top fifty women." It was a blatant lie, but what this asshole didn't know wouldn't hurt him.

It worked. Instead of fleeing, he dropped into a half crouch, his lips pulled back from his teeth in a snarl a pit bull would have been proud of. This was more like it. Unless this guy was a Krav Maga master, she had him. Not even the traditional martial arts stood up well to the vicious, dirty style of street fighting. She was going to *hurt* him now.

In a blindingly fast move, his hand jerked. But not toward her. He whipped it behind him. And whipped it back out in front of him—with a handgun in it. Pointed directly at her face.

"Die, you bitch."

2:00 P.M.

Gabe had slammed into the limousine's seat cushion as somebody landed on top of him. Jeez. That was the second time today someone had tackled him like a damned linebacker. And this time it wasn't a gorgeous, sexy blonde who made him think completely inappropriate thoughts.

But then a tremendous explosion had sounded outside the car. Really damn close.

"Are you hit?" someone barked in his ear.

"I don't think so," he'd managed to gasp, in spite of the Secret Service agent crushing him.

"Go, go, go!" a voice had shouted from outside the car, right behind him. That sounded like Owen Haas. The limousine had jerked beneath him, accelerating like an Indy race car. Who'd have thunk one of these tanks had it in them? The vehicle squealed around a corner. And around another.

The earpiece of the guy on top of him had vibrated with a

cacophony of voices shouting through it. Men down. Civilians hit. Screams for emergency response vehicles. Jesus Christ. What happened back there?

He hadn't wanted to distract the grimly silent man on top of him, but as the car screeched around a third corner and the earpiece went relatively silent for a moment, he'd taken the opportunity to ask, "What the hell just happened?"

"Satchel charge got tossed at your car. One of the guys, Haas, I think, picked it up and tossed it under the backup vehicle before it blew."

"A satchel charge?" he'd asked incredulously. "As in a bomb?"

"Yup. One of the agents on scene is estimating it was a standard military load."

"What does that mean?" Gabe had asked tersely, already not liking the sound of it.

"Twenty pounds of C-4," the agent answered.

Mother of God. Someone had just lobbed twenty pounds of high explosives at him? "How many people are hurt?" he'd bitten out.

"No damage assessments yet. One of the guys says he counts about fifty people down on the ground. So far, most of them seem to be alive."

Fifty? *Fifty?* Fifty Americans injured or killed because some crazy had it in for him? Deep in his gut, anger had begun to simmer. "I assume you guys know what to do next with me?"

The agent answered dryly, "Yes, sir. We practice scenarios like this all the time. We've got it under control."

"Fifty people down damn well doesn't sound under control to me," he'd snapped. He'd paused. Taken as deep a breath as the two-hundred-pound man on his back allowed. "I'm sorry. Stopping nutcases isn't your responsibility."

The agent replied shortly, "It is when they're coming after you. At least we did the most important part of our job. You're alive."

"Thanks," Gabe replied seriously.

"Thank Owen Haas. He's the guy who dived for that charge and lobbed it away from your car."

"I will. The moment I see him." And then a horrible thought had struck him. "He is okay, isn't he?"

"If you look up over your right shoulder, sir, you'll see him through the back windshield."

Gabe had looked up, startled. Haas was plastered across the back of the car. "Is he hurt?" he'd asked his bodyguard in alarm.

"I dunno," the agent answered.

"Well, hell's bells. Stop the car, man, and find out! If he's hurt, we've got to get him to a hospital!"

"Sorry, sir. The prime directive is to get you under cover and safely secured. Haas would have my head on a platter if I stopped this car for him right now."

Gabe had subsided underneath the agent. The guy was right. Haas was absolutely single-minded in his pursuit of keeping Gabe safe.

The car drove for what seemed like forever while those first few minutes after the blast ran through his head over and over.

He closed his eyes yet again. Jesus. Fifty people. Diana had been right. She said the Q-group would try to nail him today. Good Lord! Was *she* hurt? When he'd called her, she said she was on the parade route near the National Art Gallery, searching for the terrorists. That was right near where the bomb had gone off. Had she found the terrorists? Was she one of those fifty people lying hurt or dead on the ground?

"I've got to make a phone call," he grunted. "Any chance you could get off of me so I can do it?"

"Sorry, sir. You can't make any calls right now. But, FYI,

the protocol in a situation like this is to notify and lock down the current president. The members of both the old Cabinet and your Cabinet will be scattered and taken to secure locations, and NORAD will be notified to raise the DEFCON status. Like I said, everything's taken care of."

"It's a personal call," Gabe replied wryly. "But thanks for the information."

"Sorry. No calls. Not until you're off the streets."

"And how long is that going to take?" he asked sharply, none too pleased at being told he couldn't call Diana to check on her.

"A couple more minutes, sir. We're almost there."

Where in the hell "there" was, was anybody's guess. These guys knew what they were doing and had all sorts of contingency plans for situations just like this. It was their show until they deemed him safe. And until then, he was only along for the ride. Little more than precious cargo. Hell, he wasn't even President yet.

The bastards had tried to kill him before he took the oath of office. Why were they so damned worried about him becoming President, anyway? It wasn't as if he had any big agenda where Berzhaan was concerned, other than doing what the Berzhaani people had been screaming for the U.S. to do already. What was it about him that had these guys so pissed off?

The limousine made another sharp turn but this time it decelerated after it straightened out. The engine noise echoed as though they'd just driven inside a building of some kind. Then it stopped altogether.

"If you'll just stay put and stay down for a moment, sir, we have to secure the area before we move you."

Thankfully, the big agent got off him. Gabe drew his first deep breath since this whole thing started. The passenger door opened briefly as the agent slipped outside. Gabe caught a glimpse of what looked like an oversize garage, dim and concrete.

He lay there for perhaps a minute. A guy could get damned paranoid after someone tried to kill him a second time. First Chicago, and now this. It didn't help to have these fanatical Secret Service agents hustling him around as though the sky was about to fall on his head, either.

The car door opened abruptly, and despite himself, he jumped.

Owen Haas stuck his head in the door. "It's all clear, sir. If you'd please come with me."

He sat up, grateful to be vertical. As he slid toward Haas, he asked, "How're you doing, Owen? Are you hurt?"

"I'm fine, sir," came the implacable reply.

Right. As if the guy would admit it if one of his limbs was falling off and he had a sucking chest wound. What had he been thinking to even ask? Gabe followed the agent across the expanse of gray concrete toward a lighter gray door. A half-dozen agents ranged around the space, which was probably a small warehouse of some kind, their guns drawn. The sight of their weapons in hand reminded him sharply of the gravity of the situation.

An agent opened the door as he and Owen reached it. He reached out to touch its surface as they hustled past it. It felt like stainless steel. In a warehouse? Clearly this wasn't any ordinary warehouse they'd brought him to.

Haas, already starting down the staircase that descended away from the door, looked back over his shoulder. "Hurry, sir," the agent said quietly.

He picked up the pace, practically running down the steps to keep up with the Secret Service agent. Lightbulbs mounted high on the wall in mesh cages lit the way at regular intervals.

The stairway went on forever, down and down and down. Where in the world were they taking him?

Finally, they reached the bottom, and another stainless steel door. Haas reached for the doorknob. "Stay here, sir. I've got to go check on our train, and then I'll be back to collect you."

Gabe frowned. Train? And then it hit him. The Metro! They'd just gone down into the D.C. subway system.

Four agents closed ranks around him in a tight formation on the tiny landing. It was a good thing he wasn't claustrophobic or he'd be flipping out right about now. The door burst open, and he jumped, along with the Secret Service men. He'd never seen this bunch so edgy. And that was saying a lot. They made tense a way of life.

"This way," Haas directed the phalanx of men.

Carried along in the agents' midst, he was swept out into the dim light of a subway station, miraculously cleared of anyone except a line of police officers. They must've been sent down here ahead of time to clear out the civilians.

A sleek, white subway train sat at the platform, completely empty. Haas and company hustled him onto the train and made him lie down on the floor. They all stood around him, facing outward, their weapons still drawn, while he got a cockroach's-eye view of their shoes.

The train ride was short. It proceeded down a straightaway for just a few minutes, and then it angled off sharply.

"You can sit up now, sir," Owen told him. The agent held a hand down to help him up.

He stood up and looked outside the window. He'd never seen any subway tunnel that looked like this before. It was narrow and dark, its walls barely wider than the train. "What is this? Some sort of maintenance tunnel or something?"

Haas nodded grimly. "Something like that."

Gabe grabbed the metal pole beside him as the train

lurched, slowing down abruptly. It stopped and the doors slid open. A tiny platform, only big enough to hold maybe a half-dozen people stood before the opening. Another stainless steel door gleamed dully at the back of the cement platform.

Haas stepped forward and keyed in a code on a number pad beside the door.

The other Secret Service agents stepped aside to allow him to proceed. They were finally starting to relax a bit around the gills. He stepped forward and followed Haas into a room that could practically be a carbon copy of the Situation Room at the White House. Television screens lined the walls, and a dozen clocks announced the time in different capitals around the world. A large conference table dominated the center of the room, and telephones ranged all around its highly polished surface.

Haas walked around the table to the far end of the compact briefing room and stopped beside a closed door. "There are quarters this way if you'd like to clean up or rest a little."

He probably looked like hell. But he didn't give a damn at the moment. "Can I make a phone call now?" he asked Owen.

"To whom?"

"Diana Lockworth. The woman who had breakfast with me this morning. She was at the parade and I want to make sure she's all right."

Haas spoke a little less emotionlessly than usual. "I think she may have been the one who shouted the warning to me that the bomb was incoming."

That wouldn't surprise Gabe. She'd struck him as highly intelligent and highly competent. It would be like her to have found the Q-group cell in that crowd of tens of thousands. But it also confirmed his worst fear. She'd been at ground zero when that bomb went off, and without the benefit of an armored car to protect her. He swore violently under his breath.

Haas's eyebrows shot up at his rare outburst. "You'll have to use a land line, sir. We're too deep for a cell phone to work." Haas stepped to the table and picked up one of the phones. He spoke quietly into it and then handed the receiver to Gabe. "The White House operator is standing by to connect you if you'll give her the number."

Gabe took the receiver Haas offered him, but paused when the big man spoke again.

The agent pitched his voice in a low murmur for Gabe's ears alone. "She knew something about that attack, didn't she?"

Gabe nodded once in silence.

Haas murmured, "I'd like to talk to her when you're done, sir. I want to know everything she can tell me about what happened up there."

Gabe nodded again. He'd entrusted his life to this man, and the guy'd just saved it. If he couldn't let Owen in on his secrets, who else could he trust? Gabe pulled out his cell phone and read Diana's number off its display to the operator. He waited impatiently while the call went through.

In a moment she announced, "I'm sorry, sir. All the circuits are busy. I'll keep trying until I get through and then I'll ring you back."

"Thank you." It figured. Everyone and their uncle was calling relatives to make sure loved ones were okay.

The phone rang on the table and he picked it up eagerly. "Diana?"

A deep male voice replied, "Sorry. It's James Whitlow. You all right, son?"

For once, the term "son" didn't sound like an insult coming from his soon-to-be predecessor. Always before, President Whitlow's incessant use of the term had set his teeth on edge.

Gabe answered the guy's question. "I'm fine, Mr. President. How about you?"

"As well as can be expected in the circumstances. I'm going on television in a few minutes. You'll be able to see it as soon as they've got the bomb shelter up and running."

Gabe looked around in surprise. So that's what this place was. This facility had been mentioned in one of the dozens of briefings he'd gotten over the last couple of months to bring him up to speed on the nation's security apparatus. As he recalled, this bunker was pretty outrageously outfitted. He could run the country from down here. For a *long* time.

Gabe asked, "Do you want to contact the families of the dead with condolences, or shall I?"

"The FBI won't have a complete casualty list for another several hours, and then notifications to the next of kin will have to be made. It'll be tomorrow before the condolence calls can go out. Looks like you're stuck with the job."

Gabe winced. It certainly wasn't a duty he was looking forward to, but it was appropriate that he make the calls. After all, it was him the attackers had been after when they killed the bystanders. At least Whitlow wasn't going to try to usurp this one last Presidential duty.

The president interrupted his grim thoughts. "My press secretary wants me to tell the nation I've spoken with you on the phone and that you're completely unharmed and in good spirits. Any messages I can pass along?"

"Tell them my prayers are with the people injured in the attack, and that I share your determination to apprehend whoever did this."

"I will." There was a brief pause while he spoke to somebody nearby. Whitlow came back on the line. "As for your inauguration. How do you feel about rescheduling it for early this evening in the rotunda of the Capitol Building? My Secret Service people say that building can be made secure, but it's still big enough for the press to be there and holds enough guests so it doesn't look like we're running scared. My people think the inauguration needs to be televised live so there's no doubt about the handoff of power having happened in a smooth and timely manner. Wouldn't want any crazy rumors to get started about your presidency before you're even in office."

Right. As if there hadn't been rumors swirling around him ever since the first Q-group attack, compliments of his erstwhile running mate, Thomas Wolfe. "That sounds fine. I'll pass the suggestion on to my people and have them get back with your people. But I don't anticipate any problems with it."

Ah, the joys of changing administrations, particularly when there was a change of political party involved. It had been a tough campaign, and the outgoing president had been bitter throughout the transition phase.

Gabe asked, "Where will you be during the swearing in? I assume our security teams want us in separate locations?"

"I'll stay here in the White House until you're sworn in. And then the job's all yours, son. This mess reminds me of why I'm glad to be retiring from politics."

Gabe mentally snorted. Come tonight, Whitlow would have to be peeled out of the Oval Office with a crowbar, kicking and screaming the whole way. As it was, he had no doubt his predecessor was tickled pink to get an extra five hours on the job.

Gabe hung up the phone and turned to Owen Haas. "For lack of any of my other staff or advisors, I guess you get to be 'my people.'"

Haas grinned, although it looked more like a crack in concrete than an actual facial expression.

Gabe continued. "Whitlow's people want to hold my inauguration in the Capitol Rotunda at seven o'clock this evening. That okay with you?"

Haas shrugged. "Works for me. I'll need to get a detail of men over there to start clearing the building ASAP."

Gabe looked over at the other Secret Service agents huddled in a far corner of the room. "Would one of you guys call the White House and let them know the plans for tonight are a go?"

A burly blonde peeled away from the group and reached for a telephone. Haas gave a couple of short orders and several of the men sat down at other phones. Soon, they were in deep conversation with their people. Funny, but he didn't have a blessed thing to do. He sat down at the end of the table and noticed a small slide-out tray under the table. He pulled it open. An elaborate TV remote controller sat there, along with various writing utensils and a pad of paper.

He pulled out the remote and pointed it at the wall of monitors. One of the televisions blinked on, startling Haas. Gabe grinned at the disgruntled agent. "Down, Tonto. I just want to see how the news networks are spinning the attack."

Haas scowled and went back to his phone calls.

Gabe stared at the television screen as it replayed in slow-motion, full-color detail the last few moments prior to the attack. The voice-over and a digital arrow added by the network pointed out a blurry object sailing through the air, frame by painfully slow frame, toward his limousine. Hell of a move Owen made there. Gabe flinched as the satchel charge blew up the backup limousine in vivid living color. Good God, that was a hell of a blast! He watched the ensuing carnage in dismay, gruesome even after being edited for home viewing.

And Diana had been caught in that?

Holy Mary, Mother of God. He picked up the phone. Instead of a dial tone, a female voice said immediately, "White House secure operator. May I help you?"

"This is Monihan. Any luck getting through to that phone number I gave you?"

"Not yet, sir. We've gotten through to the phone once

and it rang, but there was no answer. As soon as the party you're trying to contact picks up, we'll forward it through to you."

"Thanks."

Dammit, where was Diana? Why wasn't she answering her phone? What had happened to her? His gaze swiveled back to the screen. He stared at the bloodied and torn bodies of dozens of victims lying on the ground in various stages of triage and evacuation. He was about to be the President of the United States, for God's sake, and he couldn't find out what had happened to the courageous, feisty, funny woman who'd been willing to sacrifice her life for him?

He picked up the phone again.

"What can I do for you, Mr. President-elect?"

This operator was slick. He replied, "I need the names of the victims of the bombing. One name in particular. Who should I speak to?"

"At the moment, that would be the Chief of the Washington Metro Police Department. By this evening, the Director of FEMA—the Federal Emergency Management Administration, and the Director of the FBI should have that information."

"Connect me to the Chief of Police."

Without comment, the operator patched him through.

"What?" a voice snapped in his ear without preamble. The poor man sounded harassed beyond belief, and Gabe felt a twinge of guilt for bugging him. But he was really worried that Diana hadn't answered her phone. If she'd indeed been the one to shout the warning to Owen, she'd saved his life. He owed her. Big-time.

"This is Gabe Monihan. I'm sorry to bother you, but do you have an initial casualty list yet?"

The police chief sputtered. "Uh, forgive me, sir. Didn't mean to be rude, there."

"You're authorized under the circumstances. I'd be more worried if you weren't short with me. How's it looking?"

"The fire's contained. Six dead and about sixty injured. Some minor, some severe. Probably gonna lose another couple more before it's all said and done. Good thing your man tossed that bomb under an armored car or we'd be looking at a whole lot more casualties. We still have some injuries trickling in to area hospitals. No suspects yet. We've got imagery of the bastard—pardon me—the perpetrator. It's at the FBI lab now getting digitally enhanced so we can make out a face and put out an APB. We'll get him, sir."

"I'm sure you will," Gabe replied smoothly. "I had a friend at the parade and I have reason to believe she was very near the blast site. Could you check her name against the casualty lists for me?"

"Of course, sir."

"Her name's Diana Lockworth."

There was a short pause. "Her name's not on my list. Either she wasn't hurt or she hasn't been reported through the hospitals to us, yet."

"But she's not one of the known dead?" Gabe asked.

"No. We've got names on all of them. Next of kin are about to be notified."

Gabe sagged in his chair in relief. Thank God. "Let me know if there's anything you need from me."

The police veteran grunted. "A small tactical nuclear strike up the ass of this SOB when we find him?"

Gabe chuckled. "You got it. Keep up the good work."

He hung up the phone as frustrated as before. Where in the bloody hell was Diana?

3:00 P.M.

Diana stared at the tiny black bore of the pistol pointed at her. Hard to believe that nearly instantaneous death could come out of something so small.

And then behind her, she heard the sound of hooves clattering on the hard ice. The police officer. The horse was coming at a dead run judging by the rapid, staccato sound of it. Albadian's head jerked up.

Now!

She took two running steps and dived for the gun. Both her hands wrapped around the guy's forearm and shoved upward with all her might. The force of her body slamming into his knocked Albadian's feet out from under him on the icy street and he crashed to the ground. She collapsed on top of him, maintaining her death grip on his wrist. At all costs, she must not let go!

Four black, equine legs scrambled to a stop beside her, and she shouted in warning, "Gun!"

A male voice behind her bellowed in response, "Freeze!"

With all due respect, she wasn't going to let go of Albadian's wrist until that gun was completely out of his hands. The terrorist continued to struggle beneath her and she hung on grimly. He tossed her back and forth, shaking his arm furiously to dislodge her.

Something heavy landed on top of her, pancaking her against Albadian. Another pair of hands came up beside hers, grasping Albadian's wrist powerfully.

The cop shouted, "Drop the gun! Now!"

Although the command didn't seem to impress Albadian, the arrival of two more cops on horseback and the sound of sirens drawing near finally took the starch out of him. He went limp beneath her. Neither she nor the cop on top of her moved, however, until several more policemen came running up, weapons propped in their fists in front of them.

Someone stepped up and plucked the gun out of Albadian's hand. The first cop rolled off her, and she followed suit, rolling onto her back, breathing hard. Lord, that had been a close call.

She looked up and blinked as a pair of pistols pointed at her this time.

"Hands over your head, lady," a policeman ordered.

She complied promptly. "My name is Captain Diana Lockworth. I'm Army Intelligence, and that's the guy who just threw the satchel charge at Gabriel Monihan. If one of you would like to reach into my left coat pocket, my wallet is in there with my military ID."

One of the cops did as she suggested gingerly, then stepped back to open the wallet. He announced, "There's a military ID in here. Defense Intelligence Agency building access card, concealed weapons permit." He looked down at her sharply. "You packing?"

She snorted. "I wish. Do you think I'd have been wrestling around hand to hand with that jerk if I were?"

The cops grinned. One of them held a hand down to her and helped her to her feet. "Care to tell us how you know who this guy is?"

"I saw him lob the backpack at Monihan's limousine. Speaking of which, is Gabe—I mean President-elect Monihan—okay? Did he get away safely?"

One of the policemen replied, "Nobody knows a damn thing. His limo drove away from the scene so it wasn't hit too bad, and there've been no calls to the cops for an escort to any hospitals. He's probably fine."

She closed her eyes. She'd done it. Gabe was still alive.

A cop interrupted her profound relief. "And how did you end up chasing this guy?"

"He had a moped. I grabbed another moped one of his accomplices abandoned at the scene and took off after him. But we were on identical machines and I couldn't make up the gap between us. When he hit the ice and had to slow down to almost walking speed, I remembered your precinct was ahead of us. I swung in to your parking lot and snagged a horse that could go full speed or close to it on the ice. By the way, I need to thank whomever I borrowed the horse from."

One of the cops smiled. "Give him a few minutes. When he's checked Red over and knows his horse is okay, he'll be friendlier—especially after he finds out why you took his baby."

Diana nodded solemnly. "His horse is responsible for capturing this guy. I couldn't have done it without Red."

She turned around and caught the tail end of a policeman carefully reading Albadian his rights off an index card. Good. These guys were going by the book every step of the way on this arrest. She watched the mob of armed policemen finish trussing up Albadian until he could barely move. They taped plastic bags over his hands so they could be swabbed for exposure to explosives later, then they handcuffed his wrists and shackled his ankles. Finally, they tucked Albadian carefully into the back seat of a squad car.

"We're going to need a statement from you, ma'am."

Diana turned to the policeman and laughed. "You, and the FBI, and the Secret Service, and every television network in creation. No problem."

She started as her cell phone rang again and fumbled for it in her pocket with frozen fingers. She pulled it out hastily and flipped open the phone.

A male voice spoke urgently in her ear without preamble. "Diana? Are you all right?"

"Gabe? Is that you? Are you okay?"

Gabe's rich voice replied urgently, "I'm fine. Are *you* all right? Tell me you weren't hurt in that blast."

"No, no, I'm fine. I just got knocked down. No injuries. And you? You didn't get hurt at all?"

He laughed, sounding vastly relieved. "I was sitting in an armored car. It didn't mess up a single hair on my head. I think the only injuries I sustained were when a three-hundred-pound Secret Service agent landed on top of me and wouldn't get off me for about a week."

Diana laughed aloud in her relief. "He was just doing his job."

Gabe groused lightly, "Well, it wasn't nearly as much fun as having you plastered all over me."

Diana blinked, startled. She replied soberly, "Well, I'm just glad you're safe."

He replied equally seriously, "And I'm glad that you're safe. I've had the White House operator trying to call your cell phone for the last half hour, and when you didn't answer, I was really worried."

"Uh, well, I was a little busy. I just chased down the guy

who lobbed the satchel charge at you. With the help of a dozen D.C. police officers, we just arrested him."

"I'll tell Owen."

She heard Gabe's voice faintly over the open phone line as he told his security chief the news. She heard exclamations in the background from several people.

Gabe came back on the line. "Owen wants to talk to you. Right away. He wants to know everything you know about what just happened and who did it."

That was understandable. "I'm with the Metro police right now. They want me to go down to the station and make a full statement to them. I expect it'll take a couple of hours."

She waited while Gabe relayed that information to Owen Haas.

Gabe came on the line again. "Owen doesn't want to wait that long. I've still got to get inaugurated today, and he wants a complete threat assessment ASAP so he can take whatever precautions are necessary." Murmured voices in the background interrupted him, and then he said, "Owen will take care of it. He's going to call the cops and explain to them that they're going to have to wait for their statement."

"I'm at Owen's disposal. I'll do whatever I can to help protect you."

Gabe answered quietly, "Thanks. I wish I had more friends like you."

Abashed, she changed the subject. "Is Wolfe there with you?"

"Lord, no. In a crisis like this, they separate us so at least one of us will survive whatever attack comes."

Of course. She asked, "So how am I supposed to link up with Owen to brief him?"

"Just a sec." Gabe went off-line again and came back. "He says to have the police drive you to your home. Owen will have one of his guys pick you up there in two hours. He's got some security arrangements to finish up for…later, and then he'll have time to talk."

"Does he know where I live?" she asked in surprise.

Gabe answered dryly, "If he doesn't, he will soon."

She laughed. "Big Brother's watching me, huh?"

Gabe laughed back. "Something like that. These Secret Service guys have nutty access to information when it pertains to a threat against the Presidency."

Gee, sort of like Oracle.

"Speaking of information, Owen says he wants to know if you had anything to do with a set of pictures he was faxed a few minutes ago of a bunch of guys."

"What sort of pictures?" she asked cautiously.

"He says they're computer printouts of fourteen guys, all in the twenty-five to forty or so age range. Some of the pictures look like they came off driver's licenses. One is marked as a student ID. A couple are immigration photos."

The sheaf of pictures she'd dropped in front of the Chaosium Café. Her hacker buddies had come through for her. They'd figured out who Owen Haas was and sent the pictures to him.

"That's the Q-group cell, or most of it I think, that attacked you today."

Gabe swore quietly and relayed the information to Owen, but came back on the line quickly. "Owen says he'll have a guy at your house in one hour. Can you be there that soon?"

She looked at the policemen milling around her. "The trick is going to be getting the cops I'm with now to release me."

Gabe retorted, "Owen will take care of that. You just be home in an hour."

She replied lightly, "For you Gabe, I'll move Heaven and Earth to be there."

Silence greeted that remark. Oops. Had she overstepped

her bounds? Her and her irreverent mouth. "I'm sorry. That was a joke. I didn't mean to make you uncomfortable, sir. I'll be ready in an hour."

Gabe retorted quickly, "You didn't make me uncomfortable. And for God's sake, please don't start calling me sir. I like Gabe a whole lot better coming from you. And Diana?"

"Yes?"

"I'm looking forward to seeing you again."

Well, okay then. It was her turn to stammer and stutter into a loaded silence. Finally, she managed to choke out, "I'd better get going if I'm going to be home in time to meet Owen's man."

She hung up reluctantly and stared at the phone for a moment after its glowing face went dark. She shook herself out of her reverie and looked up at the nearest police officer. "Who's in charge around here?"

The cop pointed to a man in a suit and she strode over to the detective in charge. "Hi, my name's Diana Lockworth. I wanted to give you a heads-up that within the next couple minutes, a Secret Service agent named Owen Haas is going to get in touch with you or your superiors. He's in charge of Gabe Monihan's security detail, and he needs to speak to me right away. I realize you guys need a complete statement from me, but Haas is going to pull rank and declare some sort of Presidential Security necessity to talk to me first."

The detective sighed in resignation. "I probably should've expected that. But I've got to have a statement out of you in the next twenty-four hours so I can charge Albadian. If Monihan's people screw that up…" He scowled in frustration and didn't finish the remark.

She felt sorry for the guy. He was just trying to do his job and handle this case perfectly so there'd be no chance of Albadian slipping through the justice system's fingers. She asked, "Would a tape-recorded statement from me work for you guys?"

"As a preliminary statement, yeah, it would."

"How about this, then?" she proposed. "You guys can give me a ride back to my house where I'm supposed to meet Haas's men, and I'll tape a verbal statement in the car on the way there."

The detective nodded. "That would work. Hey, Frankie!"

Another policeman walked up to them. "Yeah?"

"This lady's going to need a ride to her house, and I need you to go with her and take a taped statement from her en route."

The cop frowned at the highly irregular procedure.

The detective's cell phone rang, and he pulled it out. He glanced up at Diana. "Right on cue. It's the Chief of Police."

She listened to the detective's end of the short call, and sure enough, he was given orders to delay interviewing her and get her home right away. Good thing she'd given him the heads-up and an alternative plan. He didn't waste any time arguing with his boss and probably earned brownie points when he mentioned he planned to get a taped statement from her in the car en route. In a matter of seconds, Frankie had scared up a pocket Dictaphone and led her toward one of the clustered police cars blocking the street.

She passed by a squad car and glanced at it. She jumped as Albadian glared out at her. Through the glass, he mouthed, "You'll die, bitch."

She nodded back at him grimly. She might at that. But not today.

4:00 P.M.

The police got Diana across town in record time, but it was a breeze with the streets so deserted. Everyone was no doubt plastered to their TV sets or flat-out hiding from further possible terrorist attacks. Some brave new world it was turning out to be. She made a brief statement into the tape recorder her police escort shoved under her nose. She started her narrative at the point of seeing Albadian moving through the crowd with a backpack and thinking it looked suspicious. She might eventually tell the police how she recognized Albadian and how she knew to look for him in the first place, but first she needed to talk to Owen Haas and Delphi, and let them determine how much got released to whom about this threat to the President-elect.

When she got home, she had about a half hour before Owen's man was due to arrive. Thank goodness. She couldn't wait to get this awful black dye out of her hair. She jumped into the shower and turned the temperature up as high as she could stand it. As she thawed out, she edged the temperature up higher and higher until her skin turned pink and her bathroom filled with thick steam. Although she could stay in there happily for an hour, duty called. Three vigorous shampoos later, she stepped out of the shower, blond once more.

She dried off, blow-dried her hair quickly and dressed in a tailored wool pantsuit and matching turtleneck. The pale blue fabric had a touch of Lycra in it and followed the contours of her body closely. It was one of her favorite outfits. It was fully classy enough to see the President-elect of the United States in, but it was still comfortable, and just sexy enough to give a girl confidence. She put on a touch of makeup for good measure. She might not get to see Gabe when she talked to Owen this afternoon, but she wasn't taking any chances. She was going to look her best for once.

Five minutes early, a knock sounded on her front door. The Secret Service must subscribe to the same definition of what constituted being on time as the Army did. If you weren't five minutes early, you were late. She opened the door. And started in surprise. She'd expected a burly, serious Secret Service agent in a conservative suit, but instead her older sister stood there, looking better than any woman had a right to in a long, red coat.

Diana gaped. "What are you doing here?" she finally managed to say.

"Well, gee, you don't have to sound so thrilled to see me!" Josie exclaimed. "The family's been frantic about you. When Gramps' car got to the Pentagon and you were already gone, he got all worried about you. Then that bomb went off downtown, and the phone lines are all jammed, and you didn't answer your phone—let's just say Mom and Dad are panicked. They sent me over here to check on you."

She'd been gone when her grandfather's car had reached the Pentagon? Then who...? "I didn't know you were in town," Diana mumbled, stepping back from the door to let her sister inside before Josie ran her over and forced her way in.

"Diego had a couple meetings at the Pentagon and I had some shopping to take care of, so I took a couple of days' leave and came with him. Mom wanted to visit Gramps so she tagged along. They've got some...catching up...to do."

Now there was a delicate word for it. Her mother and grandfather had a huge rift to heal between them. He'd never been able to accept Zoe Lockworth's clinical depression and had railed at her irresponsibility for wallowing in it for years. Now that the antidote had been found, Joseph Lockworth had some serious crow to eat with his daughter-in-law, and she had some serious forgiving to do.

Fortunately, she and Josie had already worked out most of their differences. When she'd flown out to California to help Josie, and got shot in the process, it had gone a long way toward reminding them what was most important among families. She just wished she could've helped Josie complete clearing their mother's name. Heck, she just wished she could do something noteworthy all by herself for once without Josie coming to the rescue.

Diana commented lightly to her sister, "As you can see, I'm just fine. You can report back to the clan that I'm alive and well."

"Thank God," Josie replied fervently. "What a mess. Did you see it on TV? What do you think happened?"

Diana bit her lip and said nothing. Hopefully, Sis would interpret her noncommittal shrug as ignorance.

Josie barged into the living room, shedding her coat as she went. "We need to talk."

Oh, Lord. Not now. The Secret Service guy would be here

any second. Diana said with thin patience, "Look, Sis. I'm expecting someone in just a few minutes. Can't this wait?"

Josie plunked down on the sofa and crossed her elegant legs. "You can't keep running away from Mom forever. You're going to have to talk to her sometime."

"I have talked to her. We're fine. She's better and I'm glad." Josie rolled her eyes.

Damn. She never was any good at BSing her older sister. Josie had always been smarter, wiser, more in control in family situations.

"Diana, when are you going to stop running away from everything that's the slightest bit difficult in your life? You've got to grow up and be responsible sometime."

Right. As if she wasn't being responsible by busting her butt and putting her neck on the line to save the next President's life. That's why she'd been chosen for Oracle and was one of the leading conspiracy theorists in the country. Because she was so freaking irresponsible. Thing was, it was all so secret she couldn't tell anyone, not even her well-meaning family, about it.

"When are you going to get off my back and let me be my own person?" Diana sighed.

Josie's perfectly plucked eyebrows arched. "I'm not on your back and you know it. And when haven't you been your own person? You've always done exactly what you wanted to."

How wrong Josie was. Most of her adolescence had been shaped by doing the exact opposite of her older sister. It had never been about rebellion. It had always been about struggling to come out from behind her sister's giant shadow. The true rebellion came later. When the strictures of an Army career started to grate on her.

"Tell me something, Jo. Do you ever get tired of the Air

Force? Tired of all the rules and regulations and people telling you what to do all the time?"

Her sister frowned. "No, not particularly. Why do you ask?"

Diana remembered that flashback of her life on the Mall, the shocking realization that she rebelled within the Army because she was still angry over what the Establishment had cost her—the love of a mother, a unified family living under one roof, a normal childhood.

Diana answered belatedly, "I was thinking about everything that's happened to the two of us, and I wondered why you came out of it so calm about what happened to Mom while I...well...while I didn't."

"What ever gave you the idea I was calm about Mom's problems?" Josie exclaimed.

Diana stared. "You mean you weren't okay with it all?"

Josie snorted. "I was terrified. And furious, and frustrated and a hundred other things. But I couldn't change it and neither could Mom. So I accepted it."

And maybe that's where the two of them were so different. Josie could accept the inevitable, while she'd fight against it until she bloodied herself trying to change it. Which category did Gabe fall into? He had Josie's refinement, her controlled elegance, her ability to fit in and play by the rules. But he was also a politician. The mother of all politicians, in fact, to have run for his country's highest office. Surely somewhere beneath that polished exterior, he secretly wanted to change the world or else he wouldn't have chosen to pursue that particular job.

"What's going on with you, Die Hard?" Josie asked.

Diana smiled at the old nickname from their Athena Academy days. She used to hate the name. But this past year had seen a lot of healing between the sisters. Now she used it proudly as a computer handle. She opened her mouth to reply when a knock at the front door saved her from having to skirt the truth. Which was just as well. Josie was so sharp, she'd know for certain something big was going down.

Diana stood up to answer the door. Over her shoulder she said, "That's the guy I was expecting."

"Great!" Josie said brightly. "I can't wait to meet your latest—uh…"

It was a long-standing source of friction between her and her family that Diana managed to dredge up the scum of the earth on a routine basis, and then proceeded to date it. She grinned to herself. This should be fun. Wait till Josie got a load of a Secret Service agent. Please let this guy be built like a linebacker and have one of those severe crew cuts so many of them seemed to favor.

He was and he did. Grinning to herself, Diana opened the front door wider so her sister could get a good look at him.

"There you are! Come on in," Diana said to the agent warmly, as if she'd known this guy a long time. "I've just got to go grab my coat. I'll be back in a second. This is my sister, Josie. Don't let her interrogate you."

The agent threw her a surprised look, but nodded stolidly.

Diana broke into a wide grin as she stepped around the corner and heard her sister's startled voice murmuring a polite greeting. Served Josie right for meddling in her private life. Of course, if Josie found out she had a crush on the soon-to-be President of the United States, her sister would have a stroke. It would almost be worth spilling the beans to good ole Jo just to see it.

Diana grabbed a cream-colored cashmere dress coat from the back of her closet. It had been an extravagant gift from her mother last Christmas, but she hadn't worn it yet. When Josie had pressed her on why she never wore the gorgeous designer piece, she'd claimed it didn't fit her fashion style. But, as Diana tore off the tags and slipped her arms into its sleeves for the first time, she admitted it had probably been more about avoiding what the coat represented—a peace offering from her mother. Today she was just thankful she had something this nice to wear for Gabe.

She froze as she caught sight of her reflection in the full-length mirror. She hardly recognized herself! She looked… grown up. Fully as sophisticated and elegant as Josie. The kind of woman a President might want to meet. What was she doing? She wasn't about to change for any man, not even Gabe Monihan. She started to turn around, to head for her closet and her black leather duster. Hesitated. If she chose to look this way of her own volition, wasn't that okay?

Screw it. For once, she was going to put her best foot forward. No more hiding her beauty and trying to look like something her sister wasn't. Today she wanted to be pretty. And if that happened to be because she was hoping to see a guy she had the hots for, so be it. She turned and headed for her living room. Besides, this look would shock Josie even worse than the clean-cut Secret Service agent waiting for her. And shocking her big sister was still one of the most gratifying things Diana did in life.

Sure enough, Josie stared in outright disbelief as she rounded the corner into the room. Even the Secret Service agent did a double take. Well, sheesh. It wasn't as though she looked *that* bad the rest of the time! The Secret Service agent collected himself and headed for the front door. Still staring, Josie picked up her coat and accompanied them outside.

As she slid into the front seat of the agent's car, Diana waved cheerily at Josie. She called out, "Say hi to Mom and Dad for me. Lock up when you leave."

The agent pulled away from the curb, and Diana grinned. She hadn't seen Josie that off balance since Diego proposed to her on New Year's Eve in front of the whole family.

She turned to the agent beside her. "So. Where are we going?"

He didn't answer her question directly. Instead he said, "May I see some picture identification that proves you're Diana Lockworth?"

She dug in her purse and pulled out her military ID and driver's license. The agent glanced at them while he drove and then passed them back to her. She replied, "I don't mean to be rude, but could I see some ID, as well? I've already been kidnapped once today by someone who wasn't who he claimed to be."

The agent's head whipped her way. Fortunately, they were stopped at a red light and he didn't drive off the road. He passed her his Secret Service ID card in turn. His name was Trent Tilman. She returned his ID card without comment.

He asked briskly, "Am I correct that you have a Top Secret security clearance with a Special Background Investigation?"

She did, and that SBI clearance had been a bear to get, given her family's checkered past. Aloud, she answered, "That's correct."

"You're going to have to sign several security documents when we get where we're going regarding not revealing where I take you."

"Fair enough."

The conversation lapsed, and the agent drove in silence. He wound his way through a good chunk of Washington, D.C., and surprised her by turning into an alley that ran between a couple of vacant warehouses. She was even more surprised when he reached up to his sun visor, activated what looked like a garage door opener and proceeded to drive inside one of the big buildings. Was this guy on the up-and-up, or had she done it again and gotten into a car with someone out to kidnap her or worse? The muscles across her shoulders tightened abruptly.

She looked out the windows at the dim, cavernous space. Only a few narrow cement columns broke up the expanse, and steel girders disappeared into the gloom high overhead. Not good. She had zero options to make a break from this guy and get under cover. He'd shoot her down like a fish in a barrel with that weapon bulging under his coat in his right armpit. At least there was just the one guy in this empty shell of a building.

A sudden flurry of movement made her jump. A half-dozen men jumped out of the shadows, pointing guns at their car. Crud.

Agent Tilman turned off the ignition and sat still with his hands on top of the steering wheel. He murmured over at her, "Put your hands on the dashboard."

"What's going on here? Are we being robbed, or are you just kidnapping me?"

Tilman grinned. "Neither. It's standard procedure in a high-threat situation for the Secret Service to treat everyone who approaches as a hostile until positive ID is made."

"So you recognize these jokers?" she asked.

"Oh, yeah. If they weren't in the Service, I'd be shooting as we speak and ramming through the door with my car."

She replied dryly, "Duly noted."

She stared out at the grim-faced men advancing on their car like a SWAT team. Some welcoming committee. But then, she couldn't blame these guys for being tense after the last couple hours. Someone had just tried to assassinate their man.

An agent opened her door and ordered her to get out of the car. Slowly. She complied, handing over her identification very carefully. This time, the agent carted off her various IDs and disappeared. These guys weren't any more talkative than Agent Tilman, and she stood stock-still by the side of the car for several interminable minutes. She certainly didn't want to give any of these guys a reason to pull the trigger. Finally, the guy with her papers returned and nodded to the others. The guns went down, and all the tense shoulders in the area—including hers—relaxed noticeably.

Agent Tilman strolled up to her. "You passed muster. If you'll come with me, Agent Haas is anxious to speak with you right away."

He led her over to a door and opened it to reveal a long staircase. He descended it quickly and she followed close on his heels. But when he stopped at the matching door at the bottom without opening it, she nearly bumped into him.

He turned around to face her. "You'll need to put this on." He held out a black cloth eye mask like a traveler might use to help them sleep.

"You've got to be kidding."

"No, ma'am. You'll have to be blindfolded for the next part of this."

His tone of voice was implacable. She sighed and took the mask. She slipped it on, and started as hands touched her face, checking the security of the stupid thing. The hands withdrew, but then one of them took her firmly by the elbow. "This way."

She stumbled forward. A rush of air blew against her face as the door squeaked open. Sound echoed around her as she stepped into what must be a very large space. Underground? What was this place? But she had no more time to consider it as Agent Tilman tugged her forward. She stumbled again as he led her into some sort of enclosed space. And then he guided her down into what felt like a hard plastic chair. It lurched. A vehicle of some kind!

They rode smoothly forward for several minutes, swaying occasionally as the conveyance rounded corners. And then it hitched to a stop.

"Let's go," Tilman announced.

She stood up, disoriented in the dark until he took her by the elbow and led her forward. Out the door, and into another enclosed space this time. A door opened and they stepped through it, and then her ears popped as some sort of pressure seal closed behind her. Where in the world were they now? She walked down what felt like a short hallway, and into another room. And then, without warning, the blindfold was lifted away from her face. She blinked, squinting into the bright, artificial light.

And Gabe smiled down at her. "Welcome to the bunker, Diana."

Her impulse was to step forward and fling her arms around Gabe's neck, but she dared not. For one thing, his security detail would tackle her. Plus, he was nearly the President of the United States.

Instead, she merely sighed, "Thank God you're safe."

He murmured back, "Thank God *you're* safe."

How long they stood there, staring at each other, she had no idea. It was an eternity, but not nearly long enough. Finally, reluctantly, he looked away. "Owen needs to talk to you. I've still got to be inaugurated, and he needs to know everything you can tell him about any threats I might face when that happens."

She nodded gamely. Gabe led her into a small adjoining lounge sporting a couple of sofas, a television and—hallelujah—a coffeepot. She helped herself to a mug of its contents and sipped at the industrial-strength brew, reveling in the caffeine jolt that flowed through her veins.

Agent Haas motioned her onto the far end of the leather couch he sat on. She perched on it gingerly while Gabe sat across from her on the arm of the matching sofa, his golden eyes burning with intense intelligence. Man, he was gorgeous. Not only was he a hunk, but he was a brilliant one. A killer combination. She dragged her mind back to business as Owen asked her to start at the beginning.

The Secret Service agent interrupted with occasional questions. At the end of it, Owen sat back and stared at her for several seconds. "And you tracked down all this information about the Q-group by yourself?"

She frowned. "Mostly. I had help from some computer hackers who've probably earned a clean-up of their police records."

He leaned forward abruptly. "Good work. I'm going to go fax those pictures you sent me to the FBI and the police. We'll get APBs out on these guys and have them in custody in no time."

Gabe spoke up. "Maybe we should send those pictures to the media, too."

Owen nodded. "The FBI can take care of that. They love a good, media-blitzing manhunt. If all goes well, we'll have these jerks in custody before you have to leave for your inauguration."

She looked up at Gabe in consternation. "You're not showing yourself again in public, are you?"

He shrugged. "I have to go out sometime. I can't serve my entire presidency here in this bunker. May as well start this job the way I plan to continue doing it. And I don't plan to hide for the next four years."

"Gabe. These guys tried to *kill* you today!"

"Yes, and you stopped them. You've already apprehended one of them. We'll get the rest of them soon enough. And then I'll be perfectly safe."

She frowned. And looked over at Owen Haas. "There's more."

The agent's brows slammed together. "Like what?"

"My research indicates that the Q-group is being used as a front for someone else. Someone who's pulling their strings.

I'm not convinced that Gabe will be safe, even if you nail every Q-group guy my hacker buddies and I tracked down on the Internet this morning."

If possible, Owen frowned even harder. He uttered a single, short word. "Who?"

If only she knew. But so much had happened to her so fast that she was having trouble processing it all. Her gut said there were connections she was missing. Hints and tidbits were right in front of her, and she wasn't putting them together. She'd hoped Owen might see something she'd missed. But he looked as frustrated as she felt.

She sighed. "I don't know who could be pulling their strings. Obviously, there's a connection to Richard Dunst. A third party broke him out of jail. That says to me he's working for the same person or persons who are controlling the Q-group. Dunst is a flunkie."

Owen nodded his agreement at her analysis.

The three of them stared at each other in silence.

"Have either of you eaten since this morning?" Gabe asked suddenly.

Owen and Diana both blinked at the abrupt change of subject. "No," Diana answered aloud while Haas shook his head in the negative.

Gabe stood up. "Let's grab a bite to eat. I think better when my stomach's not gnawing a hole in my gut. Besides, I've always wondered what nuclear bunker food would taste like. How about you?"

Diana grimaced. "Are you kidding? I'm in the Army. I know exactly what thirty-year-old C rations taste like. Not to mention what they do to your gut."

Gabe laughed and held out his hand. "Come have lunch with me. I'll bet one of the White House chefs is hiding down here, somewhere."

She stood up, grinning. "I sincerely hope so."

Lunch turned out to consist of poached salmon, tossed salad and fresh snap peas—just where a person got those at this time of year in a bunker far below Washington, D.C., she had no idea. It was a far cry from C rations, but then the company was a far cry from an infantry battalion, too.

As good as the food was, her appetite was off. She was missing something important. She could feel it. And if she didn't figure out what it was in the next couple of hours, Gabe would still be in danger.

"Are you sure you want to be President?" she asked him skeptically.

He shrugged. "It's not like I have any choice at this point." He paused, then added, "And even if I did, I'd still want the job."

"Why?" she asked curiously.

"Because I can do some good in the next four years. Maybe I can make my country and my world a little better place. And that's a worthy thing to do with a lifetime."

So. Beneath all that charm and social polish lurked a reformer. A doer. Like her. The discovery was comforting not only because it was a good trait for a President to have, but because it also meant that, at their cores, they were like-minded people.

Gabe surprised her by asking, "If you had a chance to run for President, would you do it?"

She flinched. "My family's got some pretty ugly skeletons in the closet. I don't think they'd hold up to public scrutiny very well."

He snorted. "Like my family's skeletons aren't a nightmare? If you've got enough character, you can overcome all that stuff."

She leaned forward. "Is that how you did it? How you got past all the garbage in your background? You compensated by displaying extraordinary amounts of character?"

The question gave him pause. "Can't say as I've ever thought of it in those terms," he finally replied. "But I guess that's what it boils down to. If I do my best to do the right thing all the time, I believe the public will see it and respect me for who I am rather than judging me by my family and its past indiscretions."

He could say that. He only had a gambling, alcoholic father who'd had the good grace to die in his past. She was stuck with a military scandal that had disgraced her mother and even sent her into an asylum. Even though Josie had cleared their mother's name last year with her own stealth technology research, the stain lingered.

She replied, "At any rate, I think you'll make an excellent President. The American people chose well."

"Thank you," he said simply. "For the record, if you ran, I'd vote for you."

She started. "I'd be a lousy President! I'm too much of a rebel to deal with the Washington establishment peaceably for four years. And don't get me started about world leaders and their antics."

Gabe laughed. "Yes, but you'd step up to the plate and do what you had to in a crisis. Today is a good case in point."

"Nonetheless, I'll leave the job to you."

The smile faded from his face. "This is a hell of a way to come into office. I start by killing a half dozen of the very citizens I'm supposed to be serving and protecting."

She reached across the table and squeezed his hand sympathetically. "You didn't kill anyone. A terrorist named Tito Albadian did. It's not your fault."

Gabe sighed. Eventually, the tight grasp his fingers had on hers loosened.

She had to do something to lighten the mood. To distract them both from the day's events. She asked drolly, "So. How much longer are you going to be a slacker and dodge starting your new job? Honestly. Your first day of work and you're already hours late. This won't make a good impression on the taxpayers at all."

Gabe smiled, a hint of gratitude in his twinkling eyes. "I'm scheduled to take the oath of office at 7:00 p.m. in the Capitol Building. We're going to break into the evening television programming and do the deed without any advance announcements. Security around it will be insanely tight." As her brows drew together in a frown, he added, "Really. I'll be safe. In fact, why don't you come to the inauguration and you can keep an eye on me yourself. I'll put your name on the list of approved guests."

She nodded. If all went well, she'd take him up on that invitation. But after the kind of day she'd had so far, she couldn't predict if the next few hours would go well or not.

"Who all's going to be there?" she asked.

"Key members of the government, mostly. A few hand-picked guests and none of the public. The media will be there in force, of course. We need to make it clear that there's been a smooth transition of power today, and live TV coverage will get that message out the most effectively."

Crud. Seven o'clock? That didn't give her much time to figure out what was niggling at the back of her brain so tantalizingly. Maybe if she ran it all through Oracle one more time, the computer would see what she could not.

She looked up, startled. Gabe stood beside her, holding a hand out to her. She took it silently, and he tugged her to her feet, standing intimately close to her.

He murmured, "Thank you for shouting that warning to Owen. And thank you for your persistence and courage. I'm not sure I'd be alive right now if it weren't for you."

Damned if she didn't feel a blush stealing into her cheeks. "Uh, my pleasure," she mumbled abashed.

Gabe chuckled. It was a sexy sound. Private. Personal. "I highly doubt it was pleasurable chasing down a terrorist single-handed," he murmured.

She replied, "Well, I'd never have met you without the help of the Q-group."

Another chuckle rumbled through Gabe. "I never thought I'd say this, but thank goodness for the Q-group, then."

She grinned up at him. "May I quote you on that?"

He matched her broad smile. "Don't you dare."

Her humor faded. "Gabe, I'd love nothing more than to spend the rest of the day down here with you in your cozy little rabbit hole, but I need to do more research. I've got a really bad feeling about all this, but I can't put my finger on what's bugging me."

He stared down at her intently for a moment before nodding. "Your intuitions have gotten you and me this far in one piece. Go track down whatever's bothering you. And let me know if there's anything I can do to help. But you stay safe. Okay?"

She reached up to touch his cheek with her fingertips. "Okay. You, too."

"That's a deal."

But, as she donned the blindfold once more so Agent Tilman could take her back to the surface, and blackness descended upon her, she had a sinking feeling it wasn't going to be that easy.

5:00 P.M.

She dumped her cashmere coat on the couch and went directly to her computer the second she walked in her front door. She cranked up the Oracle database, praying the morning's lockdown on the system had been lifted by now. The computer monitor blinked for a few seconds after she tried to sign in, and then the Oracle welcome screen flashed up before her. Thank goodness.

She went to the data-entry screen and typed as quickly as her fingers would go, throwing in everything that had happened to her today in as much detail as she could remember. Her hands ached by the time she finished, and daylight was fading from the living room. Night came early at this time of year.

She punched the command that started the Oracle database processing the new inputs. An analysis could take anywhere from a few minutes to several hours, depending on the complexity of the computations her entries triggered. She'd seen the logic algorithms for the database once, and had been blown away by them. Whoever'd invented this system was a bona fide genius.

She wandered into the kitchen to pour herself a cup of stale coffee from the pot she'd brewed so long ago this morning. At this point, she didn't care if it tasted like battery acid. She was beat. And she suspected this day wasn't over, yet.

To kill time while Oracle did its thing, she flipped on the television and was assaulted immediately by images of the day's near miss on Gabe. She switched the channel quickly. She didn't need a blow-by-blow replay of the horror she'd gone through. She lurched as the next channel flashed up a picture of one of the Q-group members her hacker buddies had tracked down that morning. She sat down in front of the TV to hear the whole report. Apparently ten of the fourteen suspects had already been apprehended, and a massive manhunt was underway for the remaining possible terrorists. An FBI spokesman said tips were coming in from all over the East Coast and the Bureau had confidence it would have its men in custody within a matter of hours.

Now she could only hope that she and her buddies had fingered the right guys. She shoved down the moment of doubt. She'd read these guys' e-mails to each other for months, and there was no doubt in her mind that this was the cell that had planned today's attack on Gabe.

Her computer beeped. She set down her mug and turned off the TV, hustling over to the computer. She sat down at the console eagerly to read the analysis. As shock paralyzed her mind, she skimmed faster and faster, catching key phrases as they leaped out at her.

...no significant correlations have been identified...random occurrences...day's other events bear no relation to any threat to the Presidency...

This was a very different analysis from the one she'd seen in Oracle's main database this morning. Even if the Q-group threat *had* been successfully neutralized, as sure as she was sitting here she was certain there was still someone out there gunning for Gabe. How could Oracle have reversed itself so radically like this in a matter of hours? Last night, Delphi personally had been convinced Gabe was in huge danger. That whoever was after him would not give up until he was dead. And now, everything was hunky-dory? What in the hell was going on?

She stared at the computer screen in dismay, her mental wheels spinning, until she became aware of a vague noise behind her. Someone was knocking on her front door. Insistently. She stood up, went to the front door and opened it numbly.

Her mother stood on the porch, shivering in the bitter chill.

"Come on in, Mom."

"Hello to you, too," her mother replied mildly. "Did I come at a bad time?"

"Actually, yes. I'm in the middle of a crisis."

"What sort of crisis?"

Diana winced. Her mother only wanted to be part of Diana's life and be the kind of parent Diana had deserved for all those empty years. And Diana wanted to let her, get to know her as an adult. But the timing sucked. Except…what was she going to do if her mother turned around and walked out this second? She didn't have the foggiest idea what to do next. Even Oracle had given her nothing but a dead end.

"Can I get you something to drink, Mom?"

"No, thank you." Her mother sat down on the sofa resolutely. "Tell me about your crisis."

Even at the worst of her depression, Zoe Lockworth had always known when one of her girls was in trouble. It was some sort of maternal sixth sense.

"I can't talk about it, Mom. It's classified."

Her mother pursed her lips. "Are you sure you're not just avoiding me?"

Diana huffed in exasperation. "Why does everyone in the family keep accusing me of that?"

"Maybe because it's true, honey. Look, I know I wasn't there for you when you were young, and I take full responsibility for that. I chose to do dangerous work, and I chose to put myself in harm's way even though I had a family to think about. But I'm here for you, now. I'd like to help."

The fight went out of her in a rush. What was the point of being mad? It didn't change anything that had happened. In comparison to everything that had happened to her today, her childhood was starting to look pretty bland. She sat down on the other end of the couch and asked her mother, "Was your work really that important?"

Zoe shrugged. "It seemed so at the time. We were trying to save the lives of thousands of pilots by coming up with stealth technologies to protect them. I suppose you'd have to ask pilots like Josie and Diego if the research was ultimately worthwhile."

Diana'd already heard her sister's opinion on that, and the answer was an emphatic yes. "Yes, but was *your* sacrifice worth it all?"

Zoe shrugged. "I've made my peace with what happened to me. I lost a chunk of my life in the name of serving my country. I'm just grateful I didn't lose my life altogether. What I can't forgive myself for is the sacrifice you girls and your father had to make. Nobody asked you if you were willing to lose your mother for twenty years."

They'd been over this ground before. Her parents just assumed that, because she and her sister were in the Armed Forces, they'd understand the idea of serving one's country.

Of sacrifice and loss in the name of freedom. Of the price military families paid alongside their active-duty members. Josie bought into the idea hook, line and sinker. But Diana had trouble swallowing the concept. There came a point beyond which families shouldn't suffer the same way their military members did.

Although, she had put her neck on the line for Gabe today. Hadn't hesitated to do so, either. Like her mother, she'd dived into this mess without a second thought for herself. Why was that? Was it just that she hadn't found something—or someone—important enough to die for until now? At the end of the day, was she as dedicated as her mother had been? Maybe to different causes, but both in the name of defending their nation.

Startled, she asked her mother slowly, "Did you hesitate to get into such dangerous research?"

Zoe laughed ruefully. "I have to confess I leaped before I looked. I was well into the work before it occurred to me that there might be menacing forces opposed to what I was doing. But even if I had known in advance, I'd have done it anyway. I was one of only a handful of scientists who could do the research. And the need for stealth technology was bigger than me. More important than me. I did what I had to do."

Diana froze, stunned. If someone asked her if she'd considered the risks of saving Gabe, she'd have answered *the exact same way.* For the first time, she got it. Zoe was absolutely driven by her most fundamental belief in right and wrong. And Dear God, Diana was stuck with the very same set of beliefs. Was she destined to wreck herself on the rocky beaches of her morals the same way her mother had?

A chill chattered down her spine. This must be how her mother had felt once she discovered the dangers stalking her. Even if Richard Dunst or his superiors were out there waiting for her at this very moment, she still had to do this. She had to save Gabe from them or die trying.

She eyed her mother speculatively. What the heck. Her mom had been a highly intelligent scientist in her day, an expert at computer analysis of problems. "I've got a work-related question for you, Mom."

Zoe blinked at the abrupt change of subject. "I'll do my best, but it has been a long while since I did any research."

"If you were to put a set of data into a sophisticated database that has always been accurate in the past, and you suddenly got back a set of completely garbled analyses on that data, what would you do?"

Zoe laughed. "I'd recheck my data. You know what they say. Garbage in, garbage out. Computers are really just huge calculators, and databases are just big sets of mathematical formulas that get applied to your data. Those formulas never change once they're entered into the computer. The computer will do the exact same thing to your data every time you enter it. So if your output is wonky, you've got to suspect the input."

"I've rechecked the data entered. It's accurate. Late last night, the database analyzed a similar set of data and came up with completely different conclusions than it did just now."

"Well, then I'd check the database itself for bugs. Go to a backup version of it and reload the data."

Good idea. "And what might cause a bug—a big one—in a database?"

Zoe shrugged. "It could be something as simple as a maintenance technician or data-entry specialist making a mistake and hitting the wrong key. Or, it could be something as sinister as someone tampering with the database intentionally."

The sight of four men leaping into the library at the Oracle safe house this morning flashed into her mind. Oh, yeah.

The secret of the Oracle database's existence was definitely compromised. Why not the database itself?

Diana leaped to her feet abruptly, causing her mother to jump up in alarm, as well. She gave her mother a big hug and commenced herding her toward the door. "Thank you *so* much. You've been a huge help. I'm glad we talked. We have much more in common than I ever realized. We must talk more. Very soon. Right now I've got to run."

Her mother paused in the doorway, frowning. "Are you all right?"

She gave her mother a genuine smile. One of the few she ever remembered giving her mother. "For the first time in a very long time, I'm definitely all right. I know what I have to do, and I know how I have to do it. I'll give you a call as soon as this is all over." Of course, her poor mother had no idea what "this" was.

On impulse, she gave Zoe another hug. "I've got to go now. I've got a ton of stuff to do and not much time to do it."

She closed the door in her mother's disbelieving face and whirled, heading straight for the phone. She dialed Delphi's emergency phone number for the fourth time in one day. That had to be some kind of record. The usual answering machine picked up her call and she waited impatiently through the bland message.

"Hi, this is Diana Lockworth. I need an access password to get into the guts of the Oracle database. I don't need to have access to rewriting any of the code, but I need to take a look at it. No time to explain—"

The electronically altered voice interrupted her. "I'm here. What's this all about?"

"I don't have time to go into all the details, but I think the Oracle database has been compromised. I need to look at the program, itself."

"That's an alarming accusation," the voice said emotionlessly.

Diana retorted, "No more alarming than four armed men bursting into the Old Town facility and making off with what they think is the hard drive holding the database."

"We've already had a look at the database today, and it's fine."

Diana snorted. "I just tried to use it, and I got complete gobbledygook out of it. Something's wrong with Oracle, I'm telling you."

"Like what?"

"I don't know. But I do know the database should've gone nuts over the information I put into it about the ongoing threat I'm convinced exists to Gabe Monihan, and it came back with a null threat assessment. The damned thing all but called me stupid!"

A delicate pause. "You neutralized the threat earlier."

Diana gnashed her teeth as urgency nipped at her heels. Her gut was screaming at her that she was losing time. Time she couldn't afford to waste if she was going to save Gabe. "Look. You hired me. Do you trust me or not? I know we caught one terrorist but based on what I saw earlier today, I'm certain someone's still out there gunning for Gabe, and they're going to try to kill him again within the next couple hours."

"Of course, I trust you. And who do you think is going to make this assassination attempt?"

"That's what I was hoping Oracle could tell me."

"One moment."

Diana fidgeted while the line went silent. Her boss was either putting out an APB on her at this very moment, or hopefully retrieving the access code she needed to get inside the Oracle database proper.

"Enter this number into the log-in screen when you choose the system maintenance option." Delphi read off a long string of numbers that Diana scrawled down hastily. "That will get you into the code. You'll have read-only access. You will not be able to make any system changes."

"Fair enough. That's what I needed." In response to the tacit vote of confidence the sharing of that access code represented, she said, "And thank you."

"You're welcome. Call me if you need any further assistance. It is imperative that Monihan be kept safe."

Diana hung up and all but ran into the living room to sit down at the computer. She pulled up the appropriate access screen and entered Delphi's number into the correct field. Her screen went blank briefly, and then page after page of detailed, complex computer code began scrolling down her screen. Crud. This was going to be like looking for a needle in a haystack.

Time to think like a hacker. If she were going to tamper with a system of this size, how would she do it? She'd head for a low-level subroutine connected to the analysis portions of the program and she'd bury the smallest possible command she could in it that would foul it up.

She made her way to the analysis subroutines and frantically waded through the dense programming language. She couldn't help but be impressed by the elegance of the program. It was the single most intelligent piece of computer work she'd ever seen. She'd give her right arm to meet whoever'd designed this database.

And then she saw it. A bland little command sequence that didn't have quite the same feel as the rest of the code around it. She read the three-line instruction again. Her internal warning antennae wiggled wildly. She followed the instruction set to where it led elsewhere in the database and found another innocuous bit of code that didn't feel right. It led to another. And then to another. All these little pieces of code were linked together, a huge set of tiny monkey wrenches scattered throughout the cogs and gears of the mighty machine that was Oracle.

Over the course of the next couple minutes, she traced the spiderweb of commands and found them inserted all over the program. She didn't begin to understand precisely how these commands were screwing up the Oracle database, but there was no doubt the system was completely corrupted.

Something about this code tickled the edges of her consciousness. And then it hit her. She recognized the programming style of the commands. The spare, coldly logical technique of the programming was identical to the instructions the intruder in her house had put onto this very computer last night!

She opened the file of code she'd copied out of her computer's operating system and compared it to the lines of commands in the Oracle database. It was as clear as day. The same person had done both bits of hacking.

On a hunch, she called up a screen view of the code where the signature of the programmer was entered beside each line of code they'd written. She stared in shock. *Her own name stared back at her.*

The hacker this morning. Had he entered this code from her home computer? It made sense.

Somebody knew she was an Oracle agent. Why else would both her computer, and now the Oracle database be attacked by the same person on the same day? If her identity was compromised, how many other Oracle agents were exposed and in danger? And if the very heart of the Oracle agency had suffered an attack like this, was the entire agency at risk?

As alarming as that was, she had more important fish to fry at the moment. Somebody who could afford to hire a frighteningly smart hacker was trying to stop her or even kill her. From doing what? It could only be one thing. The only project she'd been working on for weeks now was the link between Q-group and Gabe Monihan. Whoever'd hacked into her computer and into Oracle was out to kill Gabe. And they were very close on not only her heels, but his.

The bad feeling in her gut exploded into panic, roiling and bubbling nearly out of control. She typed a hasty note to Delphi outlining her discovery and finished it with a warning that Delphi himself or herself could be in danger.

Now what?

She sat back and stared at her computer for a couple seconds. *C'mon brain. Come up with something smart!* The next step was to find out who was behind the Q-group and Richard Dunst.

For lack of anywhere else to begin, she typed into her computer the familiar name of the Q-group's primary chat room. It should be deserted, since most or all of its members would either be arrested by now or running for their lives.

The screen blinked. Seventeen members were present in the chat room.

Seventeen?

She signed in quickly, using her usual fake e-mail address and Arabic ID for this chat group. She scanned through the discussion, a disjointed conversation about European soccer scores. Translating the coded phrases in her head based on what she'd figured out the last couple months, she stared in shock.

Someone she'd never seen in this room before was giving this new group of people a crisp set of instructions.

On how to kill Gabe Monihan.

6:00 P.M.

Diana read frantically through the posts, looking for key phrases that meant something entirely different than their surface meaning. There. A soccer score from the Bristol Capitols. That was a reference to Washington, D.C. A mention of a soccer game date a couple of weeks from now. She reversed the date and gaped—01-20. January 20. This person was ordering another hit on Gabe *today?* Her blood pressure lurched upward significantly.

She flinched at a request for who was going to be at the upcoming game so they could get a block of tickets together. Four, no six people responded to that bit. A six-man team was volunteering to kill Gabe? Her blood pressure pounded up another few points.

The chat host, a total stranger to this room called Disco-Duck, replied that he thought he could only get tickets for one or two guys. A bunch of people clamored to be the ones chosen to go. What kind of handle was DiscoDuck, anyway? She'd lay ten-to-one odds no teenager today had ever heard of the song from the 1970s by that name. Not a kid, then. Someone older. Probably was a teen or young adult in the seventies. That would put this guy in his fifties at the youngest.

Had the mastermind behind the Q-group and Richard Dunst finally shown himself?

Quickly, she opened another chat screen and prayed some of her hacker buddies were online. They were.

She typed in, Hey guys. I need you to do another trace like you did this morning. This one's possibly more important than the last one. Anyone up for it?

A reply from a top-notch hacker who went by the handle, FantasyMan, was forthcoming almost instantly. How could it be more important than the last batch? Those idiots were out to kill the new president. What's more important than that?

She typed back tersely, Finding the idiots' boss.

FantasyMan retorted, Who are you, anyway? Why were you tracking down criminals for the FBI? Are you some sort of undercover agent or something?

Crud. She'd worked for years establishing a cover with these guys, worming her way into the good graces of the best and most dangerous hackers on the East Coast. If she confessed to being Army Intelligence now she'd spook them off for sure. But they were also highly intelligent people. Would they smell a rat if she gave them anything less than the complete truth? Ultimately, if they turned their hacking skills on her, they'd find out everything there was to know about her, anyway. Heck, for all she knew, they already had. She sighed. She had no choice.

She typed carefully, I'm not FBI. I'm not a cop, either. I'm a conspiracy theorist for the military.

The cursor blinked steadily, winking at her for long sec-

onds as she waited for a reply. C'mon, guys. Help her out here.
She couldn't do this alone.

Finally the reply popped up. You're sure you're not a cop?

Positive, she typed back immediately.

Was that arrest scene real this morning, or did you stage
it to make it look like you're on our side?

She typed in an abbreviation to indicate laughing. I'm better than that. If I'd wanted to stage a scenario to convince
you I'm legit, I'd have done a whole lot better than those
pathetic losers.

Who were those guys who hauled you off?

She didn't have time to get into this. DiscoDuck could go
offline at any moment. Army Intelligence. Long story. I managed to talk my way out of it. Hey, and thanks for getting
those pictures to Owen Haas. He says thank you, too.

FantasyMan replied, Is that Haas guy really in the Secret
Service?

She smiled. These poor hackers were having a hard time
wrapping their brains around the idea of having helped stop an
assassination attempt on the President-elect. It went just enough
against their principles to help the government that they weren't
sure they liked what she'd had them do. But, they also didn't
condone murder. It was a heck of a moral pickle for them to
find themselves in. She grinned to herself. It was good for them.

She typed rapidly, Look, I've found the guy who gives
the orders to the Q-group. His handle is DiscoDuck, and
he's online right now. I've got to track down who he is. Immediately. Are you in?

Another lengthy pause.

Please, please, please play ball.

And then FantasyMan typed back, What server is he using?

She sagged in relief over her keyboard and typed in the necessary information. In a matter of minutes, a half-dozen hackers had joined the hunt, circling in on their prey as a group. With so many hackers coming at him from so many directions at once, DiscoDuck didn't stand a chance.

But what was odd was the guy seemed to have taken no precautions to protect himself from this sort of attack. Apparently, he wasn't overly familiar with the power of the Internet and what a good hacker could do with it.

Just a couple of minutes into the hunt, FantasyMan fired off a message that he'd found something. Diana headed to the Web address he specified to take a look. She frowned as lines of programming code scrolled down her screen. He'd run into a firewall, a barrier between the Internet and a private computer network. And it was a big, nasty firewall. As tough as anything she'd ever seen.

The rest of the hackers joined them, and everyone began flinging their strongest, most creative protocols at the electronic security system. This was what hacking was all about. Except this firewall wasn't going down without a fight. The server they were assaulting began throwing back counterhacking commands, and it turned into a pitched battle to defend her own computer while trying to break into the other guy's.

In desperation, she pulled out a couple of government protocols she'd been careful never to reveal to her hacker friends, since they were designed to get into the very systems these guys most loved to invade—government computer networks. Implacably, her special protocol chipped away at the firewall in front of her.

The way her protocol was bulldozing through the layers of protection in this firewall, she'd almost guess this was a government network they were breaking into.

And then she was in.

She stared in stunned disbelief as a round logo popped up on her computer screen on a navy-blue background. Holy cow. The Central Intelligence Agency? DiscoDuck was operating from inside the CIA computer network?

She typed furiously, trying to narrow down the search parameters. Maybe get a directorate within the CIA from which the e-mails were coming, or even capture the name of this operator. But her break-in must have triggered some sort of warning. Within a matter of seconds, DiscoDuck signed off, severing the connection to the Internet and her search.

The other hackers reacted with varying degrees of disgust and dismay.

She typed quickly,

Hey, thanks anyway, guys. I owe you.

FantasyMan typed back dryly,

Nah, that Monihan guy owes us. And we're not going to let him forget it, either.

Diana grinned. She'd relay that message to Gabe the next time she saw him.

The other hackers backed away from the firewall, and she pretended to do the same, as well. Once they'd all cleared out, she opened up a file she'd never used before. It was written by an FBI computer programmer for the purpose of intercepting and opening e-mails when the Bureau did surveillance on members of the government who'd come under suspicion. She seriously was not supposed to have a copy of this program, and she'd never even hinted at its existence to her hacker buddies. They'd have a field day with it if they ever got their hands on it.

She loaded the program and watched it run.

It took a few minutes, but eventually, an e-mail log to Disco-Duck popped up on her screen. She gazed down through the mail headers of hundreds of e-mails dating back for nearly a year and nothing out of the ordinary caught her attention. Damn. She didn't have time to open all these up and read them!

The e-mail intercept program indicated that these were the nonencrypted files available. Would she like to see the encrypted messages, as well? She typed in an immediate yes command.

This program didn't decrypt the mails themselves, but she could at least look at the captions the authors had attached to their posts.

Another long list of message titles scrolled down her screen. And immediately, something odd leaped out at her. The same word kept appearing, over and over. Safe. Safe? What the heck did that signify? Was this person involved in a safety program of some kind? Maybe it was a code name for a CIA operation DiscoDuck was involved in?

But then she got that niggling feeling in the back of her head again that she was forgetting something important. She closed her eyes and wiped her mind blank. She let the word *safe* float across her mind's eye. She visualized it in various fonts and scripts, trying to place it in the context of books, newspaper and magazine articles, or even on a computer screen.

And suddenly it came to her where she'd seen it before. In small, unobtrusive print at the bottom of a title page in a book. Above the phrase, "The Society for the Advancement of Free Economies." A California-based small press that had published several of Thomas Wolfe's political and legal treatises. From what little she'd read of his deadly dull books, they professed nothing overly radical or alarming. He'd argued in the one book she'd managed to slog partway through that terror could only be effectively fought with terror and lawful societies would never defeat lawless societies, or something like that. Prophetic words a decade ago. And completely ignored, apparently, given recent past history. Could that be the same "S.A.F.E." that DiscoDuck's e-mail referred to?

The more she thought about it, the more convinced she became that she was on the right track. Safe wasn't a word at all. It was an acronym for an organization or operation of some kind.

She stared at her computer speculatively. So DiscoDuck and this S.A.F.E. operation came out of the CIA, huh? Well, it made sense. Whoever was controlling Dunst might have known him from his CIA days. And the Q-group's operation in Chicago had CIA training stamped all over it. For that matter, the break-in at the Old Town Oracle facility had classic CIA operation stamped all over it, too.

Abruptly, she recalled Oracle's analysis last night that indicated someone highly placed within the government was probably behind the attacks on Gabe. Was this the person she'd been searching for? She pulled up the list of names Oracle had generated of people in positions of power who might have had access to the information that had been passed on to Gabe's attackers. Who on that list was in the CIA?

Two names leaped out at her. Collin Scott, an assistant Director of Operations and…Joseph Lockworth. Surely not. Her brain rebelled against the idea of Gramps killing anyone. Except he'd been Director of the CIA. Of course, he'd ordered people killed on his watch. Why not order an incoming President killed?

Darryl and his Cadillac from hell had picked her up immediately after she contacted her grandfather. *After* he'd offered her a ride in his private car. Could it be? Had her own grandfather set her up to be killed?

She thought back to the times he'd bounced her on his knee, doing the same horsey-riding rhyme over and over for her. How he'd convinced her father to send her and Josie into the Athena Academy, which had probably saved both of them from ruined lives. How he'd come to visit them a couple of times a year, dropping in at the Academy without notice, pulling them out of their classes and taking them out to lunch at some outrageously expensive restaurant. He hadn't replaced their mother, but he'd by golly kept a close eye on them and done whatever he could to help them after his daughter-in-law failed them.

For that matter, most of the arguments she ever remembered Gramps having with Mom had to do with Josie and her. The one thing that had stuck in his craw was that Zoe would abandon her children. Gramps was a stickler for family taking care of family. That couldn't all have been an act. It just couldn't. He wouldn't set up his own granddaughter to be kidnapped or murdered.

DiscoDuck *had* to be this Scott guy.

But then the question arose of how in the world an active member of the CIA could get away with setting up Gabe Monihan to be killed. The Agency monitored its employees with nearly paranoid intensity. And that perennially beleaguered agency most certainly knew better than to let one of their own fool with American politics.

It made no sense at all that someone in the CIA would try to assassinate the incoming President, especially since his policies were bound to be more friendly to the intelligence community than the last administration's. This DiscoDuck had to be a rogue operator within the CIA.

Not that it mattered right now. What mattered at this very moment was saving Gabe from whatever DiscoDuck had just orchestrated over the Internet.

She went back to the Q-group chat room and scrolled through the discussion over the last few minutes while she'd been occupied tracking down DiscoDuck.

He said a pickup game of soccer was going to be played up on the hill overlooking the lake. She translated in her head, *Capitol Hill. Overlooking the Reflecting Pool.*

She read on. He said they were meeting at around six-thirty to warm up and would start playing for real around 7 p.m. Those times didn't take a rocket scientist to decipher and figure out what he was talking about.

This guy knew every last detail of when and where Gabe was going to be inaugurated tonight! How could that be? Gabe said the whole thing was a huge secret. So who'd leaked it? And how had DiscoDuck gotten his hands on the information? He had to be highly placed within the CIA, just like Oracle had forecast, to know what he did. And if that was true, it meant he was smart, powerful, and had frightening resources at his disposal.

She shoved down the panic threatening to choke her. She had to figure out who this guy was! Who all knew about tonight?

Gabe, obviously. His security detail. The Chief Justice of the Supreme Court who'd swear him in. Key members of Congress and various government agencies—enter Disco-Duck. The local police. The FBI. No doubt, members of the media had been notified so they could get cameras and crews into place to cover the inauguration. Technical support types at the networks who'd break into the evening programming with the live feed.

Crud. The list of people in the know was too big to help her narrow down DiscoDuck's identity at all.

She looked at her watch. It was after six now. These turkeys were going to meet at 6:30 p.m. to warm up. As in getting into position to kill Gabe. Some warm-up.

She shut down her computer and headed for her bedroom, or more to the point, for the safe in her bedroom that held her sidearm. Grimly, she donned a leather shoulder holster and threw her black leather duster on over it. She dialed the combination for the small safe in her closet and pulled out her rarely used pistol, a sturdy 9 mm Beretta she'd owned for years. It might not have the most firepower in the world, but its clip held fourteen rounds and a fifteenth in the firing chamber, and it never jammed. She grabbed both her spare clips of ammunition, threw them in her pocket and headed for the door.

Time to go to an inauguration.

7:00 P.M.

The Capitol was brightly lit when she pulled up a block north of it—as close as the police barricades would let her go—and parked her car. The glowing Rotunda thrust up into the night sky, a proud symbol of America in the crystalline chill of the evening. Stars glittered above and her breath hung in the air in thick clouds. She glimpsed the shadow of a pair of military choppers circling overhead just before she heard their distinctive thwocking. She'd bet there were fighter jets higher up, out of earshot, providing cover for this particular piece of real estate, too.

Ten-to-one at least one of the choppers up there was using high-resolution cameras to watch everyone and everything moving on the ground down here. From the height they were currently circling at, those cameras would be able to see ants scuttling along, if it weren't too cold for such creatures tonight.

Ducking her head and shoulders back inside her car, she

doffed her shoulder holster and emptied her pockets of ammo clips. She tucked the pistol under the front seat, out of sight. No way was she getting that baby inside the Capitol building. She could see the ground security from here, armed policemen with roving attack dogs pacing the steps in front of the Capitol.

The line waiting to get inside was blessedly short and she was only half-frozen when she stepped inside the majestic edifice. She checked her watch. Six-fifty. She had ten minutes to figure out what DiscoDuck and his cronies were up to and stop them.

She scanned the setup. A small stage had been erected on the east side of the spacious Rotunda, and rows of chairs for about a hundred people laid out in front of it. A podium stood on the stage, no doubt bulletproof, and a pair of clear, glass teleprompter panels stood on narrow poles to each side of it. A number of people were already seated in the chairs, many of whom she recognized as prominent politicians.

She scanned the exits. Every one of them was heavily covered with layers of armed guards either blocking it or carefully screening each person who entered. She looked up. The various balconies that ringed the Rotunda were also occupied by a mishmash of uniformed guards and plainclothes, men in suits. She recognized a couple of the men as Secret Service agents from the warehouse this afternoon.

Where in the heck was DiscoDuck's threat supposed to come from? She didn't see any way anyone was getting in from the outside to kill Gabe. She noticed a movement from the direction of the Senate chambers. A group of silent men in conservative suits stepped into the Rotunda and fanned out. More Secret Service. She recognized several of the men in this contingent from the bunker.

She had to give Owen Haas credit. He'd done a great job

locking down this site and securing it against any potential threat. He'd anticipated everything she could think of and more.

So how was it DiscoDuck thought he or his people could get access to Gabe?

She ticked off all the usual sources of threats. Sniper. Bomber. Close-range shooter. Attack from above. Attack from a bystander. Haas and his team were positioned to stop every last one.

She looked at her watch again—6:53 p.m. The crowd was being asked to take its seats. She hung back at the margin of the small crowd, still searching warily.

She was overreacting. Haas had this thing under control. Everything was going to be perfectly fine. She should just sit down and enjoy watching Gabe become President. A Secret Service agent herded her, last in line, toward one of the rear seats. The guy's eyes moved constantly, checking outward from the subtle cordon they'd formed around the stage.

Reluctantly, she took her seat, at the end of the last row. A group of dignitaries filed out on stage and took their places. A burst of light exploded, and she started horribly, almost diving for the floor out of sheer reflex. The television cameras had just gone on. Sheesh, she was a mess.

Several news anchors scattered around the room began to speak into microphones. In the otherwise silent space, their words swirled and echoed around her, disconnected from the people uttering them.

"In just a few moments, President-elect Monihan will be sworn in as President of the United States… After a day of terror in our nation's capital, the wheels of democracy will finally turn, and a new president will be sworn in…We're standing by for the delayed inauguration of Gabriel Monihan, which will go ahead in spite of a day of death in Washington…."

There was a rustle as everyone stood up, and she followed

suit belatedly. Over the heads of the rows of dignitaries in front of her, she glimpsed Gabe and an elderly man in a long black robe stepping into the doorway behind the stage. Almost time. In a matter of minutes, Gabe would be President, and her theories would be proven—thankfully—to be unfounded. And then she and Gabe could each get on with their lives. She was going to miss him. In the short time she'd known him, he'd made a huge impression on her. In fact, she suspected he'd left a mark on her life that would never go away. This experience had shown her it was possible to curb the rebel in her, to channel it in a positive and useful way to help her fellow man instead of fighting against the system all the time.

Owen Haas, standing beside Gabe, put a finger to his ear. Undoubtedly getting a last all-clear report from his men before he let his charge step out into the lights, alone and unprotected.

She glanced over her shoulder at the other agents in the loose ring of men converging around the stage. They, too, scanned the edges of the room. So well honed a team were they that they barely looked at one another as they moved as one through the echoing chamber.

She frowned.

The Secret Service agents weren't looking at each other.

Where better to mount an attack on Gabe than from within the very force meant to protect him?

Dunst was a master of disguise. He was ex-CIA. He'd be familiar with the standard security procedures a group like the Secret Service would use. If he took out one of the Secret Service agents—one who looked like him—replaced the guy and stepped into the cordon, none of the other agents were likely to notice. They were too busy looking elsewhere for threats to look at themselves.

She scanned the agents ranged around the floor of the Rotunda. He wouldn't be here. These men were too closely spaced, and one of them would notice a substitution at a glance. She looked up at the agents roaming the balconies above. They were operating widely spaced from each other at their various perches.

One of those guys would be a cinch to take out. As long as someone took his place and made the radio calls at the right times, nobody would notice a thing.

She looked even higher. Somewhere up there, on the very top balcony around the Rotunda, she had no doubt a team of snipers was spaced out. If one of *those* guys were taken out and replaced by Dunst…

She turned around fast and bumped into a Secret Service agent practically right behind her.

"It's time for the swearing in, ma'am."

"I have to go," she gasped. "There's a sniper in here. He's going to try to kill Gabe."

The guy glanced up. "There are several snipers in here, ma'am. They're here to protect President-elect Monihan. I can assure you, they won't hurt anyone unless they need to."

He didn't get it. He thought she was some random chick who'd spotted one of the government snipers and was panicking.

"I have to go," she insisted.

The guy gave her a hard look. "If you leave now, you won't be let back into the room."

"That's okay. I've got to get out of here," she insisted desperately. "Now."

The guy shrugged.

She raced for the nearest exit. A phalanx of security guards stepped aside to let her out. As she slipped past the men, she looked back over her shoulder at the Secret Service man standing by the door.

"Tell Owen Haas or Agent Tilman that Diana Lockworth

says one of their snipers has been taken out and replaced by Richard Dunst. Gabe Monihan is in grave danger. They have to get him out of here!"

And with that, she took off running.

She headed for the nearest staircase, flashed her military ID at a startled Capitol police officer, and ran up the steps as fast as she could. They ended three stories up, on a floor of small offices devoted to Congressional staffers. Not high enough to get into the Rotunda yet. She turned left, back toward the center of the building and its giant dome. She darted down the dimly lit hallway, looking for another staircase.

There. An unmarked door about where the wall of the dome should start. It was either the staircase she sought, or she was about to jump into a janitor's closet. She shoved on the door, and it opened to reveal another staircase winding up into the dark, narrow and steep. She raced up it, panting in her panic and exertion.

She burst out the first door she came to and lurched to a stop high above the floor of the Rotunda. Only a carved stone railing stood between her and a plunge to her death. A man to her left jolted. She looked at the guy's face. Definitely not Dunst. She looked right at the other Secret Service agent now moving toward her. Not Dunst, either.

She bolted back into the stairwell and continued her desperate flight upward. But now, footsteps pounded after her. Her feet flew over the cast-iron steps and she clattered up them two at a time, her knees pumping like pistons. God bless stair-climber machines and all the hours she'd spent on them in the last decade.

Another landing as the stairs ended. She burst out onto a narrow ledge even higher up the side of the dome. The Secret Service agents on this level were a good third of the way around the dome from her, but coming at her fast. Her pursuers must have radioed ahead. She took off running toward the nearest agent. He reached for his left armpit. Gun! She held her hands out, well away from her sides to indicate she wasn't armed. And got a good look at the guy. Not Dunst.

He hesitated in the act of pulling out his pistol, and she turned around and reversed direction. The other agent on this level was closing fast on her. African-American guy. Clearly not Dunst. Except now she was trapped between the two men!

A doorway appeared on her right. She darted through it.

A narrow, curving hallway with a sloping ceiling. She sprinted along it, frantically looking for a way higher. There was one more balcony above her, more a maintenance catwalk than an actual balcony. That's where the snipers would be, and where Dunst had to be.

Lots of footsteps pounded behind her now, and men's voices shouted, echoing in the oddly shaped space. Fighting off vertigo from the crazy slant of the walls in the near total darkness, she pushed forward. She must have run halfway around the giant dome when finally, a narrow staircase appeared on her left.

She skidded to a stop and leaped for it, scrambling on all fours for the first few steps until she regained her balance and got her feet under her again. She raced upward, her shoulders brushing the walls. Her legs burned and her lungs screamed for oxygen. But Gabe was down below, vulnerable and possibly lined up in Dunst's gun sights already.

She burst out onto the catwalk. Its iron railing looked pitifully flimsy to protect against the tremendous fall to the floor far below. She raced to the left, her footsteps rattling on the iron grillwork that formed the floor of the catwalk.

There! A man, lying prone, cradling a deadly looking rifle with a sight nearly as big as the barrel of the weapon. The barrel of the weapon poked through the iron railing and was trained on the crowd below. The sniper jerked, looking up at her in surprise as she barreled down on him. The nose was too narrow, the cheeks too high for Dunst. He sat up, wrestling to get the gun out from between the iron rails and turn it on her.

She vaulted over the guy's legs and kept on going. She raced around the perimeter of the dome, much smaller up here than down lower. And spotted the second sniper. She wasn't close enough to see his face.

As she ran toward him, he hunkered down over his rifle as if he was going to shoot. He glanced up at her once, his gaze pure malevolence directed at her. She saw his face from a range of about thirty feet. *Richard Dunst.*

His face turned back to his weapon, and his eye went down to the telescopic sight.

"Nooooo!" she screamed.

She put on a burst of superhuman speed, her gaze riveted on his trigger finger.

It squeezed in slow motion, depressing the trigger in its housing. She jumped for the rifle. But as she sailed toward it in midair, a blinding flash of light exploded from the end of the barrel. A blast of sound slammed into her a millisecond before she landed on the rifle. Too late!

The hot metal barrel crashed into her ribs, driving the breath out of her like an iron fist. She gasped in pain as she twisted to face the man scrambling to his feet above her. Screams erupted below, floating up eerily into the rafters.

The bastard had just shot Gabe and she hadn't been in time to stop it. Tearing agony swept over her, along with rage. Red-ringed, rip-someone-apart rage that boiled over, totally out of control. She rode the wave and surged upward, tackling the bastard around the legs. He went down hard, snarling as he plowed a fist into her jaw.

Oblivious to pain, oblivious to anything except her need to hurt this man, she reached for his neck, wrapping her fingers around his throat. He thrust his hands up between her forearms and gave a vicious outward chop, forcing her to release his throat or break both her elbows.

He jabbed for her eyes, and she grabbed his fingers, twisting them brutally. He roared in pain and jerked his knee upward. Fortunately, she didn't have family jewels in the same sensitive spot as a man, but the blow dislodged her from on top of him nonetheless. She rammed her elbow into his ribs as she rolled off of him, reveling in the grunt of pain that drew. But he countered with an openhanded thrust to the side of her head that made her see stars as pain exploded through her head.

This guy was no amateur thug that a few well-placed blows could drop. He was a trained killer, and furthermore, he understood that he was fighting for his life here. She, on the other hand, had only revenge on her mind. Survival wasn't of great importance to her at the moment as long as this asshole went down.

She rolled to her knees and lunged forward, grabbing the guy's ankles as he turned to flee. Oh, no. He wasn't going anywhere. They were finishing this right here. Right now. He turned and kicked viciously, his toe connecting with her throat. She gagged, choking for air, and getting none. Her grasp loosened, and he yanked free of her arms. He scrabbled away from her, swearing. Quickly going light-headed, she grabbed the railing beside her and dragged herself to her feet. She looked up at Dunst.

His lips drew back from his teeth in a grimace of fury. He reached inside his coat and came out with a pistol in hand. She stared at the bore of the weapon. Too far to reach it. And there was nowhere to dodge it. The sloping wall crowded her on the right, and to her left was a drop of many stories to a marble floor. He'd better hit her heart, because with her last breath, she was going to take the bastard with her when she went.

She flung herself forward, into the coming shot, with the intent to grab Dunst and twist over the railing with him as she went down.

The shot rang out.

She felt nothing. No impact. No burning pain of supersonic lead ripping through her body.

As she flew through the air toward Dunst, a look of infinite surprise crossed his face.

And then she hit him, a bone-grinding impact of body on body. But instead of resisting her, he collapsed, going as limp as a rag doll beneath her. Instead of carrying them over the balcony, her roll to the left slammed them into the iron railing harmlessly.

Damn!

She blinked, focusing on Dunst's face, inches from her own. His eyes were glassy. She smelled something metallic.

And then she noticed the neat, kidney-colored hole in the center of his forehead. He'd been shot? By whom?

She became aware of shouting around her. Male voices. Nearby. Adding to the chaos of sound floating up from below.

A hand landed on her shoulder from behind. Pulling her roughly away from Dunst. A pistol thrust past her nose, pointed in Dunst's face. A foot hooked under Dunst's shoulder, rolling him onto his side.

And she stared at the hand-size piece of skull ripped away from the back of his head. A spreading pool of blood and brain matter dripped through the iron grillwork floor. Dunst was dead.

She looked up numbly at the man beside her. Agent Tilman. "You okay?" he bit out.

She blinked. Was she okay? She had no idea. "I guess so," she mumbled. And then her brain kicked into gear again. Oh, God. Gabe! "That bastard shot Gabe!" she cried out.

Tilman's jaw rippled with the same adrenaline-enhanced fury still roaring through her. "He better not have."

"I've got to see him," she declared. "Be with him in case…" She couldn't finish the thought. He *had* to live. She leaped to her feet and took off running for the stairs, Tilman on her heels.

Somewhere in that interminable flight back down all those stairs, she started to breathe again. Vaguely she registered Tilman shouting into his radio behind her. Something about clearing a path and letting the two of them through. She raced past a dozen Secret Service agents and FBI men who plastered themselves against the walls of the narrow stairwells to get out of her way.

Finally, she reached the ground floor and ran for the Rotunda at full-tilt. She skidded out onto the marble floor.

A crowd of civilians were herded into one corner, filing out of the Rotunda toward the House chambers. Gun-toting men roved the space, and a cluster of news reporters chattered excitedly into microphones, huddled by the far wall. But then she spotted what she was searching for. A cluster of paramedics and Secret Service agents bending down over a prone form on the floor. *Gabe.*

She tore across the space between them and shoved through the mass of bodies.

And lurched to a halt as he grinned up at her jauntily.

"Hey, gorgeous," he said lightly.

She looked down. His shirt was open, revealing a bulletproof vest, which was also opened to reveal a four-inch purple spot low on his right side. She fell to her knees as Gabe sat up. *Thank God he was all right.* A cold wash of realization passed over her. When had this become so damned personal? For surely the sick-to-her-stomach, weak-kneed relief coursing through her was much more than professional concern.

"What in the hell were you doing out here?" she bit out.

"Owen almost had me out of here. I'm afraid I wasn't going willingly. I had a feeling you were behind all the commotion." He paused. "I was worried about you," he confessed.

"I was too late," she said. "I'm so sorry."

He smiled. "There's nothing to be sorry for. It was your scream that caused Owen to dive on me. You saved my life. Again."

A grim voice spoke from somewhere above her head. "I don't mean to intrude, sir, but I need to talk to the lady. Now."

She looked up.

Owen Haas loomed above them, his expression furious. He glared at her and gritted out from between clenched teeth, "Maybe you'd care to explain to me how you always happen to know exactly when and where these damned terrorists are going to attack. Are you their person on the inside?"

8:00 P.M.

Diana lurched. His words struck her like a fist in the face. "I beg your pardon?"

Gabe spoke up with quiet authority beside her. "Why don't we take this conversation somewhere more private?"

She climbed painfully to her feet, the aches and pains of her fight with Dunst abruptly registering with her conscious mind. She felt as though she'd been run through a meat grinder. Maybe a little stretching and twisting was in order to work out a few of the kinks. Except then she tried it. *Oww*. So much for that idea. That jerk really got some good licks in on her before Tilman shot him.

A paramedic helped Gabe to his feet and a wall of Secret Service agents closed in around him as their charge went vertical. She caught the brief grimace on his face as he started buttoning up his shirt. Even through a bulletproof vest, a slug from a high-powered rifle could break a rib. He had to hurt at least as bad as she did right about now.

"This way," Owen bit out.

"No. Wait," Gabe ordered.

Owen's head whipped around. "We need to get you to safety, sir."

"We *need* to let the American people know I'm alive and unharmed," Gabe countermanded quietly.

"This is a matter of your security," Owen growled back with quiet intensity.

"This is a matter of national security," Gabe replied impassively. "I insist. I'll take responsibility for whatever happens to me." He turned to face her and asked casually, "Could you tie my tie for me? I'm lousy at it without a mirror."

She reached up, in minor shock, and retied the red silk tie around his neck. The act was intimate and felt extremely odd in this giant room with all these people standing around, watching. She felt naked. Exposed. Like her feelings for this guy were right out in the open for everyone to see.

Gabe watched her intently as she performed the service for him, his amber gaze never leaving her face. An unmistakable heat built between them, or maybe that was just the blush burning her cheeks. She tugged the knot into position under his chin and adjusted his collar slightly. He pulled his suit coat closed, and she smoothed the lapels. Dang. She couldn't keep her hands off this guy, not even in front of a crowd of people in the Capitol Building of all places!

"There," she murmured, "You look perfect."

"It's the makeup they made me wear for the cameras. I actually feel like I'm going to puke."

"I can imagine. But you're holding up great."

He shrugged. "It's not like I have any choice. This reminds me of something I heard Ronald Reagan say many years ago about being President. He said he couldn't imagine anyone being a successful President without being an accomplished actor. I'm beginning to see what he meant."

She smiled up at him reassuringly. "Just keep up the act for a few more minutes. Then you can go somewhere private and fall apart."

Diana started as Gabe's hand closed on her elbow. "Come give me moral support," he murmured.

As if Gabe Monihan needed moral support! The guy had just faced a second assassination attempt in a single day, and he seemed totally unconcerned by any danger to himself right now. Although, that was part and parcel of being President. He was supposed to be strong and steady in the face of a crisis. And it didn't hurt that Richard Dunst's brains were splattered all over the walls upstairs. That particular threat was pretty darned neutralized at the moment.

Owen was not a happy camper, but he motioned his men to follow her and Gabe as they struck out across the floor of the Rotunda.

The cameramen facing Gabe figured out what was happening before the news anchors with their backs to him did. The lights swung away from the talking journalists as Gabe strode into their midst. She gazed up at him in shock as all the stress and discomfort of having just been shot melted away from his face.

"Ladies and gentlemen, I'm sorry to interrupt you, but I'd like to make a brief statement."

The reporters all stammered their permission to go ahead.

She blinked as the monolithic eyes of the cameras pinned black stares on them, and she shrank back as much as she could from Gabe in the press of Secret Service agents hemming her in. This was Gabe's show, and she had no interest in being seen beside him on national TV.

He began to speak, confident and relaxed. "I wanted to let the American people know that, yet again, I am fine. Thanks to the quick thinking and tremendous skill of my security team, I am safe and sound." He grinned boyishly. "I promise we will get this inauguration done one way or another, tonight. I'm thinking about dragging Judge Browning into a men's room and taking the oath right there, just to get it over with."

A chuckle from the hovering press corp.

Gabe continued, "The important thing is for the American people to remember that no matter what heinous crimes terrorists attempt to perpetrate on this nation, they will never bring down the democracy that has made this nation strong. No act of terror has ever brought down a democratic government, and no act of terror is about to do it now."

A reporter shouted out of the crowd, "When are you finally going to become President?"

Gabe grinned. "Well, we're going to take a little while to regroup and get all the right people back together, and then we'll try this thing again. You know what they say. The third time's a charm."

She simply could not believe how calm he was being about all this. She was a complete wreck, and she wasn't even the target of the killers.

As a chorus of jumbled questions got shouted at him all at once, he raised a polite hand. "I'm sorry, folks. I can't take any more questions just now. I've got a little business to take care of, but I'll be glad to speak to you at the press conference I'll be holding tomorrow."

Whether or not a press conference had been on his schedule, there surely was one now. She had visions of his staff seeing this live interview and scrambling away from their televisions frantically to arrange an impromptu press conference.

Gabe turned away from the cameras and took her elbow

again, moving swiftly with her across the space back toward the abandoned stage where he was supposed to have become President. Owen and his men closed in on the two of them, confining them in a tight cordon of big, protective bodies that moved them onto and across the stage.

"So why *aren't* you dragging Justice Browning into some office and doing the deed right now?" she asked under her breath.

"He's having a little trouble with his heart at the moment. Apparently, he's not used to getting shot at. The medics were worried about him and sent him to a hospital for observation for a couple hours."

"Too bad."

He nodded. "It would've been nice to get it over with. But I'd feel funny anyway, taking the oath of office while a dead man is lying in the rafters over my head. Even if he did try to kill me."

She could understand that. She refrained from looking up at the team of police taking pictures of the corpse on the cat-walk overhead and allowed herself to be herded, along with Gabe, through the small doorway behind the stage.

She looked over the shoulders of the agents behind her at the crowd of reporters. "Are you sure you shouldn't have stuck around and answered a few of their questions?"

Owen answered brusquely for him. "That's what press secretaries are for. Right now, you two are getting under cover and we're going to have a talk."

The Secret Service agent hustled them down a short hall-way and into a small office. Glaring sternly at her, he pointed at a chair in front of the desk. She sat down in it while he perched on the edge of the desk. Lord, it felt like being hauled down to the principal's office to be chewed out. Except this was a thousand times more serious than any accusation she'd ever faced at the Athena Academy.

As worried as she was by Owen's inexplicable leap of logic, she still waited him out. It never paid to look overeager in stating her case, no matter how innocent she was.

Owen sighed heavily. "Start talking."

She was vividly aware that Gabe stood in the corner off to her right, watching her silently. She respected both of these men immensely and had no interest in playing games with either one of them. And so, she started talking.

"Owen, I don't know where you got the idea that I'd do anything or associate with anyone who would hurt Gabe. I've been busting my butt for weeks trying to break into this Q-group, and today they finally stuck their heads up high enough for me to get a position fix on them. I have access to a top-secret, high-tech database to help me analyze their movements, and because of that, I've been able to stay only a step or two behind these jokers."

"How did you know Dunst would be on that catwalk?"

"It was the only hole in your security. You had everything else covered. But you weren't looking within your own ranks for a threat." She added hastily as a black scowl crossed Owen's face. "It's not like you should've expected a threat from the inside. I only thought to do it because I know Richard Dunst."

Gabe's brows slammed together right along with Owen's.

Surely Gabe didn't take that the way it sounded. Surely he trusted her more than that! She corrected herself. "I don't know him as in being acquainted with him. I only meant Dunst was one of the people I've investigated and I know his MO. He was caught in a Q-group takedown three months ago, and his escape from Bolling was just too timely to be coincidence. He's a disguise artist and a trained killer. Speaking of which, has the agent he replaced been found yet?"

Owen shook his head in the negative. "The FBI is searching the upper floors now."

What was going through Gabe's mind? He was standing there motionless, his expression completely unreadable. Did he believe these accusations Owen was flinging at her? Surely not! But why wasn't he leaping to her defense, then? Of course, it wasn't his job to defend her. It was his job to stay out of Owen's way and let his security chief rake her over the coals. Besides, Gabe was about to be President of the United States. He couldn't afford to let his personal feelings enter into any decision he made.

What had Gabe said a few months back in response to a press question speculating about a decision he might make? Something to the effect that, he'd rather base his decisions on facts than speculation. She ought to be pleased he'd extended that philosophy to this situation. Except all she felt was hurt and abandoned by his sudden, cold reserve.

She turned back to her accuser. "Owen. You saw me jump on Gabe this morning on that balcony. Did that look like a calculated move to get into his good graces? Or did that look like the reflex of someone fighting like crazy to keep Gabe alive?"

Owen's expression waxed thoughtful. She caught a movement out of the corner of her eye and was dismayed to see Gabe cross his arms across his chest. Was that more comfortable for his bruised ribs, or was that a defensive gesture of rejection? Oh, God. Why did the people who were supposed to care about her always leave her?

She continued in a rush. "Weird stuff has been happening to me all day. My house got broken into at oh-dark-thirty this morning. An FBI agent I'd never met before made wild accusations against me. Out of the blue, some Army Intelligence guys picked me up for questioning. Some wacko posed as my grandfather's driver and tried to kidnap me. I'm telling you, somebody's freaked out by my investigation of last October's attempt on Gabe's life and is trying like hell to stop me."

"Who?" Owen barked.

She threw up her hands. "I wish I knew! But I can tell you this. Whoever it is, he or she or they are also behind the attempts to kill Gabe today. You agreed with me in the bunker this afternoon that a third party was pulling both the Q-group's strings and Dunst's. When the Q-group failed, Dunst was sent in to finish the job."

"You can't know that for certain. Unless you're working for them, of course."

"Sure, I can. I was in the Q-group chat room on the Internet a couple hours ago when the order was sent out to kill Gabe."

Both men lurched at that one.

"I've got transcripts of it at home on my computer. A bunch of my hacker buddies were there with me, trying to track down the identity of whoever gave the order."

Owen still looked suspicious. Okay. She could see where that sounded bad. But dammit, those hackers had provided vital assistance with her investigation!

"I'm not kidding," she argued desperately. "I'm way deep inside this conspiracy, and someone knows it. If anything, I'm a security risk to Gabe because they're coming for me next, and I could draw them to him. But I *am not now and never have* worked with these jerks. I swear."

She looked back and forth between the two men. Neither one's facial expression gave away a thing.

She continued to hammer away at the stone wall that was the two men. "Let me ask you a question, Owen. Who tipped you off that I was working with the Q-group? Did it come from within the Secret Service or from outside it?"

He frowned at her implication. "My organization is not compromised," he declared forcefully.

"Oh yeah?" she challenged. "Then why was I able to trace whoever gave Dunst the order to kill Gabe to CIA Headquarters in Langley? There's a rat somewhere in the government. And he or she has to be high up. How else did Dunst know to be here, tonight? If the CIA's compromised, why not the Secret Service? It would explain how the bad guys knew so much of Gabe's plans today, particularly the details of when and where he was going to be inaugurated this evening."

Owen leaned back, as if he could distance himself from her ugly words. She wished she could do the very same thing, but neither one of them had any choice in the matter. Each in their own way, he and she were both committed to keeping Gabe alive, no matter what the risk to themselves.

He bit out, "The tip about you came from within the Service. And yes, it was from high up."

Damn! Another major government agency with possible corruption at the very top! What was going on around here?

"Please, Owen. I need a name."

He glanced over at Gabe, who nodded tersely, and then back at her. He hesitated a moment more, and then said reluctantly. "Porter. Alex Porter. He's Deputy Director of the Secret Service." Owen added angrily, "He's a good man, dammit."

That remained to be seen. She stood up, too agitated to sit still any longer. "Look Owen, if you don't trust me, kick me out of here. But for God's sake, don't arrest me. I've got to keep tracking down the third party who controlled Dunst and the Q-group while the trail is fresh, or he'll slip back below the waterline and we may not ever get another chance at him."

Gabe stepped forward. "Diana, I don't want you risking your life alone like this. It's too big for you. Turn the investigation over to Owen's men or the FBI."

She wheeled around to face him and said with terrible urgency, "There's *no time*. I've got months' worth of details stored in my head, and I could never share all those quickly enough with someone else to do any good. By the time I brought anyone up to speed on all this, it would be too late. Even if all you did was bring on board a support team for me, they'd still move too slowly. It has to be me who tracks this person down. And I have to do it now."

Gabe looked over at Owen and the two exchanged a long look of silent communication. In the palpable struggle of wills that ensued, Gabe came out on top, for Owen finally turned away and nodded shortly at her. He said bitterly, "Go."

She spun and headed for the door, but stopped with her hand on the knob. "Thank you," she said earnestly to Owen. "I swear, I'll do my best not to let you down."

He scowled. "Stay away from President-elect Monihan."

She nodded once. She paused just long enough to take one last, heartbreaking look at Gabe. Lord, she was going to miss him. She closed her eyes against the pain and stumbled out of the room.

How she made it outside and to her car, she had no idea. But she knew she was going to find DiscoDuck and pluck every last feather out of his worthless hide.

Too many coincidences had happened to her today. Too many seemingly unrelated occurrences that all added up to a big fat scheme to stop her investigation and to discredit her. This latest indignity of planting doubts about her in Owen's and Gabe's heads was the final straw.

It was time to go on the offensive. And she knew just where to start.

9:00 P.M.

Diana punched Delphi's phone number into her cell phone as she drove. Shoot, at the rate she was using this number today, she ought to put it on her speed dial. Delphi picked up on the first ring and didn't bother to say hello. Obviously had caller ID.

"I saw you on TV with Gabriel Monihan. Can I assume you had some part in foiling the latest assassination attempt?"

"Yes. Richard Dunst is dead."

"Then Monihan is safe."

"No," Diana replied sharply. "He's not."

A pause while Delphi digested that. "Now who's after him?"

"Dunst's boss. The same person or persons who were using the Q-group to get to Gabe. They're still out there."

"And do you know who they are?" Delphi asked tersely.

"No, but I plan to find out. That's why I called you. I need an address. The guy's name is Captain Hammersmith, and he's with Army CID. I don't know his first name. He's stationed here in the D.C. area. Maybe attached to the Pentagon."

"That should be plenty to track him down with," Delphi said mildly. "Let me put it into Oracle."

Diana drove west, vaguely in the direction of the Pentagon while Oracle did its thing. And in a few minutes, Delphi was back.

"You're correct. He's attached to the CID unit at the Pentagon. Here's his home address." Delphi rattled off an address in Fairfax, Virginia, not far from the Pentagon. "Keep me informed as to what you find out."

"Will do," Diana replied. She punched the address into her car's nifty navigation computer, and a map to her destination popped up on its display. For once today, she wasn't under some horrible time crunch, and she drove at a sane speed to Captain Hammersmith's home. She composed in her mind the speech she wanted to give him and practiced it a few times as she searched for his house. Ah. There it was. A modest ranch. With the cost of living in this area, it was hard to make a military man's pay go far.

She got out of the car and walked up the front sidewalk, which was neatly shoveled clear of snow and ice.

A young woman answered her knock on the front door.

Diana spoke politely. "Mrs. Hammersmith? Is your husband at home? I urgently need to speak to him about a military matter."

Mrs. Hammersmith looked surprised, but invited her in. One of the men who'd questioned her that morning rounded the corner into the front hall, wearing jeans and a sweatshirt. He blurted out, "What are *you* doing here?"

"I have a question for you. And it's a matter of national security."

Hammersmith glanced at his wife. "Step in here."

He guided Diana into a small den off the front hallway and closed the door behind her. As soon as he turned around, he lit into her. "How dare you show up at my house like this!"

Diana weathered the tirade in silence. When he subsided, she said quietly, "Are you done yet?"

He blinked.

"Look, I'm not kidding. Twice today I've barely managed to stop people from killing Gabe Monihan. But I still haven't tracked down who's behind these bastards. I need your help to do it."

He glared at her. "You're delusional."

She yanked out the personal business card Gabe had given her that morning with his cell phone number scrawled on it. "Go ahead. Call him. Ask President-elect Monihan if I'm delusional or not."

Hammersmith stared hard at the small rectangle of white and said nothing, his mouth pressed into a thin, white line.

"I don't need you to believe me, Captain," she said shortly. "All I need you to do is tell me who gave you and your partner the order to pick me up. Who tipped you off about me?"

The guy looked up at her and back down at the card in his hand. Silently, he handed the card back to her, his expression defiant.

She threatened with cool savagery, "I'm not leaving your house until you tell me, and you seriously don't want to catch the heat I'm going to bring down on your head if you don't cooperate. My grandfather was just the first of the big guns I can aim at you. You've gotten tangled up in something so much larger than you, I doubt you can even imagine it. You might as well just give me the name, because I am going to get it out of you one way or the other."

She saw him weakening. *C'mon, Hammersmith. Break already. Time's awasting here.*

She lightened her tone of voice to one of patient understanding. There was nothing like having to do a one-woman good-cop bad-cop routine. "Look. You can give me the name voluntarily, or I can call in someone way, way above you in your chain of command to give you an order. If you'd like, I can start with Gabe Monihan and let it roll downhill from there."

Hammersmith huffed hard. "Fine. A guy named Smith called us. Colonel Al Smith. He's an aide to General Pace."

"General Eric Pace? As in the Army Chief of Staff?" she asked carefully. Holy cow!

"Yeah. Satisfied now?" he snapped.

"Yes, I am. Thanks. I'll mention your cooperation to President Monihan when this is all over."

"You do that."

Not a happy camper. But she didn't have time to care. Time to move on to her next interview. She left his house quickly and repeated her call to Delphi, this time obtaining the home address of FBI Special Agent Ronald Flaherty. He'd be a much tougher nut to crack if she didn't miss her guess. The guy was a veteran agent. No way would she be able to bully him like she just had Hammersmith.

She pulled up to his house, a rambling colonial on a tree-lined street only ten minutes or so away from her home. Nice place. She walked up to the wide, covered front porch and rang the doorbell, huddling deep in her leather duster. Man, it was cold tonight. Of course, some of the chill was probably coming from inside her gut. First, a high-level Secret Service supervisor fingered her, and then someone attached to the Joint Chiefs of Staff. She dreaded hearing who'd sicced Flaherty on her.

Agent Flaherty himself opened the front door. He took one look at her and growled, "What the hell are you doing here?"

"Look. I'm sorry to bring work to your home like this. But I need to speak with you for a minute. I have a question for you. It won't take long. I promise. It's a matter of national security." That phrase usually got to men like this, whose lives revolved around the idea of protecting that national security.

Flaherty snarled, "Call me in the morning. At my office. And don't ever show up at my house like this again, or I'll arrest your ass so fast it'll make your head spin."

Damn. He wasn't going to cooperate. She'd been afraid of that. She stepped forward aggressively, shoving her hand forward, still cloaked inside her coat pocket. She jammed the barrel of her Beretta into his ribs. "Don't do anything sudden, eh, Ronald?" she purred.

His eyes widened in shock then quickly narrowed in calculation.

"Ever heard of a combat system called Krav Maga?" she asked casually. "Don't try what you were just contemplating. At this point, I really don't give a flip if I blow your head off or not."

Apparently he heard the menace in her voice of someone who wasn't lying and who could, in fact, follow through on that threat to kill him. The fight flickered out of his eyes.

"I respect your wish to protect your family. So why don't you step outside onto the porch with me?" she suggested quietly. She stepped back a pace to give him room to join her. His gaze dropped to the front doorknob.

She smiled coldly. "I'm telling you. Don't try it, my friend. I only want to ask you a question, and then I'll leave."

Flaherty stepped outside and pulled the front door closed behind him.

She gestured toward the porch swing off to her left. "Have a seat."

Flaherty did as she directed. She moved around to his right

side, partially behind him, in the best position to subdue him if he pulled any stunts. The way his eyes widened as his gaze followed her, he apparently recognized what she'd done. It was the move of a pro. Now that she'd established her seriousness with this guy, maybe they'd get somewhere.

"Who are you?" he asked.

It was undoubtedly a delaying tactic to stall her and distract her. But she was willing to give the guy that information on the assumption that he'd report her visit to the very superiors who'd set him on her. She wanted them to get the message that she was closing in on them.

"I work for Army Intelligence, and I've been investigating the terrorists who've been trying to kill Gabriel Monihan for the last several months. After they showed themselves today, I'm inches away from nabbing them. I've got names already, but I'm going to nail everyone in this conspiracy and put them all away for good. And I need your help." There. That should put the fear of God in whoever it was she was chasing.

Flaherty snorted. "That's nuts. If there was a conspiracy to assassinate Monihan, we'd have heard about it and investigated it ourselves."

She retorted, "Since when do all the branches of the government, particularly the intelligence agencies, share their toys and play nicely with the other children? Even with the Department of Homeland Security in place, you know as well as I do that interdepartment rivalries are alive and well within the government."

Flaherty made a derisive sound of agreement.

"Are you getting cold, Agent Flaherty? I figure in another ten minutes or so, frostbite's going to hit and your fingers are going to start to freeze. You know, you could lose your field qualification if you lose the tip of your shooting finger."

He didn't show any reaction to that one. Not that she'd expected him to. She spent a couple of seemingly endless minutes just standing there beside him in silence, letting him soak up the cold without distractions from her. She had a coat on. She could be patient. And silence was a hundred times more unnerving than a steady stream of conversation.

Finally, when he was shivering violently, he broke the stalemate. His teeth chattered when he snarled, "What question is so goddamned important that you'd drag me out here at gunpoint to ask it?"

"Who called you this morning and gave you instructions to detain me and interrogate me?"

His lips, black in the scant light out here, curled into a sneer. "Why the hell do you want to know that?"

He was delaying again. "Like I said, Agent Flaherty. It's a matter of national security."

"Bullshit," he spit out.

"I'm not particularly interested in your opinion on the subject. I want that name. Now."

"Go to hell."

She sighed. And leaped forward lightning fast, wrapping her right forearm around his throat and half lifting him off the seat with a vicious choke hold. With her left hand she grabbed his ear and, twisting it hard, forced his head to stay locked in a position that severely restricted his breathing.

She murmured conversationally in his ear, "This is a basic Krav Maga choke. You know, those Israelis are mean bastards. They don't care much if they kill the occasional punk in the name of doing their job. If I crank down this hold and shift it a bit, like this—" she tightened the hold across his throat and windpipe fractionally "—I can cut off your breathing altogether."

He gurgled beneath her arm and tried to struggle, but when she yanked hard on his ear, the shooting pain of it forced him to subside as it had been designed to do. She left the killer hold in place a few seconds more for good measure, then eased up with her arm enough for the guy to draw a partial breath.

"Now where were we?" she murmured. "Ah, yes. You were about to tell me who gave you the order to mess with me this morning."

He drew in another rattling breath but said nothing. She started to tighten her grip around his throat again.

"All right, all right!" he gasped.

"Talk," she commanded in his right ear.

"Janelle Parsons."

"Who's she?" Diana demanded.

"Works in the office of the Director."

Crud! What was this with high-level orders to yank her chain? "What did she say to you, exactly?"

"She said there was a loose cannon bombing around town causing problems. I was to detain you and question you, and arrest you if you gave me the slightest reason to do so."

Diana let go of him and stood up. He leaped off the swing and dropped into a defensive position before her. Didn't want her to get an arm around his throat again, did he? "So why didn't you arrest me?" she asked.

"You saved that guard's life," he answered simply. "And I didn't have due cause to arrest you other than some order from on high to harass you."

Dang. Under other circumstances, she could've liked this guy. Been honored to work with someone decent like him. Aloud, she said, "Thanks, Agent Flaherty. I appreciate the information. I'm sorry I had to rough you up to get it. But it truly is a matter of national security, and time is of the essence. When this is all over, I'll be happy to sit down with you and tell you all the gory details."

He stared at her in open disbelief as she politely excused herself and moved off the front porch. Of course, she wasn't dumb enough to turn her back to him at any point, and she kept her hand in her pocket and on her pistol. She slid into the front seat of her car and backed out of his driveway fast, peeling away into the darkness while he still stood on the porch, staring at her. Whether or not he'd call the police and get an APB put out on her was anybody's guess.

She pointed her car toward home and her computer. She had a bunch of names to run through the Oracle database, assuming it wasn't completely corrupted. The tampering she'd found had all been in analysis subroutines. Hopefully, the fact-correlation routines were still functional, and she couldn't wait to see what they said.

She parked in the alley behind her house, backing into the neighbor's driveway in case Flaherty had, in fact, called the police. She could bolt out of her house and drive away fast if someone came knocking on her door. She made her way through her yard cautiously, keeping an eye out for any company. After scanning every dark corner of the yard and finding nothing, she slipped into her kitchen. Without turning the lights on, she moved into the living room. She closed the front blinds and then moved over to her computer and turned it on.

She had a couple of incoming e-mails and she glanced through the addresses. Mostly from her family. They could wait. Nothing from the office or Oracle. She accessed the Internet and booted up the Oracle database quickly.

She entered the names she had—Alex Porter at the Secret Service, Colonel Al Smith at the office of the Army Chief of Staff and Janelle Parsons at the FBI. The computer searched for several minutes, looking for significant connections between the three people.

A response popped up on her screen. "Please enter more data to narrow the search parameters."

Damn. On a hunch, she typed in, "Find name of Richard Dunst's last supervisor at the CIA."

A cursor blinked for a few seconds and then came back with, "Collin Scott."

She typed back, "Find Collin Scott's supervisor when Dunst worked for him."

That name came back up almost instantly. She stared at it in dismay. *Joseph Lockworth.* Holy cow.

She went back to her list of names in the original search and added the names, Collin Scott and Joseph Lockworth. On a hunch, she threw in the names of the members of the Joint Chiefs of Staff, as well. Flunkies at JCS didn't do much on their own. She'd bet someone higher up had told Colonel Smith to make the call to Captain Hammersmith and friends.

Oracle took longer to think about her list of names this time. And that meant it was probably on to something. While it analyzed whatever it had come up with, she went into her bedroom and threw on a pair of warm, lined wool slacks and a turtleneck-sweater combination. No sense freezing to death tonight. And even with her coat on, that stint on Flaherty's porch had chilled her.

The computer beeped in the living room and she hastened out to see what it had come up with.

A detailed analysis scrolled down the screen. Most of the individuals on her list could be placed at various conferences, retreats, or meetings together steadily for the last three years. Oracle wasn't talking two or three meetings. It listed fourteen dates where at least four of the people on her list were in the same place at the same time. Now what were the odds of that? She read further. Oracle placed the chances of these meetings being random coincidence at less than ten percent. Maybe not enough to convict someone on, but it was enough for her.

She typed in, "Who else was at most of these meetings?"

The screen blinked while Oracle compared the various lists of attendees. And then a list of a dozen names appeared. She scanned down through it. Quickly. Nine of the names were high-ranking members of the federal government. Good Lord. Even the Army Chief of Staff himself made the list, General Eric Pace. The last three people on the list were prominent businessmen—according to Oracle two were CEOs of major corporations, and the third was a finance banker. Whoa. If this was the group behind Q-group and Dunst, no wonder they'd nearly succeeded in killing Gabe. Frankly, the real shocker was that they'd failed. *So far,* she reminded herself grimly.

She glanced further into the analysis and stared in dismay as another name caught her attention. One of the speakers at nearly half the conferences was another name she knew all too well. Thomas Wolfe. Gabe's own Vice President? Could it be? Was he involved in a conspiracy to kill Gabe and take the Presidency for himself? The very thought sent a chill racing down her spine.

She read on. Most of the conferences this gang had been at together had to do with national security issues, and three of the conferences were sponsored by the Society for the Advancement of Free Economies. *Bingo.* S.A.F.E.. *She'd found the connection.* Triumph surged through her. DiscoDuck's encrypted e-mail files had contained multiple references to the word safe in the mail titles. Now she had a positive link between the Q-group, Richard Dunst and this S.A.F.E. bunch.

Quickly she typed in the society's full name and asked for information on it. Founded a dozen years ago. Established its own small-press publishing house a few years back. Followed the teachings of…there he was again…Thomas Wolfe. Believed that terror would choke the global economy if left unchecked. Argued that terrorism was the greatest threat to the future of mankind since the beginning of history. Okay then. So this was a conservative group. Probably in favor of use of force against terrorism, given their strong opinions about it. Then why in the world would they propagate terror of their own and try to kill Gabe Monihan? It didn't make any sense. She was missing something.

She stared at her computer screen, seeing nothing but a blur before her eyes. Now what was she supposed to do? She forced her numb brain back into gear.

Four of the names on her list worked at the CIA. Maybe that was the center of this group's operations. It was worth a try. She picked up the phone on the desk beside her computer and called Delphi one more time.

Yet again, her employer picked up the phone immediately and asked without preamble, "What have you got?"

"I've got a list of names. I tracked down everyone who passed down warnings about me to the various underlings who harassed me today, and I ran those names through part of the Oracle program that's still working. I've come up with a list of twelve people who appear to have been meeting each other regularly for the last several years. They're all high rollers. You can access the analysis yourself. I saved it into the threat assessment file on Gabe that you sent me last night."

"How very interesting," Delphi said cautiously, if the toneless electronic drawl of Delphi's altered voice could be described as having any emotion at all. "What do you plan to do next?" her employer intoned.

"I'm going to start visiting these turkeys and see what I can shake out with a few pointed questions directed at them."

"Do you think it's a wise idea to shake the bushes quite so directly? Perhaps a subtler approach might be best."

Diana gaped in surprise. Her boss had never before offered any suggestions about how she should proceed with an investigation. But then, she'd never threatened to rattle the very foundations of the federal government, either. She asked Delphi cautiously, "What sort of approach do you recommend?"

"Write up a report on your findings to date. Make a few official inquiries about the purposes of all those meetings and see what you get," Delphi suggested.

Diana frowned. A written report? That would take days! Go through channels? That was the whole purpose of Oracle. To skip all that bogged-down bureaucracy! What in the world was going on? Why, all of a sudden, was Delphi backing off of this investigation? Was Delphi scared of the list of names she'd come up with? It was Delphi personally who'd green-lighted this investigation. Told her to give it all she had and nail whoever was behind this assassination conspiracy!

"Is everything all right?" Diana asked cautiously. Surely, Delphi had a good reason for all this sudden caution.

"Of course," Delphi replied quickly. "But before you proceed, I'd like to talk this over with you. Let's get together and form a plan of action before we go any further."

"Uh, okay," Diana mumbled, shocked to her core at the suggestion that she should meet Delphi in person. "When and where?"

"At the Old Town facility. In, say, a half hour?"

Diana answered quickly, "I'll be there."

She stared at the phone as she hung it up. Son of a gun. She was finally going to meet Delphi and find out who was the mysterious mastermind behind the Oracle Agency.

10:00 P.M.

It was strange to pull up to the Oracle town house in Alexandria and see lights on inside. Always before when she'd come here, the place had been conspicuously empty. She went through the usual routine of opening the automatic security gate and driving around back to park. A black Cadillac was parked behind the house, the kind a dignitary might travel in when they didn't want to be blatantly obvious in a limousine. Delphi must already be here. A tingle of anticipation raced across her skin. She was dying to finally find out who was in charge of Oracle.

She went through the tedious security protocol at the back door and let herself into the house. As always, the homey, old-fashioned kitchen struck her as incongruous in this high-tech hideaway.

She walked down the hallway toward the library and called out, "Hello?"

Nobody answered her. She opened the library door and stepped inside. A desk lamp illuminated the space softly. Wow. Someone had been busy in here today. The computer on the desk was replaced, the Queen Anne chair she'd demolished replaced with a similar chair. A new door even hung in the door frame. Had she not been here herself to witness the violent break-in, she would never have guessed the incident had happened. She backed out of the library. The front door frame showed signs of its repair in the unstained wood trim nailed up around it. But otherwise, it, too, looked completely unharmed.

She headed up the stairs and called out again, "Hello! Anyone home?"

Still no answer. Delphi was probably up in one of those plush offices on the third floor. She walked down the second-floor hallway toward the staircase to the third floor. The large conference room that sat over the library was dark, but the door was open. For some reason, she got the feeling she was being watched. Was somebody in there? Why wouldn't they have answered her if they were?

Sheesh, she was really getting paranoid. But after the day she'd had, she supposed she was entitled to being a little jumpy. Sure enough, a glow came from the top of the third-floor stairs. Delphi must be up there.

She put her foot on the first step, and all hell broke loose around her. Three masked figures burst out of the conference room behind her, while two more came barreling down the stairs. All five attackers leaped on top of her, grabbing her limbs with unbelievable strength.

She fought for all she was worth, but it did no good. All five of these assailants were trained professionals who knew exactly what they were doing. Fingers dug into pressure points in her shoulders and groin, effectively immobilizing her. Excruciating pain shot outward from the four points as her muscles went slack. In a matter of seconds, her hands were tied behind her back, her ankles lashed together, and a dark, cloth bag pulled down over her head.

Trussed up like a pig ready for roasting, she was hauled quickly downstairs and back along the first-floor hallway to the kitchen. A door squeaked open, and she was wrestled downward again. A basement? She'd never noticed before that this place had one. It smelled of dirt and mildew. The way the faint shuffles of movement were echoing, the place had a low ceiling, too. Must be an old root cellar or something.

She was flopped down onto…a bed? That's sure what it felt like. It felt like a mattress over a hard surface of some kind. A cotton sheet rubbed against the back of her hands. She registered faint surprise beneath her fury and terror. What was up with that? It was pretty darned civilized for a kidnapping or worse.

As she got over her initial shock at the attack, her brain began to function more clearly. How did these people get into this building without leaving telltale signs of a break-in? And then a terrible thought struck her. *Had Delphi been taken, too?* What had these people done with her employer? Was he or she trussed up like this somewhere else in the house?

This team had to be linked to S.A.F.E. somehow. Whether or not they were CIA operatives sent out to kidnap her or worse didn't really matter. Her Oracle search of the shadowy bunch from S.A.F.E. had obviously triggered some sort of alarm and provoked this attack on her and Oracle.

Self-preservation began to kick in. Were they going to kill her? Clearly they didn't plan to do it right away or she'd already be standing at the Pearly Gates. Crud. They probably meant to pick her brains first. Not good. She knew way too much about Presidential security and Oracle for that to be anything but very bad news. Quickly, she reviewed her training on resisting interrogations. She wouldn't be able to get away with playing dumb for these guys. Probably would have to go the "I know nothing; I'm just the hired slug following orders" route.

The pistol was plucked out of her shoulder holster, and her pockets searched. But, tied up as she was, her captors couldn't easily get her coat off her, and they left her duster on. Hallelujah. That meant she still had a few options. But not yet. Later. If and when they left her alone.

Out of curiosity to see how her captors would react, and in order to get some sort of dialogue going with them, she opened her mouth and let out the loudest, most piercing shriek she could muster up. In the low, enclosed space, it echoed impressively, paining even her ears.

Someone leaned down beside her and whispered gruffly, "This place is soundproof. Yell all you want."

Diana jolted. If she didn't miss her guess, that was a female voice. So, S.A.F.E. was an equal opportunity employer. Well, ducky for it.

The whispering voice said, "You're going to be detained here overnight. Someone will be here in the morning to talk to you. Until then, I suggest you try to get some rest."

Her hands were untied and retied high over her head. Someone actually put a pillow under her head while they were repositioning her, too. Since when did kidnappers give a hoot for their victim's comfort? Confusion swirled even more deeply around her.

Her feet were untied and retied to opposing corners of whatever they had her lying on. All in all, she wasn't particularly uncomfortable except for the stuffy bag over her head.

"Any chance you could lose the bag over my face?" she asked in a normal speaking voice.

"Sorry, no. Got to protect our identities," the woman whispered. "Wouldn't want to have to kill you."

Diana would swear that was humor infusing her captor's voice. Okay. This was, bar none, the weirdest kidnapping she'd ever heard of. If these people were so confident that they could joke around with her, then they must have Delphi in custody, too. If that was the case, that probably meant she was just a little fish they weren't all that interested in. No wonder they could afford to make her comfortable and joke with her. Damn. Damn, damn, damn.

There were a few more rustles in the direction she'd come from, and then what little light seeped in around the edges of her bag disappeared. Complete darkness closed in around her. And then silence. She held her breath and strained to listen for even the faintest sound of breathing. She wouldn't put it past her captors to park someone in the dark nearby to keep an eye on her.

But as hard as she listened, she couldn't hear any evidence of anyone else down here. Furthermore, she didn't feel anyone's presence. Did she dare make her move now, or should she wait a couple of hours until the coast was definitely clear? Were it just her in trouble, she'd wait. But there was Delphi to think about. Who knew what was happening to her boss? She had to go now.

She wriggled and squirmed, working the decorative belt buckle at the right wrist of her duster around to the side. It took some fancy wiggling of her elbows, but she managed to point the buckle at the cloth strip securing her wrist. How many times she stabbed the sharpened tip of the buckle through the fabric, she had no idea. But eventually, she felt frays begin to tickle her wrist, and the cloth began to weaken. She yanked on it hard a few times. Not quite there. A few more good pokes, and another mighty jerk of her arm, and her hand ripped free. Thank God.

She tore the bag off her head and looked around. It was nearly pitch-black in the cellar, but her eyes were fully adjusted to the dark from inside the bag. The room looked empty. She was lying on an old table with a mattress laid across it. Assorted odds and ends of furniture filled the corners, and cardboard packing boxes were stacked along the far wall.

She rolled on her side and quickly examined the bonds tying down her left wrist. By straining against the ropes around her ankles, she was able to reach the knot that held her left wrist down. It took a few minutes to pick loose the knot by feel, but eventually she got it. She sat up and had her feet free in under a minute. She eased to her feet, relieved to be off that table. Now to go rescue Delphi.

She headed for the stairs. She'd heard one of the steps creak as her captors left earlier, so she took her time, easing her weight slowly onto each step. There. The squeaker. She backed off it fast, and waited several seconds, holding her breath for some reaction to the first, faint squeak of noise it had made.

Nothing.

Stepping over the squeaky step, she glided up the stairs to the basement door. Crouching on her hands and knees, she peered out from under the crack at its bottom. A single pair of black leather boots sat at the kitchen table. Facing the door, dammit. But at least they were narrow and small boots. The woman, then.

She wasn't going to be able to surprise this lookout. And if they got into a noisy fight, the others would come running. She could probably burst out of here and get out the back door before the other attackers got here. But then, she'd have to leave Delphi behind. And that went against every fiber of her being.

She turned over other possible options. None of them were good.

A chair scraped. Diana lurched back from the door and plastered herself against the wall. Heels tapped quietly on the floor as the woman walked quickly out of the kitchen.

This was her chance! After a quick peek under the door to verify that the room was empty, Diana tested the doorknob. Unlocked. Pretty confident, her captors were. She opened the door quickly and spun out into the kitchen low and fast. She was alone. She moved to the drawer where she'd fetched a knife this morning and did the same again, arming herself with a couple butcher knives and a paring knife stuck in her boot.

She raced down the dimly lit hallway, stopping before the library door. Closed. She eased past it, running up the stairs as lightly as she could. Her heart pounded a mile a minute, and her breath came fast and shallow. The second floor was still dark, and the third floor still glowed with light.

She glided up the third-floor stairs, her knife held out before her.

Murmurs of sound came out of the front office. Its door was cracked open about one quarter of the way. She glided forward along the wall. The voices were too quiet to make out the words, but it surely didn't sound like a forced interrogation.

The desk and its high-backed leather chair, situated facing the window, were occupied. She caught a glimpse of silver hair over the back of the chair. Delphi, maybe? A couple chairs in front of the desk, between it and the window were also occupied. Black-clothed figures lounged in the chairs. *Her captors.* Minus their masks.

She gaped in disbelief. She recognized every one of the women she saw. They were all old classmates of hers from the Athena Academy. They were part of S.A.F.E.? How was that possible?

And then the truth hit her, a sledgehammer blow right between the eyes. S.A.F.E. hadn't kidnapped her at all. *Oracle had.*

Delphi had set up the meeting with her to deliver her to this team of her fellow Oracle agents. A single question screamed across her brain. *Why?* What had happened? Why had Delphi turned on her? Unless…

Of course. Her signature next to the altered Oracle programming code. Delphi thought *she* was part of the plot to kill Gabe. But who'd pointed it out to Delphi? Surely someone had. With everything else that had gone on today, there was no way Delphi had been randomly sitting around browsing through Oracle's programming code. Who could turn Delphi on one of his or her own agents?

It had to be someone Delphi trusted implicitly. Someone in a very high position of power. Someone who knew Diana very well. Well enough for Delphi to believe out of hand. Like her grandfather.

Oh. My. God.

One of the agents shifted in her seat inside the office, and Diana lurched back to awareness of her surroundings. She had to get out of here.

She headed back toward the stairs, but heard footsteps below her. Headed this way. Crud. She turned and raced on silent feet toward the back of the house. She slipped into the small room there and closed the door noiselessly. She waited behind the door as the footsteps climbed the stairs and headed away from her. Toward the meeting in the front office.

She was poised by the door, just about to sneak out of the room, when another set of footsteps froze her in place. They headed downstairs. She strained to hear them, and thought she heard them descend the first-floor stairs, as well. So much for that escape route.

She locked the door—a pitiful defense against the highly-trained team of operatives outside, but it would slow them down a little. Buy her a few seconds, maybe. She took stock of the room she was in. A bedroom. Furnished not like a room someone lived in, but rather a resting spot for someone who'd worked too long or too late. But the bed had sheets and blankets, and that's all she cared about.

She tore the bedding off the bed and used a knife to saw through the bedspread as quietly as she could. It took several minutes, but eventually she had enough thick lengths of bedspread and wool blanket to reach nearly to the ground. At least she hoped it would reach. She tied the strips of cloth together and measured them one last time. Her improvised rope should get her within ten feet or so of the ground. No problem.

She tied the end of her blanket rope to the foot of the bed nearest the window. The bed wasn't heavy enough to hold her weight and would slide over toward the window, but the double-bed's frame shouldn't come out the window after her. At least that was the plan.

She checked the window for an alarm and found the inconspicuous metal disk at the side of the frame. She didn't have the tools to disarm it readily. No help for it. She'd just have to go fast.

She gathered up her blanket rope in her arms and flung up the window sash. As she'd expected, a loud, high-pitched alarm whooped through the house. She tossed the blanket out the window and climbed out after it before the thing had even finished unfurling. She grabbed onto it and began to shimmy downward fast, hand over hand.

It gave an ominous lurch as the bedframe gave way and slid over toward the window with a loud scraping noise of wood on wood. Shouts erupted from inside the house, audible through the open window.

She slid down the blanket to the next knot, burning her hands on the scratchy wool. She shifted grips to the next strip of cloth and slid down that, as well, ignoring the raw pain in her palms.

One more knot to go.

She slid down the last length of cloth, checking her descent only enough to break her fall. And then she let go. She executed a parachute-landing fall as she slammed into the asphalt, carrying her momentum through the rolling impact and popping back up on her feet all in one movement. She leaped into her car and hit the gate opener clipped to her sun visor. The back door opened and the women raced outside. Time to go.

She hit the accelerator. The gate started to open as she backed her car around in a tire-squealing J-turn and pointed it toward the driveway. She watched in horror as the gate, not quite fully open, reversed direction and began to close again.

She stood on the gas pedal of the German sports car. It shot forward as the gap in front of her narrowed. She bolted through it, wincing as metal scraped horribly against her right rear door. But thankfully, her car made it through the gate.

She bounced out into the street and slammed the steering wheel into a hard right turn. Her back end skidded out and she bumped a car parked across the street with her left rear fender, but her tough little car righted itself and straightened out, accelerating like a bat out of hell. She tore away from the Oracle house, slowing down only when she turned corners, so as not to leave telltale tire marks.

She watched her rearview mirror in a panic. No sign of a follower. That Caddy couldn't begin to keep up with her coupe, assuming it had even gotten out of the driveway anytime soon after her. The way that gate had been closing, they'd have lost precious seconds waiting for it to open again.

She made it out to a major highway and slowed down to a reasonable rate of speed. No sense getting pulled over by a policeman right now.

And then the delayed reaction to being kidnapped and escaping hit her like a ton of bricks. Adrenaline still screamed through her body, ordering her to defend herself from the life-or-death peril she'd just experienced. Her hands started to shake, and then her large muscles. Her legs trembled until she could hardly keep her foot on the accelerator, her knees were knocking together so uncontrollably. God, she felt cold. She shivered all over. Probably another side effect of the scare she'd just had. She drove blindly for several minutes, trying to breathe normally and bring her pulse down below, oh, two hundred beats a minute or so.

And as the adrenaline slowly drained away, making rational thought possible, the anger finally set in. How could Delphi have turned on her? Her own employer! A person who'd handpicked her to serve her country in a very special way!

She started the stopwatch in the dashboard of the car and punched Delphi's number into her cell phone. Furious, she slammed the instrument to her ear.

The line picked up and Diana didn't wait for anyone to speak. She snapped, "Very cute. Care to explain why you tried to kidnap one of your own agents tonight?"

At least Delphi had the good grace not to deny it. "You've become a possible threat."

"To whom?" Diana exclaimed. "I'm out here busting my butt to save Gabe Monihan's life, like you ordered me to I might add."

Delphi replied patiently, "You tampered with the Oracle database. We checked the logs, and the changes came from your home computer."

"The hacker who broke into my house last night inserted that code! I'd never turn on you or Oracle, I swear."

Silence met her impassioned declaration.

Diana said slowly, "Tell me something. Did someone call you, too? Put a bug in your ear that I'd lost it? Who called you?"

The silence that greeted her question was eloquent. Someone *had* called Delphi. Dammit. "Was it my grandfather?" Diana demanded.

Time was up. Thirty seconds. All she could afford to talk to Delphi without her phone being traced. She couldn't stay on the line any longer waiting for Delphi's response. And maybe she didn't need to hear it anyway.

She disconnected the line and tossed the cell phone on the seat beside her.

Time to go have a little conversation with good old Gramps.

11:00 P.M.

Her grandfather had sold his Chevy Chase estate a couple years back and usually stayed in some posh hotel when he came to town these days. But, as had been his habit for all the years he worked in the CIA, he kept to no set routine and changed hotels every time he came to town. She had no idea where he was staying this time.

She dialed Josie's cell phone number. "Hey, Jo. It's me."

Her sister sounded inordinately grumpy. Must have interrupted a romantic interlude with Diego. "Diana. It's after eleven. What do you want?"

"Where's Gramps staying?"

"The Shoreham in Rock Creek Park. Why?"

"He and I need to have a little talk tonight."

"Now?" Josie asked in surprise. Abruptly, Sis sounded at full alert.

"Don't ask," Diana said sharply.

"I'm asking," Josie retorted. "What's up?"

"I think he turned me in. Called my boss and said I've lost it and gone over the edge."

"Have you?" Josie asked seriously.

All the frustration built up over years and years of wrong and negative assumptions about her flared up and finally bubbled over. "Why is it everyone in this family thinks I'm such a screwup? How long am I going to have to be Superwoman before you people get off my back and accept the fact that I've grown up into a responsible adult?"

A long silence met that outburst. Long enough to startle Diana. Was her sister actually seriously considering the question? By rights, they ought to be in the middle of a screaming match right about now. Maybe both of them had done some growing up recently.

Finally, Josie said slowly, "Maybe you're right. Maybe I still do think of you as my baby sister who's in need of protection."

"Protection? Me?" Surprise coursed through Diana.

"You were so little when Mom went away. And you never knew her. You didn't remember how much she loved us. I had the memory of that to sustain me, but you didn't. I felt so sorry for you. I tried to make it up to you. To love you the way she would have. But you always pushed me away. You wouldn't let me."

Remorse slugged Diana, a heavy fist straight to the gut. Is that what Josie had been trying to do all along? She'd always thought Josie was trying to smother her. To keep her little sister from shining as brightly as she did. She'd thought it was sibling rivalry, for goodness' sake! Could she have been wrong for all those long years of simmering ill will? She stammered, "I didn't know. I thought you resented me. Were trying to boss me around."

"Good Lord, no! I was trying to be a substitute mother to

you. But I was too young. I didn't know how to do it. You were so hurt. So shut down. You closed me out. You closed everyone out."

The words were daggers to her heart. She *had* closed everyone out. In her pain and loss and misunderstanding, she'd pushed away the one person who'd reached out to her in shared pain and loss. And it must have been so much more difficult for Josie. She'd really known their mother. Remembered her. Suffered an even greater loss. But, in spite of that, she'd still reached out to Diana.

In return, she'd mistaken generosity for dominance, love for resentment. And she'd rejected Josie. Rejected everyone. Revelation broke over her in a cold wave. She was still rejecting everyone. Even a great guy like Gabe who'd opened himself up to her. Reached out to her. *Trusted her with his life.*

She mumbled, "I didn't know. God, I'm so sorry…." Unable to speak anymore, she disconnected the line. What a mess she'd made of everything. And she'd never realized it. What a selfish brat she'd been. She'd been so busy feeling sorry for herself, she'd never looked beyond her own suffering to see the pain she'd caused the people around her.

Was she doing the same thing now? Was she so caught up in herself she wasn't seeing the bigger picture? Did it really matter if she tracked down this S.A.F.E. organization—if it even existed at all? Was she Don Quixote, tilting at windmills in her own elusive chase after glory?

Maybe she should just give it up. Stop pretending she was capable of saving Gabe single-handedly. That's what the entire Secret Service was for. They could handle the job.

Her phone rang, startling her out of her funk. She picked it up. "Hello?"

"Hey. It's me."

Gabe. What in the world was he doing calling her now? "Are you all right?" she asked in quick concern.

"I'm fine. I was worried about you. You seemed pretty upset after Owen raked you over the coals. I'm sorry about that."

"He was just doing his job. I can't blame the guy."

"Still, he was pretty rough on you. You put your neck on the line for me today and I really appreciate it."

Was that all he felt for her? Gratitude for her work? Had she blown it with him, too, and somehow shut him out as she did everyone else? Soberly she replied, "I was just doing my job. No different than Owen."

Gabe chuckled. "I don't know about that. I'd say you're quite a bit different than Owen."

His remark startled her into a laugh. She retorted, "Well, I should hope so."

Gabe replied quietly, "That's much better. I needed to hear you laugh."

He'd needed it? Needed something from her? Aloud she said, "Well, then, did you hear the one about the boy who got the bicycle after he had sex for the first time?"

Gabe laughed again. "I don't need a laugh *that* bad."

They lapsed into silence for a moment.

She said hesitantly, "Thanks for believing in me today. Not many people would have. They'd have figured I was some sort of nutcase."

"I suppose you are a nutcase."

"What?" she blurted out.

"You like me, don't you? I figure you have to be a little bit crazy to do that."

"Gabe Monihan, you're one of the most eligible bachelors in the entire world. Women are swooning over you by the thousands in case you hadn't noticed."

He snorted. "They're swooning over my job description.

You're the first woman I've met since I ran for President who looked at me and really saw me."

She stammered, flustered at the compliment.

He said earnestly, "Just promise me you won't change after I become President."

"You're not sworn in, yet?" she exclaimed.

"Nope. Owen's really wired tight. He's worried that someone way up in the government may be a crazy bent on taking me out. He's got me locked down. Again."

She said seriously, "I have to agree with Owen on this one."

Gabe absorbed that in silence. Did he think she was crazy after all? She took a deep breath. She had to stop looking for reasons to push people away. She'd be engaging in long bouts of silence, too, if someone told her a close associate of hers was out to kill her.

She said lightly, "Well, look at it this way. A day's delay in taking office will make for an interesting footnote in the history books about you."

"Gee, thanks," he said dryly. "There's nothing like being reminded that my every word and move for the next four years is going to be recorded and commented on for generations to come."

She couldn't help but chuckle. "Hey, you're the numbskull who volunteered for the job." Lest he take offense she added quickly, "You're going to be a great president."

"Why's that?"

She answered sincerely, "Because you care. Because you want to make the world a better place. Because you're decent and honorable and will do the right thing."

A long pause. Then he said quietly, "I think that's about the nicest thing anyone's ever said about me."

"So, are we taking turns embarrassing each other tonight, or what?" She laughed softly. "I think it's your turn, now."

"Tell you what. I'll take a rain check on that. I have confidence that in the next few months, I'll have ample opportunities to embarrass you."

Months? As in he wanted to see her again? For months? Whoa. "Okay," she managed to choke out.

"So what are you up to right now?" he asked her.

"Well, I thought I'd try to track down some of those high-ranking crazies who might be out to kill you. I'm on my way to see my grandfather."

"Joseph Lockworth, right?"

"How did you know he's my grandfather?"

"Owen ran a background check on you after breakfast this morning. He mentioned it to me."

"Oh." She cringed. He'd heard all the gory details of her checkered past, eh? So much for him ever respecting her.

Gabe added, "I didn't ask to hear the details. I'd rather learn about you myself. From you directly."

If only she were half that noble. She cleared her throat. "In the interest of being honest, I should tell you that I've done quite a bit of research into your life over the course of trying to figure out why the Q-group was so determined to kill you."

"Did you find anything in my past that bothers you?" he asked cautiously.

"Well," she drawled, "there was that whole French 101 debacle in college. You really are hopeless at foreign languages."

He laughed. "I plead guilty as charged."

"In the interest of honesty, I should also tell you that my past won't stand up to scrutiny nearly as well as yours does. I was…a bit of a rebel in my youth."

"Well, whatever went into making you the person you are today is fine with me."

"Okay. You've embarrassed me, now. I guess that makes it my turn again."

He laughed. "I can't wait. Unfortunately, I've got to go now. We're going to have yet another planning meeting to set up an inauguration for me. I think we're going to bag trying to do it publicly and just do it at the White House. One of the official photographers can film it and then we'll release the film to the public tomorrow.

"Sounds like a plan," she replied earnestly. "At this point, I don't think the nation cares about a fancy ceremony. They just want to get you safely installed in office."

"Agreed. My cabinet and a few key advisors are going to assemble in a couple of hours to witness the oath."

A chill of foreboding trickled down her spine. Why was she still so bloody sure that he was in mortal danger? It was a certainty lodged deep down in her gut, and no matter what she did, she couldn't shake it. "Well, I'd better let you go to your meeting. I wouldn't want to keep the nation waiting."

"Take care, Diana."

"You, too, Gabe. Be careful."

She set down the phone gently. She had no choice. She had to see this thing through. For him. And for herself if she was ever going to have a chance at love. She had to push through the fear, the vulnerability he provoked in her. Resolutely, she picked up her phone and asked a mobile operator to connect her to the Shoreham.

"Joseph Lockworth's room, please," she told the hotel operator.

"One moment please."

The phone rang a couple times, and then her grandfather's deep voice answered. "Lockworth, here."

He answered that as if he expected this to be a work call. But he was retired. Of course, if he was involved with S.A.F.E. he might answer that way if he expected the call to be one of his partners in crime.

"Grandfather. It's Diana. We need to talk. Now."

"Do we, indeed?" he answered. "About what?"

Gramps was definitely in full CIA Director mode. She answered coolly, "About a man named Richard Dunst. He used to work for you. And about the Q-group. Do they work for you, too? For S.A.F.E?"

"Well, now. We do need to talk, don't we? I'm a little tied up at the moment. I'll call you in a few minutes and we'll meet. We have a lot to talk over."

A lump of lead formed in her stomach. He didn't deny it. She'd been right. He was involved in S.A.F.E. Was he the one who decided Gabe Monihan shouldn't be President? That S.A.F.E. somehow had the right to pick and choose the nation's leader? Had he sent that hacker to her house to frame her? Then fingered her to Delphi, too. *Why?* Who was this S.A.F.E. group that they could turn a man against his own flesh and blood? Especially her grandfather, to whom family loyalty was so important? Did they have something on him? Some hook to blackmail him with?

He'd delayed setting up a rendezvous with her. He needed time before he met her, eh? Why? Who was he frantically calling right now? What was he doing before they met? Arranging another kidnapping, maybe? Her murder this time?

She glanced up at a road sign overhead listing upcoming exits. Langley, Virginia. Home of the Central Intelligence Agency. Was it also the headquarters of S.A.F.E.? Her jaw tightened. There was one sure way to find out.

She steered her car onto the exit ramp and followed the unobtrusive signs pointing the way to CIA headquarters. She pulled up at the front guard shack. "I'm Diana Lockworth. I'm here to meet with my grandfather, Joseph Lockworth. He told me to meet him at the front reception desk." She flashed her military ID and DIA identification for the guy.

He put a parking pass inside her car on the dashboard and waved her through.

One hurdle down.

She pulled into the parking lot, which was surprisingly crowded for this time of night. But then, after the day's double terrorist attacks, the CIA probably had every analyst on staff at work tonight trying to track down leads on the men who'd done it and who was behind them. Was there someone inside right now, equally furiously covering those very tracks?

She parked her car and walked toward the white, modern structure, vividly aware of the cameras and guards watching her progress toward the building. She stepped into the brightly lit glass foyer, with its modern art and the eloquent wall of anonymous stars, one for each agent who'd fallen in service of his or her country. Of course, she didn't even make it to the CIA seal on the floor before she was directed in no uncertain terms to a visitor's reception area. Crud. She had to get into the building somehow. Fortunately, her job gave her occasional exposure to people who worked over here in the Spook House. She needed the name of someone who worked here, and who might conceivably be here, working late tonight.

A couple names of people she'd dealt with in the last few months popped into her head. Except she hesitated to call on anyone she'd worked with on her Q-group investigation. She wouldn't put it past her grandfather or whoever was sabotaging her research to have gotten in contact with all of her recent colleagues.

Samantha St. John.

The petite, Slavic beauty was one of Josie's best friends from Athena Academy. Sam worked for the CIA as a linguist—and undoubtedly more, although they'd never spoken about that aspect of her work. Of course, Sam traveled a ton and might not be here, but it was worth a try.

Diana stepped up to the receptionist, if the cold-eyed man sitting behind the counter could be called that. "I'm here to see Samantha St. John. Could you ring her office for me?"

"Is she expecting you?" the man asked coolly.

"No, she's not. But it's a matter of some urgency."

The guy gave her a condescending look that said everything that passed through this building was a matter of some urgency. Nonetheless, he typed briefly in his computer and then dialed an extension on his phone. He spoke into his wireless headset, a quiet murmur Diana couldn't hear. Which was impressive since she was standing only a foot away from the guy.

He looked up at her. "She'll be right down."

Hallelujah. Now maybe she'd get to the bottom of what and who S.A.F.E. was and stop it once and for all.

12:00 A.M.

Diana spied Sam's arrival before she could actually see her by the way people's heads were turning at her passage. Sam was one of those women who was so strikingly beautiful that people couldn't help but stare at her.

"Diana! What a surprise! What brings you here at this hour of the night?"

She smiled warmly at Sam. Ever since she'd gotten together with Riley McLane, Sam had been a different woman. Warmer. More open. It was good to see. Made a girl kind of wish she could find a guy like that for herself. Diana sighed. She *had* found a guy like that. There was just the small problem of him becoming President of the United States at any second.

Diana replied, "How about we go up to your office? This is actually a business visit. I have something…sensitive…to discuss with you."

Sam arched one eyebrow questioningly but made no comment as she signed Diana in and got her a visitor's badge. "This way," she said.

Diana followed her classmate across the giant CIA seal inlaid in the floor and down a long glass-enclosed hallway beside a courtyard. They went upstairs, past a series of unmarked doors, and through another anonymous door into a cluster of glass cubicles. Sam wound her way through the maze of people and desks to a tiny office in the back, thankfully with solid walls. She picked up a stack of files off the second chair in her office and offered it to Diana.

Diana closed the door behind her and sat down.

"What's up?" Sam asked.

Diana frowned. Now wasn't that a good question? Aloud she answered, "I don't know how much to tell you. If I say too much, I could put your life in danger. But, I need your help, so I owe you some sort of explanation."

Sam grinned. "Sounds interesting. And I can handle a little danger."

Diana grimaced. "This could be a lot of danger. I've already had my house broken into today, been arrested, been kidnapped and nearly shot twice."

Sam's eyebrows zinged up and her demeanor abruptly became serious. Focused. Intense, even. Sometimes Diana forgot just how smart Sam was behind all that exotic beauty. Diana continued. "Here's the thing. I need to break into an office in this building and search it for some information. ASAP. That's what I need your help with."

Sam didn't bat an eyelash. It confirmed Diana's suspicion that she was a covert field operative for the CIA in addition to her overt duties as a linguist. No simple desk jockey reacted that calmly to a suggestion that she assist in a breaking-and-entering job.

"Whose office?" Sam asked.

"A guy named Collin Scott. Have you heard of him?"

Sam laughed. "It's kind of hard not to have heard of him around here. He's the number two guy in the Plans Section. Why on earth do you want to break into his office?"

"I have reason to believe he's involved with a secret group called S.A.F.E."

Sam chuckled. "I'm sure he's involved with a number of secret groups. That's his job."

"How many of them are trying to kill Gabe Monihan?"

That sobered up Samantha in a hurry. "You think Collin Scott's trying to kill the next President of the United States?"

Diana closed her eyes for a moment. Spoken aloud, it sounded absurd to her, too. "I don't have time to go into the entire investigation I've done. But I think Scott is involved in a clandestine conspiracy of a few high-ranking government officials and civilians who want to kill Gabe."

"That's preposterous," Sam retorted.

"So go with me to his office and see if we can find any information on this S.A.F.E. bunch."

Sam asked thoughtfully, "What does it stand for?"

"Society for the Advancement of Free Economies."

Sam stood up. "Honey, I'd love to help you, but I just can't. Not on this one."

Diana nodded in disappointed understanding. As she recalled from their martial arts training at the Athena Academy, Sam was as fast as greased lightning in a hand-to-hand fight. "I didn't think you could help me, but it was worth a shot." She stood up facing her old friend. "Just keep an ear to the ground, eh? If you hear anything about this S.A.F.E. group, could you give me a call? And be careful. They're dangerous."

She leaned forward to hug Sam. And chopped her across the back of the head beneath the back of her skull. Hard.

Enough to knock her out. She caught Sam as she sagged, un-conscious, and lowered her to the floor. God, she hated hav-ing to do that.

She taped Sam's hands and feet behind her back using a roll of wide masking tape she found in Sam's desk drawer. She put a couple strips of tape across her mouth, too. She taped Sam's trussed hands and feet behind her to the legs of her desk, as well. That should keep her immobile for a few min-utes. Working fast before Sam woke up, Diana tore off a strip of clear, cellophane tape from another roll of tape in Sam's desk and pressed it hard against the pad of Sam's thumb. She tore the tape off quickly and held it carefully, sticky side out. She grabbed Sam's ID badge and fished in Sam's pocket for the access card she'd used to get into this office area. Got it.

Last, she opened up the employee directory she found in Sam's desk and thumbed through it until she found the name, Collin Scott. She noted his office number and located it on the map inside the back cover of the book.

She clipped Sam's ID badge to her collar, picked up a stack of files off Sam's desk and headed out. Here went noth-ing. A breaking-and-entering job inside one of the most se-cure buildings on the planet. If there was any doubt about her having completely lost her mind, this sealed the deal.

She walked back through the cubicles briskly, not looking at the people working at desks inside them. Out the door and into the hall. She oriented herself quickly and headed left. Up one more floor and down another long hall. Then, around one more corner. Bingo. There was the office she was looking for. She tested the door. Locked.

She pulled out Sam's access card and swiped it through the magnetic lock pad. She started violently as a two-inch square pad lit up on the face of the lock and a voice intoned, "Right thumbprint, please."

Diana pressed the piece of tape against the pad.

A green light flashed and the door lock clicked.

Holy cow. It had been a total long shot to try Sam's access code here, but Diana wasn't about to look a gift horse in the mouth. She stepped inside, closing the hallway door behind her. A secretary's desk dominated the center of the room. A single door stood behind it. Colin Scott's private office. With another elaborate electronic lock beside the door. No wonder it had been so easy to get into this outer office.

She took a look at the number pad beside this door. Similar to the one outside, except when she swiped Sam's card this time, nobody asked for her fingerprint and the lock didn't open. She pulled out her pocketknife and, using the screwdriver attachment, unscrewed the stainless steel cover over the guts of the electronic lock. Who'd have thought that her electrical circuitry class at the Athena Academy would ever come in so handy? She traced the circuit quickly and identified the wires that had to be crossed to open the system. Once she did that, though, she had no doubt it would trigger an alarm somewhere else in the building. She gave it two, maybe three minutes until someone would bust in here, guns blazing.

She organized herself quickly for the break-in. Her target would be any paper records Collin Scott had in his office. They were what she'd use if she were running a conspiracy to kill the President. Electronic files were just too easy to break into. He'd probably have a filing cabinet of some kind. And it would be locked. Agency policy was that all desks were cleaned off and all papers put under lock and key every night. The infamous policy had actually cost employees here their jobs.

She'd need a sharp, tough metal object of some kind to bust into the filing cabinet. She would never have enough time to pick the lock before security got here. She looked around the outer office. Perfect. A gold-plated shovel from some ground-breaking ceremony or other. It laid in a glass cabinet in the far corner. She snatched it out of its case and hurried back to the lock. Her other time constraint was Sam waking up and calling security. And that could happen any second.

Ready or not, here she went. She set her watch alarm for two minutes. And went to work. It only took a couple seconds to slice through the pair of wires, strip their ends and twist them together. A touch with the tip of her knife to the right switch, a spark, and the door lock clicked open. And the clock was ticking.

She leaped into the office, looking around for a filing cabinet. Bingo. In the corner behind the desk. She raced over to the two-drawer console. Top or bottom drawer?

Definitely a top-drawer kind of operation.

She smashed the shovel into the side of the cabinet. It dented and made a hell of a lot of noise, but didn't give. Again. Paint chipped away and the dent got bigger. It took another half-dozen blows before the metal finally weakened and gave way. A tiny slit appeared in the cabinet. She slammed the shovel into it and pried the hole larger. One more big heave, and a piece of metal the width of the shovel peeled back to reveal the sides of several files stuffed with paper. Most of them were red. Probably indicated they were classified. She took the extra several seconds to widen the hole to the entire height of the drawer.

Then, frantically, she knelt by the cabinet and started pulling out files as fast as she could. She read the tabs at the top and tossed them aside by the fistfuls. Come on, come on. It had to be in here, somewhere. Please God, let the file not be in the bottom drawer.

The pile of papers lying all over the floor behind her grew, and the seconds ticked by. A quick glance at her watch. Thirty seconds to go. Oww! Slashing pain ripped through her left hand. She'd cut her hand at the base of her little finger on the ragged edge of the hole. No time to do anything about it. She continued yanking files out and tossing them aside.

Twenty seconds to go.

And then, without warning, there it was. A thick, red file marked Classified. The Initials S.A.F.E. were typed on the white label glued to the top tab. No time to look at it. She had to get out of here. She stuffed the file inside her coat and froze. A beeping sound came from the outer office. Someone was using the keypad to enter it from the hallway beyond.

She leaped to the inner door to the office, scooping up a clock from Scott's desk on her way past. It was embedded in a grapefruit-size marble sphere. She stuck her arm out the door and slammed the marble piece down on the door lock to the inner office. Sparks flew and sizzled as she slammed the door shut. Good Lord willing, this door failed to a locked position. She tested the knob and it wouldn't turn. Now she could only hope the security man outside had no quick way to override the fried lock. And then, of course, she had to figure out how in the hell to get out of a third-floor office of a supersecure facility like CIA headquarters.

Fists pounded on the door. She ignored them. Then a male voice shouted through the door. She ignored that, too. She turned on the overhead lights to better see any possible escape route, since it was no longer a secret that she was in here. No man-size ventilation shafts opened up onto this room. Just a couple small registers. The window didn't open. She tested it with her hands. Not glass. It was no doubt made of tough, bulletproof polymers. She might conceivably be able to break it out of the frame, but the fall to the concrete below—or rather, the landing on it—ruled that out as an option. Bookcases lined both of the other walls of the office.

She was so hosed.

She was not going to get out of this one alive. But that didn't mean she couldn't get done what she'd come here to do before she went down in flames. She sat down at Collin Scott's desk and pulled the S.A.F.E. file out of her coat. Working hard to ignore the heavy pounding on the door, she read as quickly as her eyes would travel across the pages.

In the very front was a CIA analysis of a legal treatise written by one Thomas Wolfe a decade ago, predicting the rise of global terrorism and criticizing the open society America maintained. He argued with great mental agility that the only way to defeat terror was with terror. He claimed that as long as law-abiding societies were constrained by law in their fight against terrorists, they were doomed to failure. The CIA analysis found the arguments sound.

Diana frowned. A lot had changed in the last decade. The rise of huge, powerful terror networks worldwide, 9/11 and the American overthrow of entire governments in response to terror. Huge armies of American soldiers had been thrown into the fight, along with billions upon billions of dollars of resources. Was Wolfe's premise still valid? If she lived more than the next couple of minutes, she'd have to spend some time thinking about that one. She thumbed on to the next document.

Transcripts of a conversation Collin Scott had at a Defense consortium with a couple of the men on her list of S.A.F.E. suspects from Oracle. They expressed concern at the direction the United States was going with terror policy or its lack thereof.

She read on, tracing the evolution of S.A.F.E. from a loose bunch of like-minded people to a cautiously organized interest group to a conspiracy committed to action.

The pounding at the door became even louder. Heavier. As if they were using a battering ram of some kind. The entire wall began to shake, and a picture of Collin Scott shaking hands with a giant yellow duck wearing a polyester leisure suit fell to the floor with a crash. DiscoDuck. Collin Scott had to be DiscoDuck.

She skipped most of the rest of the file and moved close to the bottom of the stack of notes and documents. She stared in dismay at a note in the margins of a meeting transcript. "If Monihan and Wolfe win the election, Monihan must be removed from his position so that Wolfe may assume leadership of the nation."

She stared in horror. There it was. Her proof. This group was behind the assassination attempts on Gabe.

She thumbed through the pages again, noting names wherever she spotted them. Janelle Parsons. Al Smith. And then another name started popping up. At least she thought it was a name. Freedom One. Whoever this Freedom One person was, he or she was clearly the engine that drove formalizing S.A.F.E. from a loose association of individuals into a full-blown conspiracy.

But who was Freedom One?

She thumbed through page after page, but nowhere was an actual name ever attached to that mysterious entity. She read further. Whoever he or she was, Freedom One was definitely the leader of this motley crew of sickos. Orders came down to the rest of the group from Freedom One. The purse strings were controlled by Freedom One, and operations like the two Q-group attacks were largely planned by Freedom One.

She turned one of the sheets of paper over and began to write down on it every name she came across in the file. With a few exceptions it almost perfectly matched the list Oracle had given her. She ran across more names. Two in particular caught her attention. Richard Dunst and Tito Albadian. Bingo.

Proof that her hypothesis had been correct. Both men were flunkies of S.A.F.E. and operating on that group's orders.

And then a name she'd dreaded seeing started to pop up in documents dated just a few months ago. Joseph Lockworth.

She closed her eyes against the pain of a betrayal so deep, so close to her heart. She looked through the documents regarding him, but found no reference to any blackmail or coercion of her grandfather. Apparently, he'd approached someone in the group and expressed identical views to S.A.F.E.'s. Freedom One had dispatched several group members to approach him separately and see if he was S.A.F.E. material. It appeared Gramps had passed muster, because his name was included in all the most recent correspondence.

She jumped as her cell phone rang. She looked at the number on its face. Unknown Caller. She put it to her ear. "Hello?"

"Hey there, Diana. It's Sam."

Wow. She had sure gotten loose fast. But then, Diana expected no less of an Athena Academy girl. "Hi, Sam. Are you okay? I'm so sorry about bonking you like that."

"No problem. I walked into the blow on purpose." Sam had let her knock her out on purpose? Aloud she gasped in shock. *"Why?"*

"You're an Athena girl. We stick together. You had to have some absolutely dire need to get into Collin Scott's office or you wouldn't have come here at all. I thought I'd give you a chance to find what you were so sure you would. But, while we're on the subject, would you care to tell me what it was you were looking for so desperately?"

"Have they assigned you to be the hostage negotiator here?" Diana asked dryly.

Sam answered equally dryly. "Something like that. I'm supposed to distract you while they figure out a way to get through that door." Diana heard a squawk of voices in the background at that one. Apparently, the real hostage negotiators hadn't wanted her to share that tidbit of information. Not that it took a rocket scientist to figure it out.

Sam commented, "You really did a number on the lock."

"Thanks. It's all that wholesome Athena Academy training, you know."

Sam laughed. "So. Can you tell me why you did something this crazy?"

Diana sighed. No harm in being honest, now. And, she could stand to do a little stalling of her own. She glanced around the room and found exactly what she was looking for. A fax machine.

She tucked her cell phone between her shoulder and ear while she dialed up Oracle's fax number. She started feeding documents from the S.A.F.E. file into the machine while she spoke to Sam.

"I found the file on S.A.F.E. It's all here in front of me. These guys are certifiable. They follow the writings of Thomas Wolfe from some years back when he argued that the only way to defeat terror is with terror. He proposed that the U.S. can't win that war unless we resort to lawless violence ourselves. I've identified about a dozen guys in S.A.F.E. at a first glance through these documents. Wanna hear their names? It's a Who's Who of high rollers and big dogs. I figure I need to tell someone before the yahoos with you bust in here and kill me."

"Sure," Sam said cautiously.

Diana kept feeding papers into the fax machine, but rattled off her list of names at the same time. She finished her recitation and Sam was silent for long seconds. Finally her classmate breathed, "Are you serious?"

"As a heart attack," Diana replied. "Do you think I'd be dumb enough to pull a suicide move like this if I weren't certain of what I was going to find and that it was worth dying or going to jail over?"

She had about ten more pages to send to Oracle and Delphi. She needed to stall the crew outside just a few more seconds. Quickly, she asked Sam, "So, how many security thugs does a break-in to Collin Scott's office rate?"

"A couple of dozen," Sam answered.

Diana commented, "If I were the suspicious type, I might make note of who all responded to the break-in that weren't strictly required to do so. Could be a second, lower layer of S.A.F.E. types. With four CIA agents known to be in the group, it would make sense that there are more where they came from in this spy palace."

"A most interesting observation," Sam said thoughtfully. "Duly noted."

Five more pages to go. "Sam. Do me a favor. If I don't make it out of this alive, tell Gabe Monihan thank you for me. For everything."

"As in almost President Gabe Monihan?" Sam choked.

"Yup. Long story." She fed the last sheet of paper into the fax machine. Thank God.

Sam murmured under her breath, as if she didn't want the agents around her to hear what she said, "Diana, your grandfather is in the building. Said he wants to talk to you. But if he's one of them…"

Diana whirled, dropping her cell phone as a panel of one of the bookcases slid open behind her. A concealed door!

A man's silhouette loomed in the space.

And before she could dive for cover behind the desk, Joseph Lockworth stepped fully into the room.

1:00 A.M.

The file of S.A.F.E. documents crashed to the floor and Diana dropped into a defensive crouch. What a hell of an irony it would be if her own grandfather killed her.

He held his hands out carefully away from his sides. His *empty* hands.

She straightened cautiously but continued to stay light on the balls of her feet and at the ready. He might be silver haired and eighty years old, but she held no illusions about Gramps being an easy takedown. He'd been one of the toughest covert field agents in the entire OSS and its later iteration, the CIA.

Her grandfather said easily, "Hi, kiddo. How about we have that talk, now?"

She stared in surprise. "Now?"

"I think this is as good a time as any, don't you?"

She laughed without humor. "I don't have much else to do, I suppose, except go out there and die."

He waved a casual hand at the door. "Don't worry about that bunch. I can handle them."

Her eyes narrowed. "And what's your price for that little trick going to be?"

She started as her grandfather laughed heartily. "You're good for an old man's heart. A real chip off the old block, you are. Just like your mother."

"My mother?"

He nodded. "You two are both stubborn and wild and opinionated, and maddeningly lovable."

She had a hard time imagining her haunted, silent mother being any of those things. "I'll take your word for it. I've never seen that side of my mother."

"And it's a damned shame. But now that she's better, you mark my words. She's a pistol. She's going to make your life a living hell."

A genuine smile spread across her face. "I'll look forward to that."

Gramps nodded. "Yup. Just like her." He changed subjects abruptly. "So. What's this about S.A.F.E.? How did you find out about that?"

She sure as heck wasn't telling him about Oracle. That was the last thing S.A.F.E. needed to find out about! "I did it the old-fashioned way. Months of investigation and legwork, and a bit of deductive reasoning. It took me a while to make the connection between Dunst, Q-group and S.A.F.E., but it all fell into place today. Along with the identities of S.A.F.E.'s members and their true agenda."

He shook his head. "How'd you make the connection?"

That she was willing to tell him. It wouldn't hurt S.A.F.E. to realize they couldn't hide any longer, now that the rock they'd been hiding under had been turned over. "I analyzed the Q-group attack on Monihan last October. It matched up with a CIA training scenario too perfectly to be coincidence. So, it was an easy leap to figure Richard Dunst was training them. He was using his former CIA agent status to do a bunch of illegal arms deals with the Q-group in Berzhaan. It was in the news when Q-group took over that TV station in Chicago. When they tried to blow up Gabriel Monihan."

Gramps nodded. "I actually fired him from the CIA before I retired."

"When Richard Dunst got broken out of jail this morning, it was clear that someone with a whole lot of power and re-sources helped him. And that wouldn't be the Q-group. They're a shoestring covert op all the way."

"Sound reasoning."

"So, it became clear that a third party was in the picture. Someone pulling both Dunst's and the Q-group's strings. And that's when I went looking for S.A.F.E. I intercepted some-one on the Internet instructing Dunst to kill Gabe Monihan this evening. Again, it had to be someone with inside access to the highest levels of the government. I tracked down the e-mail address of the guy giving Dunst orders, and funny thing, I ran smack-dab into a CIA firewall on the Internet."

"So, you put two and two together and fingered Dunst's old boss at CIA, Collin Scott. And you just waltzed in here, broke into his office and found…what?"

Diana gestured at the papers scattered all over the floor at her feet. "I found it all. The entire S.A.F.E. dossier. And lest you think you're going to get away with this, I've already faxed the entire file to the authorities."

Her grandfather stared down at the papers in shock.

And then a slow smile spread across his face. He looked up at her in jubilation. "You did it!"

She blinked. "I beg your pardon?"

"You broke open S.A.F.E. We've been after these bastards

for going on two years, and you did it in a single day! Simply amazing. Congratulations!"

"Who exactly has been going after S.A.F.E. for two years?"

"A group of…concerned citizens. A few people, highly placed in the government complex have been aware of a subtle force at work behind the scenes, pushing events in…dangerous directions. I've been helping them investigate who's behind it all."

That was a convenient story. "Not to be rude, Gramps, but you could easily be changing your tune to try and dodge the ton of bricks that's about to land on S.A.F.E. Why should I believe a word of what you just said?"

He grinned broadly. "Bravo. You really are a Lockworth through and through."

Okay, this conversation was just getting strange. She was barricaded in the CIA building, about to get thrown in jail for the rest of her natural life if she was lucky, and her grandfather was crowing about her calling him a liar.

"Tell you what, Pumpkin. I'll make you a deal. I'll get you out of this building in one piece—not under arrest—if you'll go for a ride with me. I want to take you to meet someone."

"To meet whom?" she asked cautiously.

"Someone you'll believe when he tells you I've infiltrated S.A.F.E. on his behalf in order to expose it and take it down."

"Why would I believe anyone you take me to?"

"Oh, I think you'll believe this person."

"And why should I trust you? You could just as easily take me to some deserted spot so more of S.A.F.E.'s thugs can kill me and feed me to the sharks. I'm not getting in any car with you."

He nodded. "I commend your caution. You'd make a hell

of a field operative. Good instincts. I'm going to reach into my pocket and get my cell phone. I'm going to do it nice and slow. Okay?"

She nodded once. And watched him like a hawk as he did exactly what he said he'd do.

"May I dial it?" he asked.

Another short nod.

He held the instrument to his ear for a moment. "Hello, it's Lockworth. There's someone here I'd like you to speak to. She's reluctant to get in a car with me and go for a ride. Rightly so, I might add."

He held the cell phone out to her. There was an outside chance it was a stun weapon of some kind. If she put it to her ear, she could be zapped and dropped. But, she was also curious just whom he could call on who would convince her to go with him.

She took the phone. Held it near her head but was careful not to touch her ear with it. "Hello?" she said cautiously.

"Hello. It's Gabe."

Her jaw dropped.

"Diana? Are you there?" His voice came as if from a great distance. Her grandfather was working with Gabe Monihan? Had Gabe played her for a fool all along?

"Diana? Talk to me. Are you okay?"

"Uh, yes," she managed to mumble.

"What's going on? What's your grandfather talking about? What does he mean that you won't get in a car with him?"

"Is my grandfather working for you?"

"Yes, as a matter of fact he is. And that's classified information, by the way. Please don't reveal it to anyone. He's working on something extremely important for me."

Gabe *knew* about the existence of S.A.F.E. or something like it and was using Gramps to smoke it out? And all of a sudden, the pieces started falling into place. This was the real reason why Gabe had insisted on it not being publicized before the election that the Q-group attack in Chicago last October had been aimed solely at him. Why there was so much enmity between him and Wolfe. Why he'd been so willing to trust her—another Lockworth—on sight.

Good grief. Did this also mean that Gabe hadn't felt any instant connection with her as she'd thought? Was his easy familiarity nothing more than an extension of his acquaintance with her grandfather? Had she read a great deal more into their bantered exchanges than was really there? Had he merely tolerated her as a favor to Gramps? Had she made a *colossal* fool of herself?

"Diana?" Gabe spoke worriedly in her ear. "What's going on?"

"I'm sorry. I'm a little busy at the moment."

"Doing what?" He asked that in a way that suggested he'd push until he got an answer.

"Well, I broke into the office of a high-ranking CIA official a few minutes ago. I'm barricaded inside it right now, and there are a couple of dozen security types outside who are jonesing to kill me. They're trying to figure out how to break down the door as we speak."

Gabe gave a snort of laughter.

But when she said nothing, he added in dawning dismay, "You're kidding, right?"

"Sorry."

"Jesus H. Christ, Diana. The CIA? What were you thinking?"

She laughed ruefully. "Well, the good news is I found out who's been trying to kill you. I just faxed the entire dossier on the conspiracy to my superiors. If I live more than a few more minutes, I'll ask to have it all sent to Owen Haas."

"And the Attorney General, it sounds like," he bit out.

"There's only one problem," she said.

"Only one?" he retorted. "It's sounds to me like you've got several problems at the moment."

She replied impatiently, "I'm not talking about me. I'm talking about you. I couldn't find out who's in charge of the whole conspiracy. It has to be someone way up in the government, though, based on the kind of information and resources they seem to have access to. You watch your back."

"That's what both of you Lockworth's have been doing for me."

"So Gramps is really on the up-and-up when he says he's been investigating this bunch for you?"

"Absolutely," Gabe answered firmly.

No hesitation. And that was a definite ring of truth in his voice. Well, okay then.

"So, are you President, yet?" she asked lightly.

"No," he laughed. "But soon. Less than an hour."

"Sheesh," she groused teasingly, "Who'd have guessed this nation elected such a slacker? It's about darn time you took the reins."

"We'll get there. One step at a time. Although, if you've busted this shadow group as wide-open as you say you have, my job just got a whole lot easier."

"Not to mention that you might live to do your job now," she added.

He waxed abruptly serious. "Exactly. I can't thank you enough. So. What can I do to help you out of your current predicament?"

"I do have a way of getting into messes, don't I?" she asked ruefully.

"Indeed."

"Actually, Gramps seems to think he's got it covered. How about we give you a call back if we get into a jam?"

"All right. But you call me if you need help, all right? I owe you an enormous debt."

She winced at his words. Is that what she was to him? A debt? Her stomach roiled, more nauseous than it already was. She hung up the phone and handed it back to her grandfather.

"It seems I owe you an apology, Gramps."

He waved a dismissive hand. "Put that thought right out of your mind. You were doing your job. I completely understand. And frankly, if you hadn't been cautious with me, I'd have chewed your butt."

She had no doubt he would've, too. No wonder her mother had been wild and stubborn with this man for a father-in-law.

"Exactly how were you planning to walk me out of here past all those guys out there?" she asked.

"That's the thing. We're not going past them." He nodded at the hidden door.

"Surely those guys out there know about that connecting door. They'll have agents posted outside the adjoining office."

"Well," her grandfather drawled, "I had a little chat with the Director when I got here, and he arranged for there not to be agents on the door that opens to a separate hallway that runs behind the adjoining office."

"We're going to escape?" she asked in disbelief.

"Yup. Just like the good old days." He was grinning like a mischievous six-year-old.

"What about the security cameras? The hallways are lined with them!"

"Not being monitored for the next—" he glanced at his watch "—four minutes. It really is time to go."

"If those guys in the outer office figure out what we're doing, they'll shoot to kill! If—and that's a big if—we manage to make it out of the building, they'll put out an APB on us so fast it'll make your head spin."

"Nah. Think how foolish they'll look when they finally get into this office and there's nobody inside. You'll have vanished into thin air. They can't very well put out an APB on an invisible woman."

Her eyes narrowed. "They won't put out the APB because you're going to take down Collin Scott, and they won't want to draw any more attention to him and the reason for what happens to him than they have to."

"Ah, my girl, you'd be a natural in the agency. Can I possibly tempt you to transfer over here from Defense Intelligence?"

"Not on your life. You can keep all these political games and maneuvering. They make my head hurt."

He guffawed. "And that's why you're a conspiracy theorist, right? You like to think about simple, straightforward things."

She grinned back at him. "Exactly."

He knelt down and began picking up the scattered S.A.F.E. documents. "We'd better take this stuff with us, don't you think?"

She knelt down and began helping him. "Definitely. We wouldn't want there to be an unfortunate accident with a paper shredder."

In a few seconds, they'd gathered up all the papers and stuffed them back into their red file.

"Better stick that under your coat," her grandfather advised. "If someone sees you leave the building with a red file, you could get into big trouble."

She replied dryly, "That will be the least of my problems if we're stopped on the way out of the building."

"True. Here. Put this on. Just in case we run into anybody in a hallway." Her grandfather held out a light brown wig to her. It was a chin-length pageboy-shaped thing, not terribly different from her own hair, but its smooth shape and chestnut color were enough off that nobody would give her a second glance.

She tucked the last of her wavy, golden locks under it. "How do I look?"

"Not nearly as pretty as my granddaughter," he replied. "Let's get out of here."

She followed him to the hidden panel and stepped through it into a darkened office. Light and noise came from the other side of the door as some of the security team from next door spilled over into the outer office of this suite. She and Gramps moved quietly across the carpeted floor, toward another door on the opposite side of the office. Yup, just as she'd thought. Her grandfather moved with the grace and stealth of a cat. The old guy must have been something else in his prime.

She waited in the shadows behind him as he opened the second exit silently. He glanced both directions down the hall, then gestured for her to follow him. They slipped outside. She walked beside him, moving purposefully, but without undue haste that might draw attention to them.

They wound down hallway after hallway, moving ever farther from the front door and the fiasco behind them. They went down an elevator and stepped out into a small vestibule.

"If each of us doesn't swipe an ID card as we leave, it's going to set off an alarm. We'll have to run for my car once we get out of here," he instructed in a low murmur.

"I can do you one better than that," she murmured back. She fished Samantha's ID card out of her coat pocket and dangled it from her fingers.

Gramps shook his head admiringly. "Lockworth, through and through."

They duly swiped their ID cards and stepped out into a dim parking garage. Perhaps twenty feet away, a limousine lurked in a dark shadow, its long, sleek shape menacing. Pantherlike.

They moved over to it swiftly, and the rear passenger door opened from inside as they approached it. Someone was inside waiting for them? Startled, Diana ducked into the vehicle and slid across the leather seat to make room for Gramps, who was close behind her.

"Let's go, Jens," he said into an intercom before the door was even fully closed.

The vehicle pulled out smoothly while Diana's eyes adjusted to the dark interior, lit only by a few small running lights along the floor. Not only was there one someone inside the limo, there were five someones.

She jolted as a voice said out of the darkness, "Hi, honey. Are you all right?"

"Mom? What in the world are you doing here?"

"You know us Lockworths. We stick together. I was with your grandfather when you called his hotel room. As soon as the call came in that you'd just gone into the CIA building, and we realized you were probably in trouble or about to be in trouble, wild horses couldn't have stopped me from coming along."

So that explained how Gramps had gotten to the CIA building minutes after she broke into Scott's office. She leaned forward and squeezed her mother's hand. "Thanks. That means a lot to me."

Her mother's startled gaze met hers and tears abruptly filled her mother's eyes. The lady never had been slow on the uptake. Zoe saw her overture for what it was. And dang it if her own eyes didn't start to fill with tears, too. Twenty-five years without a mother. And now she finally had one who'd worry over her and fight her battles beside her. The lonely little girl inside her was feeling better by the minute. As though she was growing up.

"I'd do anything for you, you know," her mother whispered. "I love you so much, sweetheart."

"I love you, too, Mom." That was the first time she could ever remember saying that. And it felt good. Really good. As if her heart was opening up and blooming like a big, bright, overblown sunflower.

She sniffed surreptitiously and said as briskly as she could manage under the circumstances, "We have a lot of catching up to do once this whole mess is taken care of. Gramps tells me you were quite a hellion in your day. I want to hear all about it."

Zoe gave her a watery smile. "No way am I telling you *everything*. I wouldn't want to give you any crazy ideas."

One of the other people spoke up. "As if breaking into CIA headquarters wasn't crazy enough."

Diana's head whipped up. She knew that voice. Allison Gracelyn, daughter of one of the Athena Academy's founders, Senator Marion Gracelyn. When that eminent lady passed away several years ago, Marion's son, Adam, took her place on the Athena Academy's board of directors, and Allison had become a consultant to that same board. What in the world was she doing here?

Diana glanced at the other occupants of the car, now that she could make out their faces. Allison's father, Judge Adam Gracelyn, another Athena Academy board member. Beyond him was a gray-haired man she'd never met, but who could only be Charles Forsythe, the billionaire who helped fund the formation of the Athena Academy. His portrait in the front lobby of the school was of a younger man with thick, dark hair, but the patrician features and burning intelligence in those dark eyes left no doubt as to his identity.

The last man wore a military uniform. She gaped as he leaned forward slightly and came into clear view farther down the long bench seat from Forsythe. The Chairman of the Joint Chiefs of Staff himself, General Bart Snyder. What the heck was *he* doing with this bunch? Everyone else had a strong connection to the Athena Academy that her grandfather had also helped found. But why was Snyder along for this little joyride?

The limousine pulled out of the CIA building's parking lot, sailing past the armed guard patrolling the gates on high alert. Looking for her, no doubt. She managed not to slink lower in her seat—the windows were blacked out, after all—but it was a struggle not to dive for the floor and hide her face.

Her grandfather broke the silence that descended over the vehicle as it accelerated into the night. "Diana, I think you are familiar with, if not acquainted with, everyone in the car, are you not?"

Yikes. That was his business voice. "Yes, sir," she replied crisply, putting on her military professional voice, as well.

Gramps turned to the vehicle's other occupants. "Our girl, Diana, was kind enough to retrieve a very interesting dossier for us this evening. It's the classified S.A.F.E. folder out of Collin Scott's office."

Without exception, everyone in the car lurched at that news, and there were general exclamations of surprise and, if she wasn't mistaken, pleasure. And why was it, exactly, that he would mention something so sensitive in this car full of government outsiders with no security clearances, with the exception of General Snyder, of course?

Allison Gracelyn spoke up. "Diana, have you had a chance to look through the file, yet?"

"I've glanced at it," she replied cautiously.

"Are there names?" Allison sounded tense. Urgent.

Diana nodded. "All except the leader of the whole conspiracy. That person is only referred to as Freedom One in the various documents. It may have been above Scott's pay grade to know who that person is."

"And is there evidence to tie S.A.F.E. to the assassination

attempts on Monihan?" Allison asked tersely, leaning forward intently in her seat.

Diana's gaze whipped over to her grandfather in no little surprise. How in the world did a consultant for a girl's prep school know about that possible connection? He nodded his permission to answer the question, a tacit endorsement of Allison's right to ask it.

Nonetheless, Diana replied to the woman carefully, "I'm afraid that's a matter of national security. I'm not aware of your need to know that particular information, so please forgive me if I decline to answer the question."

General Snyder chuckled. "I'm authorizing you to answer the question, Captain."

She nodded crisply at her boss. General Snyder might be way up the chain of command from her, but he was certainly able to give her that authorization to answer the question.

She looked down the length of the limo's interior at Allison. "Yes, there is direct evidence linking S.A.F.E. to the assassination attempts on Gabe Monihan. There's a planning document in the file outlining the details of the attempt to kill him last October. There are also records of funds transfers to Tito Albadian. And it's clear that Freedom One planned the bombing earlier this afternoon. There are payments to and correspondence with Richard Dunst. There can be no doubt that he worked directly for S.A.F.E. and was poised to be the backup assassin if the Q-group attack at the inaugural parade failed."

Allison sat back in her seat with a grim, but satisfied, look on her face.

Forsythe spoke up from the other side of the car. "They'll crack. If we bring in all the people we do know about and interrogate them hard enough, someone will give up the identity of this Freedom One character."

Diana retorted, "Yes, but will it be in time to save Gabe's life?"

Her grandfather replied cryptically, "That's what we're on our way to find out, now."

Judge Gracelyn, Allison's father and husband to the woman whose brainchild the Athena Academy was, commented, "It's only fitting that you be with us after you saved Gabe's life twice today."

Now what did that mean? She was damned confused, here. And this wasn't exactly the kind of crowd with whom she could just blurt out a demand to know what in the hell was going on. "Where are we going?" she asked carefully.

"You'll see soon enough," her grandfather answered.

Great. Now they were all grinning at each other as if they had some hilarious joke between them that she wasn't part of. Or maybe was the brunt of. She crossed her arms with a huff and leaned back in her seat. The grins got even wider, dammit!

Pointedly, she turned her gaze to the window and stared outside as the limousine wound through the northwest streets of downtown Washington, D.C. After the day she'd had, she severely didn't feel like dealing with anybody laughing at her right now.

Her grandfather asked the group in general, "Anyone have any guesses as to who this Freedom One person is?"

Allison Gracelyn said wryly, "That is the question of the hour, is it not?"

When no one else spoke up, Diana said into the silence, "Whoever it is has to be extremely highly placed in the government and work close to the office of the President."

"Why do you say that?" Allison asked.

"Freedom One knew about the second inauguration attempt for Gabe today at the Capitol Building. Admittedly, a fairly wide circle of people were aware of that ceremony, but it still was far from public knowledge. Yet, Freedom One had the details in enough time to send Richard Dunst over to the Capitol Building to kill Gabe."

Allison nodded her agreement with the analysis.

The atmosphere in the car grew noticeably more tense as everyone jumped to the next logical conclusion. And whoever that person was, he or she was still on the loose. And potentially still capable of ordering another assassination attempt on Gabe Monihan.

The same sense of impending doom that had filled her all day surged anew. Her worry for Gabe was a tangible thing, swirling within the limousine's interior to join the controlled panic now filling the enclosed space.

The limousine decelerated smoothly. Diana looked outside, curious to see where they were going. She gaped as the vehicle made a left turn into a driveway famous the world over. They were at 1600 Pennsylvania Avenue.

The White House.

2:00 A.M.

For it being two o'clock in the morning, the place was lit up like a torch. Of course, under normal circumstances, an inaugural ball would be in full swing. But today had been anything but normal.

The limousine stopped, and a uniformed guard leaned down to peer in the window. The driver turned on an overhead dome light, and Diana blinked at the sudden light.

"Who's in the vehicle?" the guard asked.

Her grandfather leaned forward. "The Athena party."

The guard looked down at a clipboard in his hand. "Ah yes. Delphi and associates." He stepped back and waved the driver through.

Delphi? One of the people in this car was Delphi? She managed not to gawk in open shock, but it was a close thing. Which one? Her curiosity raged, but their limousine pulled up under the East Portico and came to a stop before she could demand to know which one of them was her secretive boss.

A uniformed military officer opened the door at her elbow and held out a gloved hand to assist her from the vehicle. She stepped out into a rush of blessedly warm air blowing down from a vent in the porch ceiling. The entire party was handed smoothly out of the car.

A social aide in a white ceremonial uniform with Air Force insignia on it handed her a comb and held up a palm-size mirror. "Would you like to fix your hair, ma'am, before you go inside?"

She peered into the tiny mirror. Good thing she couldn't see more of her face. She looked like hell. She repaired her hair and handed the comb back.

A suited Secret Service man she'd never seen before said, "If you'll come with me, ladies and gentlemen. They're expecting you inside." He slipped white cotton gloves over his hands and opened the double French doors that led directly into the East Room.

Who was expecting them? Were they all going to attend Gabe's inauguration? Her heart leaped in consternation at the thought. She wasn't at all sure she was ready to face him yet. Her thoughts and feelings were a jumbled muddle where he was concerned, and she needed some time, some distance, to sort them out before she could face him again with equanimity.

But as she stepped into the room full of people, her thoughts were swept aside as foreboding slammed into her with all the force of an Abram's tank. Gabe wasn't President, yet. And S.A.F.E. wasn't finished, either.

She stumbled along in the middle of the group of Athena dignitaries and General Snyder into the spacious and gracious East Room. Its butter-yellow walls were warm and inviting after the deep cold of the night outside. Several hundred formally dressed people milled around the sumptuous room.

Dear God, she could smell it. The malice seething below the surface of someone in here. She caught a fleeting frown that crossed her grandfather's features. She leaned close to him and murmured, "You can feel it, too, can't you?"

He nodded infinitesimally.

"How about you and I take a little stroll around the room," she suggested sotto voce. "You take the right, and I'll take the left."

"Done," he replied through clenched teeth.

"I'll be back in a minute, Mom. I want to take a quick look around."

Her mother smiled knowingly at her. "Protective of him, are you? I'm sure the Secret Service has it well in hand this time."

She didn't have to ask which "him" her mother was referring to. She rolled her eyes, embarrassed, and turned away from Zoe. Using her intelligence training, she melted into the crowd of people, which was a bit of a trick given how violently underdressed she was. This crowd must be the guests who'd been invited to the mother of all inaugural balls, the White House Ball. They would be top officials from the incoming administration and the very largest donors to Gabe's campaign coffers. She recognized many of the faces in the room. A few people gave her strange looks at her casual attire, but she ducked her chin and slid past those people as unobtrusively as she could. No time to explain herself just now.

She started as a heavy hand landed on her shoulder from behind. She whirled, her hands coming up defensively.

"Agent Tilman," she exclaimed under her breath. "How's everything going?"

"I was about to ask you the very same thing. I figure it can't be a good thing that you're here."

She smiled humorlessly. "I was just talking with Gabe earlier about how trouble does seem to have a way of finding me."

He shrugged. "Maybe you just have a good nose for finding it. Smelling anything interesting this evening?" he asked lightly.

"Actually, I am," she replied with quiet significance.

His gaze snapped to hers, questioning. Concerned. "Come with me."

She nodded and fell in beside him as he politely elbowed his way out of the room. It was a whole lot easier to move through this dense crowd with a grim-looking linebacker at her side. They stepped out into a broad, elegant hallway, stretching away from the East Room all the way across the ground floor of the stately building.

As soon as they were clear of the East Room, Tilman's stride stretched out to a near run. It was all she could do to keep up with him without breaking into a trot. He turned a corner and stabbed a button for an elevator. One of the doors in front of them slid open immediately. He dragged her inside the small cubicle.

As soon as the door closed, he asked tersely, "What have you got this time?"

She answered grimly, "Less than before. I think someone very highly placed in the government may try to have Gabe killed again. Maybe not tonight. Except…"

"Except what?" he prodded.

"Except I've had this gut feeling all evening that it would happen before he became President."

"We're big believers in gut feelings in the Service. And a whole lot of us have been getting gut feelings, too. Do you have any idea at all what's planned?"

She shook her head regretfully. "None."

"He's about to be sworn in."

She asked, "How many people is he exposed to?"

"No more than two dozen. He's in the Situation Room, now. No assassin could possibly penetrate it."

Her intuition jelled into screaming certainty all at once. No assassin could penetrate that group unless Freedom One was in it, and Freedom One had decided to personally knock off Gabe. *And that's exactly what was about to happen.*

"Who's there with him?" she demanded urgently.

The elevator came to a stop and they stepped out into a narrow corridor. Tilman turned to face her. "His new cabinet. The Joint Chiefs. A couple members of the Supreme Court."

She said around the tightness in her jaw. "That may do it. Within that bunch may very well be the final assassin."

Tilman's jaw sagged for an instant before it snapped shut and fire lit in his eyes. "Let's go," he bit out.

They took off running down the hall, shoving aside everyone and everything in their path. They skidded to a stop in front of a closed door guarded by a pair of burly men. "Let us in," Tilman snapped.

"Nobody's supposed to go in or out," one of the agents protested. "Haas's orders."

"Monihan's in danger. There's a killer in there and this lady may know who he is."

The men's faces registered shock as the roster of people in the room passed through their minds. But, to their credit, they didn't waste time arguing about the absurdity of Tilman's claim. One of them punched a number code in the keypad beside him and Tilman shoved the door open. Diana leaped past him and burst into the room.

Startled faces turned toward her. There was Gabe at the far end of the room, in an open space beyond a long conference table. His left hand rested on a Bible and his right hand was raised in the air. An elderly, black-robed figure stood in front of him, holding the Bible. Justice Browning. Thomas Wolfe stood just behind Gabe. And as Tilman had said, members of Gabe's inner circle ranged around him in a loose arc.

In the millisecond it took her to register all that, several faces in the room registered her identity, as well. Gabe's eyes lit in pleased surprise followed by alarm. He knew full well what her bursting into the room like this meant.

Owen Haas leaped to the same conclusion as Gabe did when he saw her and Tilman come bursting through the door. She watched, as in slow motion, his elbow came up and he shoved aside the new Secretary of State to take a step forward toward Gabe. His face creased into lines of grim determination. He didn't know where the threat was going to come from, but he was as certain in that endless instant as she was that it *was* going to come. Please, God, let Owen be in time to get his body in front of Gabe.

And then she registered the only two other faces in the room whose expressions shifted away from surprise to something else. They both darkened in displeased recognition of her. Thomas Wolfe. And General Eric Pace, the Army Chief of Staff.

And both of them reached into their coats.

Which one of them was it? Which one was Freedom One? She couldn't take out both men. There wasn't time and they stood too far apart, Wolfe on Gabe's right and Pace to Gabe's left. Like Owen Haas, she took a slow-motion step forward, preparatory to leaping for one of the men.

Eric Pace's name had only shown up once, on a list of frequent attendees to defense conferences along with some of the known S.A.F.E. members. Wolfe's writings, on the other hand, were the foundation of S.A.F.E.'s work. He'd opposed

Gabe in a bitter primary campaign, much of it centered around their wildly differing views on dealing with terrorism. He'd tried to unseat Gabe after the election on the grounds of mental unfitness for the job—to steal the Presidency. He'd waylaid her this morning and attempted not to let her see Gabe, as if he already knew who she was and what she'd been there to warn Gabe about.

She leaped for Eric Pace.

The leader of S.A.F.E. would never make himself as obvious a target as Wolfe had.

She flew through the air, tackling the barrel-chested general, slamming him into the ground and landing squarely on top of him. He fought beneath her, twisting and turning in an effort to throw her off. She hung on to him grimly. It was like wrestling a bear. A big, strong, angry one.

Without warning, a deafening sound echoed in her ears, so loud it took her a moment to identify it as a gunshot. A huge jolt of force exploded between her and Pace.

Out of the corner of her eye, she saw Gabe stagger as something or someone struck him.

And then all hell broke loose, people shouting and Secret Service agents diving all over the place. Gabe went down under a pile of agents, and she was abruptly crushed by several men, herself.

"Gun!" one of them shouted practically in her ear.

"Blood!" another one of the men on top of her yelled. "Someone's hit! Medic!"

Good Lord willing, the bastard had shot himself in the gut. The other people in the room were shoved back, and the chaos resolved itself into two piles.

A voice bellowed beside her, "I've got the weapon." That was Agent Tilman. "Hold him down!"

The pile around her squirmed and heaved as Pace fought

like a madman beneath her. It felt like the time she rode a wild
bronc and nearly broke her neck. Her lungs started to burn,
and she was having trouble breathing. With all these two-hun-
dred-twenty-pound jokers on top of her, it was no wonder.

She turned her head, searching for a pocket of air in the
smothering pile of wool suits and brawn. And came face-to-
face with Eric Pace. At a range of about two inches. His eyes
blazed with insane fury.

"Freedom One, I presume?" she managed to gasp.

His eyes glazed with manic intensity. "You bitch," he
snarled. "You have no idea what you've just done."

"I believe I've prevented you from assassinating the President of the United States."

"You've weakened our nation. You've made us vulnerable
to terrorism. I was going to win the war against it, going to
protect this nation the way it ought to be protected. But you've
ruined it all."

"I think…that's a decision…for the people…of this nation…to make at…the polls." She forced the words out of her
flattened lungs.

Dang, she was having a hard time breathing.

"I've got his arms," someone shouted.

Pace gave a violent heave beneath her and she felt his legs
kicking out beneath hers. Spittle flecked the corner of his mouth.

"Give it up, Pace," she ground out. "It's over." She dragged
air into her protesting lungs. She blinked a couple times to
clear the pinpoints of light dancing in front of her eyes. She
was starting to feel light-headed. "S.A.F.E. is finished."

Pace froze for an instant, staring at her in shock. Didn't
think anyone knew about his secret little conspiracy, did he?
Surprise, surprise.

Apparently, that brief moment of advantage was all the Secret Service needed to finally subdue him. Someone bel-

lowed that they had his legs immobilized. The guy on top of her blessedly rolled away from her. Hands lifted her roughly to her feet as she was yanked away from Pace. She took a staggering step back as a phalanx of Secret Service agents rolled Pace over, jerked his hands behind his back and slapped handcuffs on his wrists. They dragged him none too gently to his feet.

Gabe and Thomas Wolfe stood shoulder-to-shoulder, and Wolfe mopped at his forehead with the handkerchief he'd pulled out of his coat. Gabe snarled, "Why, Pace? Why me?"

The general growled back, "You're weak. This country needs a man like Thomas Wolfe at the helm. This was all about putting him into power, where he belongs."

Gabe's gaze snapped to his vice president.

The look of stunned disbelief on Wolfe's face had to be legitimate. He stared in shock at the Army general and then turned to face Gabe. "I had no idea. No idea whatsoever that he was planning something like this. Of course, I'll step down. I'll tender my letter of resignation first thing in the morning."

The guy sounded completely shell-shocked, as if he could be knocked over by a feather right about now.

Gabe said shortly, "Don't send me any letters, yet. We'll talk about this tomorrow."

Wolfe nodded, his gaze bewildered.

Agent Tilman, who still held her elbow, jolted beside her. And looked down. "Jesus, Miss Lockworth. You're bleeding."

She looked down and saw a large bloodstain spreading down the right side of her sweater.

Gabe leaped past Owen Haas. "Where's that medic?" he shouted.

His arms went around her, and he picked her up, carrying her over to the conference table. He laid her down on it gently.

She looked up at him in blank surprise. "I'm shot," she said rather obviously. But it was the only thing that came to her mind.

"Everything's going to be okay," he murmured reassuringly. "Don't worry."

Hands raised her sweater and eased her slacks down to her hips. Something wet and cold that burned like acid was pressed against her side. "Ouch!" she exclaimed, lurching with unpleasant surprise.

A gray-haired man that eyed her side like a doctor commented, "Well, we know her lung isn't collapsed if she can yelp like that."

He swabbed at her side, tossing away several bloodied gauze pads. She lifted her head, twisting her neck to look down at her injury, but the doctor ordered her to lie back down and stay still.

The doctor fussed around for another minute or so, smearing a cream of some kind on her skin. It numbed the growing burning sensation a fair bit, and she sighed in relief. The sound of tape tearing accompanied the doctor pressing a thick wad of gauze against her side. After he'd finished bandaging the wound tightly, the doctor pronounced, "It's just a graze. She's going to be fine."

Gabe leaned down over her and his palms came to rest on her cheeks. "Thank God," he said fervently.

She gazed up into his worried eyes. She reached up and smoothed away the lines of worry from his brow. And smiled. He smiled back.

Owen Haas cleared his throat from over Gabe's shoulder, breaking the spell of the moment. It probably wasn't proper Presidential protocol to sprawl all over the Situation Room briefing table making goo-goo eyes at the commander-in-chief.

She sat up, wincing at the sudden, sharp pain in her side. Gabe's hand was right there on her elbow, steadying her.

She flashed him a look of gratitude. Then she demanded, "Are you President yet?"

He laughed aloud. "Not yet."

"Well, good grief, Gabe Monihan, let's get on with it. You can procrastinate like nobody I've ever met before."

Laughter filled the room.

Gabe held her arm solicitously, helping her gently to her feet. Her side stung sharply, but she wasn't going to lie around on some table while he became President, darn it.

"Let's do it, Wendall," Gabe said.

The elderly man in the black judge's robe stepped forward. "Now where were we?" he asked drolly.

More chuckles sounded around the room. But they faded away, and a solemn silence enveloped the space. Gabe took the Bible out of the Justice's hands and turned to face her. He cleared his throat. "Diana, it's traditional that the first lady holds the Bible for her husband when he's sworn in. My mother was planning to do it this afternoon, but the day's events have been a little much for her. Would you do me the honor of holding it for me?"

Her eyes opened wide. That wasn't the sort of request someone made of some random hot babe they wanted to have a casual fling with. She looked up questioningly into his eyes. "Are you sure?"

He gave her a smile that melted her heart right there on the spot. "I get feelings about things sometimes. I just know when they're right. And you're the one for the job. I'm sure."

She had no idea whether or not he was talking about simply holding the Bible or much more. But it was clear he intended to give them a chance to find out. And so did she. "It would be my great honor to hold the Bible for you, Gabe."

He held out the book. Their fingers brushed as she took it

from him, and as he laid his palm on the leather cover, he flashed her an intimate smile.

And then, standing by her side, Gabe raised his right hand, vowed to uphold and defend the Constitution, and became President of the United States.

* * * * *

Can't get enough of ATHENA FORCE
and Silhouette Bombshell? Every month
we've got four fresh, unique, satisfying reads
to tempt you into something new....
Turn the page to read an exclusive excerpt from
one of next month's thrilling releases,
the final ATHENA FORCE adventure,
CHECKMATE
by Doranna Durgin
On sale June 2005
at your favorite retail outlet.

"Ambassador—" Selena Shaw Jones rubbed the bridge of her nose, right above the little bump Cole liked so much. *Don't think about Cole just now.* Fatigue washed over her in a startling rush. She closed her mouth on indiscreet words, a warning from the super secret Oracle database—the alarming intel from the CIA, along with other military and agency listening posts with which an FBI legate such as Selena should have no direct connection. Word that the Kemeni rebels of Berzhaan were desperate in the wake of what they thought was lost U.S. support—that they had to grab power *now,* or concede it forever.

"Selena?" Ambassador Allori set his teacup in the saucer, brow drawing together. "Are you quite all right?"

And just like that, she wasn't. Her stomach spasmed beyond even her iron control, and she blurted, "Excuse me!" and bolted from the room, briefcase clutched in her hand. She remembered the bathroom as a barely marked door down the embassy hall and only hoped she was right as she slammed it open. *Thank God.* Most of the room was a blur but she honed in on an open stall door, grateful for the lavish, updated fixture—

Better than a hole in the floor. Been there, done that.

And when she leaned back against the marbleized stall wall, marveling at the sudden violence her system had wreaked upon her, the thought flashed unbidden and unexpected through her mind: *We were trying to start a family.*

No. Not here, not *now.* Not with Cole half a world away and an even bigger emotional gap between them. She knew he hid things from her; she thought she could live with that. *Maybe not.* Selena clenched down on her thoughts the same way she'd tried to clench down on her stomach, and stumbled out to the pristine sink to crank the cold water on full and splash her face and rinse her mouth. When she dared to look at her image, she found that it reflected what she felt: she looked stronger, less green. This particular storm, whatever the cause, was over.

What if she were pregnant in a strife-torn Berzhaan, her estranged husband not even knowing he was estranged? Theoretically he was still deeply undercover in wherever it was that he'd gone, unable to do more than send a sporadic e-mail or two. *Theoretically.*

Except she'd seen him in D.C.

Kissing someone else.

If she were pregnant…she'd have to stay here long enough to stabilize this new legate's office, in spite of the unrest. And then she'd have to go home…she'd have to tell Cole. To decide if she trusted him, or if she'd merely contribute to the long line of broken branches in her family tree.

And if this is any taste of things to come, I'll have to carry around a barf bag wherever I go.

The water still trickled; she scooped another handful into her mouth, held it and spit it out. Her eyes stung, sympathetic to her throat. It wasn't until she coughed, short and sharp, that she stiffened—and realized that the uncomfortable tang didn't come from her abused throat, but from the air she breathed.

Tear gas.

Trickling in from the street outside? From somewhere in the building?

Damn. Damn, damn, DAMN.

Listening at the bathroom door revealed only silence, and she went so far as to peek out. The smoke hung thickly in the abandoned hallway. Selena ducked back inside, took another deep breath—this one to hold—and eased out into the hallway, running silently to the waiting room where she'd left the Berzhaani ambassador so precipitously only moments before.

Empty. Allori's teacup lay broken on the floor, tea soaking the priceless carpet.

Son of a bitch.

The door leading to the prime minister's office stood slightly ajar, and Selena made for it, her chest starting to ache for air. But breathing meant coughing, and coughing meant being found.

She didn't intend to be found until she understood the situation. If then.

Razidae's office proved to be empty as well, the luxurious rolling office chair askew at the desk, papers on the floor, the private phone out of its sleek, lined cradle—and the air relatively clear. Selena closed the door, grateful for the old, inefficient heating system, and inhaled as slowly as she could, muffling the single cough she couldn't avoid.

All right, then. The building was full of tear gas, and the dignitaries were gone, and Selena had somehow missed it all.

They could have blown the building out from under you while you were throwing up and you wouldn't have noticed.

Think, Selena. She pressed the heels of her hands against her eyes and calmed the chaotic mess of her mind. She could call for help from here—Razidae's private line might have an in-use indicator at his secretary's desk, but it wouldn't show up on any of the other phone systems, so she wouldn't give her presence away by picking it up.

But there was no point in calling until she understood the situation. No doubt the authorities were already alerted.

You still don't know what's going on.

Well, then, she told herself. Let's find out.

Selena laid her briefcase on the desk, thumbed the token combination lock and flipped the leather flap open. She'd left her laptop behind in favor of her tablet PC, and the briefcase looked a little forlorn…a little empty.

Not much to work with. No Beretta, no extra clip, no knives…

Maybe she wouldn't need them. Maybe by the time she discovered what had happened, it would actually be over.

Nonetheless, she took a quick survey: cell phone, battery iffy; she turned it off and left it behind. A handful of pens, mostly fine point. She tucked several into her back pocket. A new pad of sticky notes. A nail file, also worthy of pocket space. Her Buck pocketknife, three blades of discreet mayhem, yet not big enough to alarm the security guards. It earned a grim smile and a spot in her front pocket. A spare AC unit for her laptop, which garnered a thoughtful look and ended up stuffed into the big side pocket of her leather duster. A small roll of black electrician's tape. A package of cheese crackers—

Selena closed her eyes, aiming willpower at her rebellious stomach. *I don't have time for you,* she told it. Without looking, she set the crinkly package aside and then looked at the remaining contents of the briefcase. A legal pad and a folder full of confidential documents. She supposed she could inflict some pretty powerful papercuts. A few mints and some emergency personal supplies she wasn't likely to need if she was actually pregnant.

No flak vest, no Rambo knife, not even a convenient flare pistol.

Then again, there was no telling what she might find with a good look around the Capitol. Almost anything was a weapon if you used it right.

Selena jammed the rejected items back in her briefcase, automatically locking it; she tucked it inside the foot well of Razidae's desk and checked to see that she'd left no sign of her presence, except there were those *crackers*—

She made a dive for the spiffy executive wastebasket beside the desk, hunched over with dry heaves. Mercifully, they didn't last long. And afterward, as she rose on once-again shaky legs and poured herself a glass of the ice water tucked away on a marble-topped stand in the corner, she tried to convince herself that it was over. That she could go out and assess the situation without facing the heaves during an inopportune moment.

She dumped the rest of the water into a lush potted plant that probably didn't need the attention, wiped out the glass and returned it to its spot. She very much hoped that she'd creep out to find an embarrassed guard and an accidentally discharged tear gas gun.

A stutter of muted automatic gunfire broke the silence.

So much for that idea. Selena's heart, already pounding from her illness, kicked into a brief stutter of overtime that matched the rhythm of the gunfire. "All right, baby," she said to her potential little passenger, pulling her fine wool scarf from her coat pocket and soaking it in the pitcher. "Get ready to rock and roll."

But as she reached for the doorknob, she hesitated. She could be risking more than her own life if she ran out into the thick of things now. As far as she knew, whoever had pulled the trigger of that rifle didn't even know she existed. She could ride things out here with her lint-filled water and her cheese crackers.

Or she could be found and killed, or the building could indeed blow up around her, or whoever'd fired those shots could succeed in their disruptive goal, and Selena and her theoretical little one could be trapped in a rioting, war-torn Berzhaan. Her mind filled with images of frightened students and dead Capitol workers and a dead Allori. She closed her eyes hard.

It really wasn't any choice at all.

Silhouette® BOMBSHELL™

**BRINGS YOU THE LATEST BOOK
IN THE EXCITING CROSS-LINE
MINISERIES BY READER FAVORITE**

Maggie Price

LINE OF DUTY

Where peril and passion collide

Forensic statement analyst Paige Carmichael has crossed swords with a sexy homicide cop and been mugged...all by midmorning. Now she must use her unusual skills to investigate a murder that could blow the police department apart and make her the target of a deadly—and desperate—killer.

The hunter will become the hunted...but is more than one man after her? There's only one way to find out! Don't miss

TRIGGER EFFECT
June 2005

Available at your favorite retail outlet.

If you enjoyed what you just read,
then we've got an offer you can't resist!

Take 2 bestselling love stories FREE!
Plus get a FREE surprise gift!

BOMBSHELL™

COMING NEXT MONTH

#45 DOUBLE VISION—Vicki Hinze
War Games

U.S. Air Force captain Katherine Kane had been sent to the Middle East to look for a suspected terrorist weapons cache, but stumbled upon much more than she had bargained for— American hostages, biological weapons and the most feared terrorist in the world, a man Kate could have sworn was locked away for good. But seeing was believing, and Kate suspected the criminal mastermind was no double vision after all....

#46 CHECKMATE—Doranna Durgin
Athena Force

Her marriage on the rocks, FBI legal attaché Serena Jones took refuge in an assignment to a foreign land only to be caught when rebels took over the capitol. Trapped in the building but free to move inside, Serena would take on the crafty rebel leader and lay a trap using the weapons at hand—her dying cell phone, her wits and an unexpected ally, her estranged husband....

#47 TRIGGER EFFECT—Maggie Price
Line of Duty

Hours after arriving in Oklahoma City, Paige Carmichael had clashed with a tough homicide detective, had her briefcase stolen and wound up in the E.R. And when she was asked to consult on a murder case, things didn't get any better. Because the killer knew Paige held the key to solving the mystery, and was determined to keep her from revealing the truth—by any means necessary.

#48 AN ANGEL IN STONE—Peggy Nicholson
The Bone Hunters

Archaeologist Raine Ashaway was determined to beat her rival, Kincade, and buy a precious rare fossil. But when the fossil's owner was murdered, Raine was plunged into a mystery that led her to the other side of the world. She had to join forces with Kincade. And with a killer on their heels, they'd have to learn to get along....

SBCNM0505